MW01093615

A MARCH FROM INNOCENCE

A C.T. FERGUSON CRIME NOVEL (#6)

TOM FOWLER

TOM FOWLER WRITES

Do you love free books?

I know—probably a silly question. Presuming you said yes, I'm giving away the prequel novella to the C.T. Ferguson mystery series. If you've wondered what happened to C.T. In China and how he wound up on his unusual path, this book holds the answers.

It's called *Hong Kong Dangerous*, and I don't sell it anywhere. It's available only to my VIP readers. To get your copy, please go here.

A March from Innocence: A C.T. Ferguson Private Investigator Mystery is copyright (c) 2019 by Tom Fowler. All rights reserved. No part of this publication may be reproduced, distributed, or transmitted in any form or by any means, including photocopying, recording, or other electronic or mechanical methods, without the prior written permission of the publisher, except in the case of brief quotations embodied in critical reviews. For permissions, please contact: tom@tomfowlerwrites.com.

Cover design: 100 Covers

Editing: Chase Nottingham

❀ Created with Vellum

For Lisa and Isabel, as ever.

CHAPTER 1

"Every life is a march from innocence, through temptation, to virtue or vice."

~Lyman Abbott

BLUE IS AN AMAZING AND UNDERRATED COLOR. DUST and water droplets scatter and diffuse light, making the blackness of the sky take on a vibrant hue. Three of my favorite colors of dress shirts are shades of cyan. Some people have eyes blue enough to have stolen the color from precious gems. At the current moment, my favorite shade was the perfect and endless blue of the Pacific Ocean in Hawaii.

Gloria Reading and I had been here on vacation over two weeks. My last case resulted in the suspension of my PI license for thirty days. It was only fair—I assaulted the bastard, but in my defense, he murdered my sister thirteen years prior. The fact I hadn't emptied the magazine into his body didn't merit much consideration from the panel deciding my fate. I chose to get away from the emotion of the whole thing and take my beautiful girlfriend to the loveliest place on earth.

I lay on the beach, having applied enough sunscreen for two normal people. Early December in Baltimore is cold, sometimes rainy and snowy. In Hawaii, we enjoyed perfect beach weather. I lay on a *chaise longue* with a book, letting the sunscreen soak into my skin before I ventured into the water. Gloria, who wore a bathing suit which hugged her curves better than it absorbed water, swam in the pearlescent waves. Our resort featured a private beach and lagoon. It had pools, too, but why bother with a pool when the ocean is right there? Gloria and I swam laps every day we'd been to the beach.

A few minutes later, I decided the sunblock soaked in as much as it was going to, and I joined Gloria to race out to a manmade barrier reef. Gloria's athleticism usually manifested itself in tennis, but she was also a good swimmer. I, however, happen to be a great swimmer, and I beat her to the barrier. We then moved to a rock formation to our right about 200 yards away. As we got closer, the ocean got darker, shallower, and colder. Jagged stones made walking on the bottom painful, so we swam slowly up to a section of beach before exploring the formation.

We didn't have shoes, but we did have a powerful desire to climb, and we each harbored enough competitive fire to want to get there first. The slipperiness of the stone made it slow going, and we paused to give each other a hand now and again. Nothing like a little friendly cooperation among lovers in the middle of a competition. After a few minutes, we got over the rocks and found a virgin tract of beach. Here, we could swim past the man-made barrier if we chose. Instead, we lay on the warm sand, each of us breathing heavier than normal from our expedition.

Gloria kissed me and then rested her head on my chest. "I could get used to being here."

"Me, too," I said, "but I think it would make my job harder."

"How?"

"Well, I'd be more interested in going to the beach than working for one."

"I can see that."

"And I'd have to compete with Dog the bounty hunter. I don't think his show is still on, but a lot of people know him. Too much of a headstart."

Gloria humored me with a polite chuckle and kissed me again. "Yes, but his show was terrible."

"You watched it?"

"I had an ex who was into it. The relationship didn't last long."

"How could it?" I said.

LATER IN THE DAY, we took our rental car and drove to Waikiki. I'd made a reservation at Duke's. Originally, I tried to get a table the same night I called, and the fellow who answered the phone retained his composure enough so he didn't laugh at me. Duke's took reservations days in advance, he told me, so I conformed to custom. We headed to Waikiki early, both because of traffic and because Gloria wanted to shop. I parked in a garage, Gloria headed for stores from which she needed absolutely nothing, and I walked into Honolulu Coffee Company.

One steaming cup of java in hand, I sat at a small table and scrolled through emails on my phone. Before we left the mainland, I had sent all of my business calls to my office phone. My cell remained refreshingly quiet. Even my parents only bothered us once so far. The fact I'd used their time-share weeks—which would've only languished in their account, but still—to take Gloria to Hawaii tugged at my underdeveloped sense of guilt and compelled me to talk to them. I offered to take home souvenirs and my mother reacted as if I'd promised to bring scurvy back to Maryland.

I checked my messages to see how things were faring. Part of running a free detective service is being in the good graces of the press. My last real case before jetting to Hawaii involved locating the missing daughter of a wealthy Baltimore magnate. She had disappeared at eighteen, been a prostitute for five years, and I remain convinced her father knew where she was the whole time. Their interesting family dynamics aside, the case provided me a nice jolt of publicity which I promptly squandered by going on vacation for four weeks. Oh, well. We can't time everything perfectly.

A few of my messages were interview requests from local media outlets. Even on vacation, I managed to find time to talk to the reporters, usually while Gloria pampered herself in the spa. The rest had been from a persistent woman who wanted me to know her niece was a troubled lass, and would I be able to help rescue the girl from a life of who-knows-what? I probably would, but the troubled lasses of Baltimore would need to wait for me to fly back home. The unnamed woman left two more messages. I deleted them both. If her niece still needed help in a week and a half, we could talk. I finished my coffee. Gloria came into the shop carrying two bags full of clothes and shoes.

"You're going to have a dozen checked bags at the airport," I said.

She shrugged and smiled. "Clothes and shoes are the best reasons to check a lot of bags."

"Are you ready for dinner, Imelda Marcos?"

"All this shopping has given me an appetite."

"Good. Let's go eat too much."

"It'll give us an excuse to work the calories off later," Gloria breathed into my ear.

I loved this woman.

* * *

AFTER A TERRIFIC AND filling meal at Duke's, we drove back to the resort, valeted the car, and entered through the sliding glass front doors. A few police officers walked away from a middle-aged woman who shook her head and wiped her eyes. She sagged into a chair in the lobby. Gloria squeezed my hand when we saw the drama play out. We approached the woman. "Is everything OK?" I said.

The woman shook her head anew. "It's my husband," she said. "He's missing, and the police won't do anything!" This led to a new round of tears. Gloria fetched a box of tissues from the concierge desk and handed one to the woman, who accepted it with a grateful nod.

"Why won't they help?" Gloria said.

"They say he hasn't been missing long enough."

"How long has it been?" I asked.

"Since earlier today. I know something is wrong. I don't know if he's in trouble, but I know my husband. He would never disappear without a call or a text."

"I hate to ask, but . . . "

"Is our marriage OK?" The woman flashed a rueful smile. "Sort of. We're here to rediscover the magic and all that. Our counselor's idea."

Gloria stood beside me again and gave my hand another squeeze. I stared at her while large eyes pleaded with me.

"Ma'am, will you excuse us?" I said as Gloria and I took a few steps back.

"This is right up your alley," she said in hushed tones.

"I thought we were on vacation."

"You heard her, C.T. She knows something is wrong."

"No, she *suspects* something is wrong. Because she and the hubby are in counseling, she's assuming the worst."

"What if she's right?" I didn't answer. "You could help her. You could find her husband. Hell, you might even save their marriage."

"Now you're ascribing powers to me I don't possess," I said.

"You know you could step in when the police won't."

I pondered it for a moment. "I'm sure I could."

"You probably wouldn't even have to work very hard."

"True."

"Have you missed doing your job?" said Gloria.

I shrugged. "A little. I never thought I would, especially on vacation."

Gloria smiled at me. "Then you know what you should do."

I took a deep breath and smiled in spite of myself. "You're lucky I love you." I went back to the woman, who sat in the chair and stared at the floor. "Ma'am? I'm on vacation, but back in Maryland, I'm a private investigator."

She looked up quickly enough to strain her neck. "Do you think you can find my Francis?"

"I'll do my best."

"Do you need to know much about him?"

"A little information wouldn't hurt."

She spent about five minutes telling me about her husband. She smiled when she mentioned his (or their) successes and winced at any mention of troubled times. This was a woman who still loved her spouse. When she finished, I went to the concierge desk, grabbed a pen, and tore off the top sheet of a memo pad.

"Write his full name, date of birth, and cell phone number on here," I said.

"What do you need that for?" she said as she handed the filled-out paper back to me.

I smiled at her. "Let me worry about the details."

* * *

JOANIE BAKER HAD GIVEN Gloria her cell phone number and gotten mine in return. She operated under the assumption Gloria was my secretary. I found this much more amusing than Gloria did. When we got back to our suite, I pulled out my laptop and turned it on for only the third time since we arrived in Hawaii.

"Here you go, boss," she said.

"Does your being my secretary prevent me from sexually harassing you?"

"I certainly hope not."

I logged in and began anonymizing my traffic right away. Long ago, I wrote scripts to do this for me. I updated them as the Internet landscape changed, but the scripts worked every bit as well today as they did when I first wrote them. Armed with Francis Daniel Baker's information, I could access any record of his I needed. First, I wanted to know what he looked like so I would recognize him when I found him. Facebook proved to be a swing and a miss, but I found his profile on LinkedIn. Joanie told me Francis recently turned fifty-two. He looked a decade older. Loose skin hung from his slender face. I got the impression it was fuller up until recently. The suit he wore in his picture looked at least one size too big. The profile identified Francis—from Columbus, Ohio—as a senior manager in a large sales conglomerate I'd never heard of.

The combination of Francis' full name plus his date of birth made finding his Social Security number an exercise in simplicity. Armed with it, I gained access to his bank records in a matter of moments. Francis and Joanie did well for themselves, though their credit card history showed a bunch of frivolous charges. They'd struggled to get by for a while before making out much better starting about three years ago. Francis' LinkedIn profile told me he earned a promotion around the same time.

I pored over the Bakers' money situation for a few minutes. To my untrained eye, they looked like a middle-aged couple of good means. I'd hoped to find evidence Francis skimmed money from somewhere but saw nothing of the sort anywhere. He made four ATM withdrawals of three hundred dollars each earlier today—after Joanie said he disappeared. I punched up those ATM locations on a map. Did a criminal force him to withdraw over a thousand dollars? If so, I doubted I would find either the criminal or Francis, who may not have survived the encounter. I worked on locating his cell phone.

Cellular towers make finding people easy, and the phone companies make breaking into their towers easier than it should be. The Bakers' financials told me who provided their service, and a couple minutes later, I obtained Francis' current location as well as his movements for the last few hours. His phone hadn't moved from its current spot in Waikiki for about two hours. Before, Francis moved around the area after departing Ko Olina. I jotted down the address where his phone reported its location. "I may have found him," I said to Gloria.

"Already?" She looked up from her paperback.

"We'll see." I grabbed the rental car keys off the dresser and kissed her. "I'll be back."

"What if he's in trouble?"

"Then I'll get him out of it."

"You don't have your gun."

"If someone else has one, I'll borrow theirs." I gave her a smile I hoped conveyed confidence. The results were mixed.

CHAPTER 2

Waikiki Beach is a tourist trap. It's a strikingly beautiful one in spots, but it's earned its status nonetheless. Visitors from America, Japan, and the rest of the world crowded the streets and sidewalks and spilled out of the densely-packed shops and restaurants. Like most cities, Waikiki has its more upscale areas and its neighborhoods best avoided by civilized folks. Francis Baker's phone reported a location somewhere in between. I'd hoped to avoid the seedy part of the city. Despite my confident parting declaration to Gloria, I didn't relish the idea of walking into a potential gunfight unarmed. I still hoped to avoid it as I zeroed in on the prodigal husband.

I walked the block a few times, looked in every restaurant and shop at least thrice, and never saw him. The timing of my popping into the various places eliminated the possibility I had missed him in the bathroom. I checked my phone again. His location beaconed out as the restaurant and bar I currently occupied. I walked the entirety of the inside again —sans the ladies' room and other areas which would raise suspicion—and saw no signs of Francis. When I was about to leave, a door near me opened. I happened to glance at it, saw a set of stairs going down and heard enough noise to indicate a congregation of several people. I slipped through the door before it closed and went below.

The stairs ended at another door, this one locked. I knocked. A panel slid back and a set of eyes looked out at me. "Who are you?" said a deep male voice.

I didn't know the password, so I took out my badge and pressed it right to the opening. I took it away quickly. Letting the fellow on the other side of the door see I was not a police officer and traveled some seven thousand miles out of my jurisdiction struck me as a lousy idea. The guy on the other side grunted and slid the window shut. I heard two heavy locks disengage. The door swung into the room.

Cigar smoke was the first thing I noticed. I frowned and coughed as I entered the room. While I might enjoy an occasional cigar—especially with a nice glass of port—I did not relish walking into a basement of people smoking them. Casinos at least piped in fresh air. The room featured six large poker tables packed with players. Dealers shuffled up and dealt, and men the size of offensive linemen patrolled the room. "Someone refer you?" the guy who opened the door said. He looked like he could play on the line for the Ravens, and maybe even do a better job than some of the gents who currently toiled there.

"Yeah," I said, "he's at the far table."

"You want a seat . . . you gotta wait. And you gotta pay a higher seating fee."

"Why?"

"We don't like cops much."

"Me, either." He gave me a funny look. "Can I go say hi to my friend at least?"

The large man waved me off. I made my way across the smoky room. Rock music blended into the background noise.

A girl emerged from another door carrying a tray of drinks. Her skirt was short enough to allow everyone a peek at the bottom of her panties. She slinked across the floor, dropped off a drink, and collected both a tip and a pat on the ass. She didn't seem to mind either. I made my way over to Francis' table. He sat to the left of the dealer with an above average stack of chips. I stood across from him as the dealer shuffled, got his attention, and gave the universal "go over there and talk to me" head jerk.

I met him past the end of the table. "Who the hell are you?" he said.

"Your wife is concerned about you," I said.

"So? What's it to you?"

"She called the police. They couldn't help her because you haven't been gone long enough. She was crying. I offered to help."

"How'd you find me?"

"I'm really good at what I do."

"Sir?" the dealer called to us. The other players at the table all turned and stared at Francis and me.

"Fold me this hand," Francis said. He turned back to me. "So you found me. Good job. Now what?"

"Your wife is worried. I think she'd like you to go back to the hotel."

"I'm doing pretty well here."

"Cash game?"

"Yeah, why?"

"Your stack size could be from buying in big. Say with . . . twelve hundred dollars. If you were on a good streak, you wouldn't have folded your hand so quickly."

Francis stared at me. "How the hell do you know how much money I came here with?"

"Like I said, I'm really good at what I do."

"Yeah? Why don't you do it somewhere else?" Francis snapped his fingers at the guy who let me into the room. "Get this asshole outta here, will you?" He dismissed me and returned to his seat.

"Let's go," the big guy said.

I'd done what I said I would do: I found Francis Baker. If he wanted to toss his wife aside for a poker game, I doubted an impassioned speech from me would sway him. I nodded at the lineman. "Is he really your friend?" he said.

"Maybe I don't know him as well as I thought," I said.

"I figured." The guy moved behind me and shoved me in the back. I staggered forward a couple of steps, stopped, and gathered myself. The room quieted. I turned around.

"Seriously?" I said. "I was about to leave."

"Not fast enough, pig." The lineman moved toward me. He threw a strong right. I stepped inside his reach, deflected the punch with my left forearm, and drove my right elbow into my large attacker's face. His eyes closed, and he stepped back. I did it again. This time I heard the satisfying crunch of his nose snapping. Blood poured over his mouth and chin. My large friend's compatriot noticed our scrum and moved toward us. I needed to wrap this up.

While my assailant struggled to see past the stars in his eyes, I gave him a strong right to the solar plexus and a chop on the side of the neck. Then I put one leg behind him, punched him in the stomach, and shoved him backward. He toppled over my leg and hit the cheap carpeting hard. Just in time for his friend to step close. "You might want to think twice about this," I said.

The straight left he threw at me expressed the sum of his thoughts. This guy was a little smaller and quicker than the first but not as strong. I blocked his first two punches, then sidestepped the third enough to put him in a wristlock. Like most people do, he struggled against it. I applied more pressure. "Your wrist bones can't take much more," I said. "Stop struggling. I'll walk out of here in peace with my friend over there if you do. Understand?"

The large man nodded. "Yeah, sure," he said past a wince.

I let him go. To his credit, his machismo didn't compel him to attack me again. I left with Francis Baker in tow a couple minutes later. The games already resumed.

* * *

"You HAD no right taking me outta there," Francis protested from the passenger's seat.

"I didn't force you to come with me," I said.

"You didn't? You beat the heck out of those two guys—"

"Technically, I only put the second guy in a wristlock."

"Whatever," he muttered. "What was I supposed to do then?"

I shrugged. "I didn't care either way. Your wife was worried. I told her I would find you. I found you. She could have come and collected you herself for all I care."

"She probably would have, too."

I got back onto the highway headed toward Ko Olina. While I understood the reason Hawaii had interstate highways, the signs still amused me. "I don't mean to pry, but what were you doing there, anyway?"

Francis stared out the window a few seconds before he answered. "I like playing poker. Hard to find a legal game. And I wanted to win money to buy Joanie a nice bracelet."

"You don't seem to be hurting for money."

"Big difference between investments and cash on hand. It's also a lot more fun to win the money than hand someone a fucking credit card. I figured I could turn my twelve hundred into at least three grand."

It would be an impressive profit, but possible in a no-limit cash game. Presuming Francis possessed the skill, of course. "Sounds like some serious winning."

"It woulda been."

We made it back to Ko Olina quickly. Gloria sat with Joanie in the lobby when Francis and I walked through the doors. She smiled and came to greet me. Joanie remained seated and scowled at her husband. I pulled Gloria toward the elevator as Francis grabbed a seat beside his wife. "I think we'll want to give them some space," I said as we got on the elevator.

"Where was he?"

"An illegal poker game."

"How'd you get him to come along?"

I smiled. "Don't you know my powers of persuasion by now?"

"That's why I'm asking."

"Fair. I flashed my badge to get in. Then—"

"You brought your badge?"

The elevator dinged, and the doors parted. Gloria and I walked down the hallway to our suite. "Force of habit," I said. "The place had two guards. They probably played football at Aloha Stadium. There . . . might have been an altercation."

Gloria shook her head as I opened the door, and we walked into the suite.

"So what happened?"

"Francis came with me. We didn't really disrupt the games much, but I still think I'm banned from the poker room for . . . probably forever."

"Did you have any interest in playing poker out here?"

"Thankfully not."

Gloria walked up to me and pressed her body against me. "Did you have any other more immediate plans?"

"Lots more vacation sex?"

"I like those plans," Gloria breathed onto my neck.

* * *

THE NEXT MORNING, I checked my messages. Once again, the persistent lady with the disturbed niece left me a long and rambling voicemail. I felt tempted to call her back and spout a string of uncharitable words. A year or two ago, I may have done it. Instead, I deleted the voicemail. She would end up leaving a bunch more anyway. I couldn't help her from Hawaii, so she'd need to wait for me to get home. By now, she probably stalked my office waiting for my return.

Gloria went shopping. I got my fill of it the previous day, so I stayed back in the suite. If our homebound flight ran low on fuel, the pilot could dump Gloria's luggage and enjoy a significant weight reduction. After running about four miles on the mean streets of Ko Olina, I showered and took breakfast at the resort's restaurant. Thirty minutes later, I was on the beach. After fifteen more minutes, I swam laps out to the breaker and back. Once I completed a dozen, I relaxed in the *chaise longue* again and watched with interest as girls in bikinis arrived. The life of a detective is rarely dull.

After a half-hour of lying out in the futile hopes of overcoming my European ancestry enough to tan, I went back inside. When I walked into the suite, Gloria had returned. A large box, wrapped with a bow, sat on the bed. Gloria herself lay next to the box, in a teddy perfectly highlighting every curve. She gave me a come-hither grin. "Did you think I'd forget your thirtieth birthday?"

"I held out hope," I said.

"You're an old man now."

"I'm in my prime."

Gloria put the box on the floor, reclined on the bed, and crooked her finger at me. "Show me."

So I did.

CHAPTER 3

AFTER WE FINISHED LUNCH, MY PARENTS CALLED. I GOT treated to my mother sniffing and tsking over the fact I dared celebrate my thirtieth birthday in Hawaii. Relations with my parents acquired an air of frostiness since the whole flap over my sister's death turning out to be a murder. We agreed to meet for dinner after I returned to the mainland. They would take me someplace fancy and expensive, which wouldn't melt all the frost, but it would help.

A little while later, my cousin Rich called. He worked as a detective the Baltimore Police Department, and his rise through the ranks of the BPD coincided with my career as a private investigator. I don't normally believe correlation means causation, but Rich—though he would be loath to admit it—saw his career greatly aided by mine. In balance, he'd shown me a lot about what it means to be a detective, something I would never admit to him. We got along most of the time, but we were still a distant kind of close. "Hello, favorite cousin," I said.

"You're damning with faint praise, considering the competition," said Rich.

"But it's praise nonetheless."

"Happy birthday. How does it feel to be thirty?"

"About the same as it felt to be twenty-nine," I said, "except the dread caught up to me."

Rich chuckled. He'd be turning thirty-seven in a few months. "You'll get used to it."

Gloria took away our glasses and busied herself in the kitchen. "Honestly," I said in a hushed voice, "I'm not sure how to feel about it. I know it's just a number, but it's a pretty significant one."

"Where did you think you'd be at thirty?"

"I don't know. Traveling the world. Having fun. Not working."

"Well, you're on vacation in Hawaii. I think you've come pretty close."

"You know what I mean," I said.

"I do. I remember how you were back then. It's much better to have you around like you are now."

"Really?"

"Yeah," Rich said. "You've grown up a lot. You're still careless and reckless, but you've matured since you've been working . . . and since you've been with Gloria."

"Wow." I paused. "I guess I never expected to hear something like this from you."

"Don't get used to it. You won't hear anything like it again until you're forty."

"Fair enough."

"You having fun out there?" he said.

"Pretty hard not to. We still have another week-plus. You should fly out and join us."

"Some of us actually have to work."

"Take vacation," I suggested.

"I'm actually working on something now. Otherwise, I probably would."

I didn't really want to talk shop with Rich—a feeling I was confident he shared—so I changed the subject. "What did you do for your thirtieth?"

"Hmm." Rich paused as if in thought. "Went drinking. I had been with the BPD a year or so by then. Some of my fellow cops took me out."

"Sounds nice."

"It was a hell of a lot better than my twenty-fifth. I spent it in Afghanistan."

"Despite the bad rep Baltimore has, I'm sure it's much better than Afghanistan."

"It is," Rich said, his voice acquiring the faraway tone of distraction. "Look, I need to go. We can do dinner when you get back. I won't take you to a place as nice as your parents will. Hope you don't mind."

"As long as we sit down and order from a menu, wherever will be fine."

"All right. Have fun out there. Happy birthday."

"Thanks, Rich." As he always does, Rich hung up on me without saying goodbye. On rare occasions, I got to turn the tables on him and hang up on him first. Today would not be one of those days. Maybe my reflexes were already slowing down in my dotage.

After I talked to Rich, Gloria insisted I open the large box next to her on the bed. Inside, I found a carry-on sized suitcase. It went well with the rest of my luggage, and—true to form for Gloria—sported a designer label. I doubted Ralph Lauren had much input on the design of the carry-on bearing his name. "Open it," she said as I inspected the suitcase. I unzipped it and looked inside. Gloria packed it with sweaters and shirts. "I figured you could use a wardrobe refresh this winter," she said with a smile. The garments were as designer as their container. I tried everything on. The garments fit like someone stitched them just for me. Gloria was a shopping ninja when it came to clothes.

"I guess I have a few older things to donate now," I said.

"Get rid of those young man's clothes in your closet," Gloria said with a wink.

"I'll remember this when you turn thirty."

"I still have almost two years."

I thought about it. Gloria and I knew each other going on two years. For a while, ours was a relationship of convenience. Neither wanted a commitment, but both wanted to have fun. Eventually, she confessed she loved me. I couldn't blame her. I told her I loved her, too, and we've been an official couple ever since. Would we still be together in another two years? Would she expect a ring if we were?

Were these the kinds of thoughts men harbored once they hit thirty?

"You OK?" Gloria said.

"Yeah," I said. "Just getting used to being thirty."

THE REMAINDER of our time in Hawaii passed without any incidents worth mentioning. We came back on another nonstop flight to the mainland at Dulles Airport outside of DC. Nonstop flights between Baltimore and Honolulu were impossible to find. We each watched a couple of movies on the journey before napping the rest of the way. When we landed, it was about noon local time. We collected our luggage, retrieved my Audi from long-term parking, and stuffed it with more bags than we brought upon departure. I almost needed an SUV just for Gloria's stuff.

My plan for the day was to stay awake until a normal bedtime. Gloria napped in the middle of the afternoon. To fight off the temptation of resting beside her, I decided to run around Federal Hill Park. I hadn't seen the familiar sights in a month. As much as I love running in Baltimore, the backgrounds in Waikiki and Ko Olina proved much more scenic. If I lived in Hawaii, I would be a marathoner.

When I got back, Gloria was awake and watching a sappy movie on TV. I couldn't tell if she looked sad from the film or tired from having to adjust to eastern time again. I took a shower, then came down and looked in the fridge. Before we left, I pitched most of my perishable items. My grocery situation is normally lacking, and today's was the worst it's ever been. I still owned a pantry, however, so I made some whole wheat pasta with sauce. The sauce would be boring without any meat or sausage in it, but at least it was lunch. Gloria joined me, and we chatted about being home.

After our meal, my phone rang. I looked at the number. It was the same one which plagued me in Hawaii. There is something to be said for persistence. In reality, there are many things to be said for it, and not all of them were kind. I spun a few of the more uncharitable ones through my head as I answered. "Hello?" I said, summoning my professionalism from its long retreat.

"You're a hard man to get a hold of," the woman on the other end said.

"I was on vacation as my voicemail told you about a hundred times." So much for professionalism. Sometimes, I wondered how I kept the clients I found.

"I wouldn't keep calling if it weren't important."

"Of course not."

"Can we meet at your office?"

I frowned. I didn't expect to dive back into work so soon. A day or two adjusting to being on my normal time zone would have been nice. Sensing my ambivalence, the woman continued. "I think any more delays would be bad for my niece."

At least a month passed. Her niece was probably dead. My professionalism reared its head again when I decided not to share this fact with her. In this age of easy information, she must know it already. "All right," I said. "I'll be there in a half-hour."

"Thanks," she said and hung up.

"I'm going back to work," I said to Gloria.

"Already?"

"Better than getting fifty more calls from this woman."

She nodded. "True. She certainly left enough messages while we were gone."

"I might as well hear what she has to say." I grabbed my keys and threw a jacket on. I looked at the two guns in shoulder holsters on my coat rack. My license would be valid again by now. I could carry a gun and not get in trouble for it. Did I need one to meet an annoyingly persistent woman at my office? I didn't know where the case would lead if I chose to accept it. I took off my coat and slipped the 9MM in its shoulder holster around my body. On a colder day, wearing a heavier coat, I would have gone for the .45. I hoped I wouldn't need either.

It is my custom to be late. I routinely feel I have plenty of time even when I don't, and I've always felt being prompt is overrated. The drive from my house in Federal Hill to my office in Canton was short, made longer only by traffic lights along the way. I sat in my office in the CareFirst building ten minutes early. I wondered if turning thirty would give me a new perspective on time and timeliness.

I hoped not.

Eight minutes later, I heard the elevator down the hall ding. Footsteps tracked along the corridor toward my office. I saw a woman walk through the outer door, then right through the inner door. If I were a more conventional detective, I would have a secretary and a waiting area. I had the room for both and the use for neither.

The woman was white and looked to be about forty, with blond hair graying at the temples and at the top of her head. She was slender without looking unhealthy. Her face would make people take a few years off her age. She sat in my guest chair without waiting to be invited.

"Welcome back," she said. Enough sarcasm dripped from her voice to stain the carpet.

"Thank you," I said, not taking the bait. "I needed some time away." I figured adding in my suspension would not help me land a client.

"I'm Madeline . . . Madeline Eager."

I offered my hand, and after a moment of indecision, Madeline shook it. "Nice to meet you, Madeline." I hoped I sounded sincere.

"Do you want to hear about my niece?"

"It's why we're here."

"She's a good kid. That's the first thing. She doesn't deserve what's happened to her."

"Why don't you tell me about it?"

"I don't know. Not all of it, at least. Her mother—my sister—is a mess. We've tried to get her cleaned up, but it never lasts for long."

"Drugs?"

Madeline nodded. "She just can't stay clean."

"What's your sister's name?"

"Karla. Karla Parsons. She was married at one point."

"Husband left her because of the drugs?" I asked.

"Yes."

"And I suppose she hasn't been the best parent?"

"I love my sister," Madeline said, "but she's a terrible parent. Libby would get money for things, and Madeline would use it to buy drugs. Libby would get nice gifts for Christmas or her birthday and same thing. The poor kid." She paused and shook her head. "It's tough to admit, but I've basically given up on my sister. I spent a lot to send her to rehab. It didn't work. I can't afford it again."

"Grandparents?"

"Our parents died a few years ago. Karla's ex's parents don't want to have anything to do with her. They live out west somewhere."

I nodded. "Tell me about Libby."

"She's fifteen. She's a good kid. I think she blocks my sister out most of the time and tries to live her life, you know? That's a lot for a kid to have to do."

"And you're worried she's missing?"

"I usually hear from her every few days. Sometimes she stays with me when Karla gets to be too much." Madeline's voice cracked. I pushed a box of tissues toward her. She took one and held it in her hand. "I think I've done more to raise that girl the last couple years than Karla has. Libby stayed with me while her mom was in rehab a few months ago. I've barely seen her since. Only heard from her a few times. That stopped about six weeks ago."

"What do you think happened?"

"I don't know. Karla doesn't know, either . . . not that I'd expect her to know, or care." Madeline dabbed at her eyes with the tissue. "I just want to find out. I hired a detective but could only afford a day. He didn't find anything. I've heard about you on the news, so I figured I'd ask you to help."

"Do you have a picture of Libby?" I said.

"Yes, from a few months ago."

"Good. Text it to me."

"You'll help me, then?" said Madeline.

"If I didn't, you'd keep calling me. This seems easier." I gave Madeline a small smile to soften the blow, even though I meant what I said.

She smiled in return. "I suppose it is."

"I have to warn you, though . . . if your niece really is missing, this might not have a happy ending."

"I know." Madeline dabbed at her eyes again. "I've seen enough movies and TV shows to understand that her odds of being found go down every day. I guess I hope she's not really missing. Or that she'll be easy to find if she is."

"I hope so too. I'll let you know what I find."

"Where are you going to start?"

"With your sister," I told her.

"Do you need her address?"

"I can find it."

"OK," she said. "Good luck with her. She didn't know shit when she talked to me. Maybe you'll have better luck."

"I doubt it, but I'll try to remain hopeful."

"Me too," Madeline said. "For my niece."

CHAPTER 4

KARLA PARSONS, NÉE EAGER, PROVED AS EASY TO FIND AS
anyone else. She possessed a spotty employment history
consistent with drug problems, and she hadn't worked in
almost a year. I ran a quick financial search and discovered
she collected disability. Unless drug abuse got reclassified,
there must've been some fraud at work. She lived in a mobile
home village off Pulaski Highway, near what used to be
Golden Ring Mall and is now a bunch of stores which almost
form an outdoor mall or two.

Because Karla didn't work, I didn't feel bad popping in
on her in the middle of the day. I drove the Caprice to the
mobile home park. The Audi would stick out way too much,
and besides, I liked the nicer car and wanted to keep it. I got
on the Beltway, took it to Pulaski Highway, and turned into
the community. No pink flamingoes greeted me from what
passed for people's yards. My disappointment was palpable.

I drove to the second street and found Karla Parsons'
home. A dilapidated car exuding disuse sat in the yard. I
parked near it. Trash and assorted detritus lay strewn about.
A few quick glances didn't reveal any syringes. Despite the
chill in the air, Karla kept a window open; I heard the TV

inside through it. I walked up to the slapdash door and knocked.

No response. I knocked again, louder and longer this time. An inarticulate voice grumbled something. Maybe I'd awakened Karla from a bender. I summoned my professionalism again. Drug addiction was a disease. I'd studied enough psychology and sociology in college to learn and believe it. Karla Parsons had her problems, and many were of her own making. Still, her daughter could be missing. I took a couple of deep breaths as I waited for the door to open.

A minute later, it swung toward me. Karla Parsons stared back. The information I uncovered said she was 37, but she'd done an awful lot of hard living in those years, and it all showed on her face. Her eyes were sunken and marked by crow's feet. The beginnings of wrinkles marred her cheeks. Her pale complexion reminded me of someone infirm for months. My first thought upon seeing Karla was she wouldn't make it to forty.

My second was she would be useless when it came to finding her daughter. I hoped I would be proven wrong on this count. Pessimism—more like realism, really—bled into my professionalism. "Who the hell are you?" Karla said.

I took another deep breath and showed her my badge and ID. "My name is C.T. Ferguson. I'm a private investigator."

"You got any drugs?"

I hadn't expected her question. "No," I managed to say.

"I didn't do nothing."

I didn't believe her for a second, but arguing with Karla at her door would not be productive. "No one said you did. I'm here about your daughter."

"Daughter?" Confusion clouded her eyes and pulled her brows into a frown. Great. Now I hoped she remembered having a child.

"Yes. Your daughter, Libby."

"Libby. Right." The clouds in Karla's eyes cleared somewhat. I figured some always remained.

"Can we talk about her? Maybe inside?"

"OK. Come on in."

She opened the door and I followed her. As disheveled as the outside of the mobile home looked, the interior managed to be worse. Clothes lay strewn about the floor and furniture. They smelled dirty, but it also could have been the prevailing aroma of Karla Parsons' home. Dirty dishes full of crusted ingredients threatened to spill out of the sink. Mold grew in a few containers badly needing to be thrown away. Three pizza boxes lay atop the counter. I had no interest in knowing their contents.

The kitchen led to the small living room. The furniture looked like Karla found it free at a curbside one day. She sat in a recliner I wouldn't have trusted to lay me down or sit me back up again. I pushed a few loose articles of clothes aside and sat on the cleanest section of the sofa I could find. I also made a mental note to take a bath in a tub full of hand sanitizer later.

"What do you wanna know?" Karla Parsons said.

"When did you see your daughter last?"

"I dunno. What's today?"

I looked at my watch. "December ninth."

"Hell, it's been a few months, then."

"A few months?"

"Yeah. She don't always stay here."

"Sounds like an understatement," I said.

"Why you interested in her, anyway?"

"Your sister Madeline is concerned about her." I should've mentioned this outside. Of course, if Karla resented Madeline for some reason, she may not have let me in.

"Madeline's a good lady," Karla said. She spent a few seconds nodding about it. I didn't need convincing. "She can be nosy, though. Libby ain't her problem."

"She's no one's *problem*," I said. "She's your daughter."

"Sometimes, I think she's better off without me."

I agreed with her unexpected bit of self-awareness but didn't say so for fear of piling on. Karla might still be a resource for me. I didn't need to burn the bridge, though incinerating her trailer might've been a mercy. "You said it's been a few months since you've seen Libby. Do you know where she might go?"

"No."

I paused, expecting a follow-up there, but none came. "Does she have any friends she might stay with?"

"I dunno. Libby didn't have a lot of friends. She never brought anyone over."

The reason why was not a mystery to any sane person. Again, I summoned my professionalism and bit the thought down. "Did she visit anyone, then? People she talked about, maybe a relative other than Madeline?"

"I ain't too close to my family. I doubt she'd be with any of them."

"What about your ex-husband's family?"

Karla shook her head hard enough to dislodge it from her shoulders. "She don't have nothing to do with them, and they don't have nothing to do with her."

I understood why, even though I wished the grandparents tried going around Karla rather than throwing up their hands. "So you have no idea where she is?"

"None," Karla said.

This woman would not win any mother-of-the-year awards. The lack of concern she showed for Libby surprised me. The woman couldn't express less care. The only time

Karla had even mentioned her daughter's name was to say Libby wasn't Madeline's problem. "She hasn't contacted you since you saw her last?"

"Ain't heard a word."

"You don't even know if she's alive," I said.

"I guess not."

I waited for some emotional acknowledgement, but this was a visit packed full with disappointments. "It doesn't seem to upset you."

"Ain't nothing I can do about it."

"I suppose not."

"That's all you need?"

"Unless you remembered something profound to tell me?"

"Nope," Karla said. "You got any drugs?"

"No."

"What the hell are you here for, then?"

"I've been wondering, myself," I said.

I GOT HOME, took off my clothes, and got in the shower. I resolved to have everything I wore to Karla Parson's mobile home dry cleaned, including my underwear and socks. Anything the cleaner refused to take would get tossed into the incinerator. The interior of the Caprice could also use a good detailing. I stood under a hot shower for about twenty minutes until I felt clean again. Once I got out, I put on fresh clothes and went back downstairs.

I called Madeline Eager. "Madeline, it's C.T. Ferguson."

"Oh! Do you have news already?"

"Not really, but I have a question. I visited your sister a little while ago."

Madeline sighed into the phone. "I'm sorry."

"So am I," I said. "She tells me she hasn't seen Libby in a few months and—"

"What?"

"It's what she said."

"Good grief. That's just like her. I love my sister, but she's done nothing except waste her life for years. Now she might have wasted Libby's too." Madeline's voice cracked again.

"I was wondering if you knew anyone Libby might stay with . . . any friends she talked about, another relative who might take her in?"

"I would have taken her in if she had asked," she said

"But is there someone else she could have gone to?"

"I don't think so. We're a small family. No one else is in the state."

"Could you try Karla's ex's family?" I said.

"They want as little to do with Karla as possible."

"And Libby?"

Madeline sighed again. "I think they've painted her with the same brush. It's a shame. Libby's a good kid. She's smart. She still has a chance." Madeline paused. I could hear quiet sobs through the phone. "Promise me you'll find her."

I didn't want to hear those words. They would create such an expectation in Madeline's mind. Then I would feel obligated to find Libby no matter what. I wanted to find her, but I also realized I might have to deliver some awful news to Madeline along the way. "I'll do my best," I said.

"That's all we can do," Madeline said.

* * *

LIBBY PARSONS HAD BEEN off the grid for at least a couple months. For an adult, I could buy it. For a fifteen year-old girl who came from a drug-addled mother, not so much. She must've been somewhere. Libby hadn't turned to friends or family as far as anyone knew. Problem: no one seemed to know if the girl had any friends, nor who they might have been. A quick search through Baltimore County's records showed Libby last attended Kenwood High School not far from where her mother lived. I could have called but preferred to do things like this in person. I took another drive to the Rosedale area. The school day wrapped up by the time I got there, but administrators would still be around.

I parked in the lot and walked into the school through the front doors. The main office sat to the immediate left. I strode in and approached the secretary, who offered me a small smile. She looked like a schoolmarm in her late forties and bore an uncanny resemblance to the secretary in my high school. "I'm looking for some information," I said, showing her my badge and ID. "It's about one of your students . . . or former students. Is there someone I could talk to?"

"Who is the student in question?" She even sounded like a schoolmarm. I half expected her to rap me across the knuckles with a ruler if I asked an intemperate question.

"Libby Parsons."

"Is Libby her given name?"

"I doubt it, but Parsons is."

The secretary frowned and conducted a search on her computer. Her desk was crowded without being messy. I couldn't see a nameplate on it. "Miss Parsons has not come to school in quite some time," she said after a moment.

"I figured she hadn't," I said. "Has she withdrawn or been expelled?"

"No. She just has a large number of unexcused absences. Her mother has been no help."

"To me, either. Is there someone I could talk to about her? A counselor, maybe?"

"I'll see if Mr. Kropp is still here." She made a phone call and talked to someone on the other end in a quiet voice. A moment later, she hung up. "Mr. Kropp is still in and would be happy to see you."

"Great. How do I get there?"

She blanched as if I suggested tarring and feathering the good Mr. Kropp. "He will meet you here and escort you to his office," the secretary said. "We can't have you simply roaming the halls."

"I could only class them up," I said.

She tsked at me and went back to her work. It felt almost like dealing with my mother. Mr. Kropp came to rescue me a minute later. I did not bid adieu to the secretary as I left, nor she me.

* * *

Mr. Kropp must have been seventy years old. He looked it and sounded like it, with thin leathery skin and a voice made gravelly through years of smoking. I could still smell faint traces of it in his office. He must have sensed my suspicion. "I quit six years ago," he said.

"Good for you," I said.

"George Kropp." He extended his hand. I shook it.

"C.T. Ferguson."

"Might I see your ID?" I showed him, and he scrutinized it over the top of his wire-framed glasses. "All right. What can I do for you?"

"I'm looking for anything I can find out about Libby Parsons."

"Did something happen to Libby?"

"Her mother . . . to no one's surprise . . . doesn't know where she is and hasn't for months. Her aunt is concerned about her and asked me to try and find her."

"I've heard of you," he said.

I shrugged. "I make the news sometimes. It keeps the business going."

Kropp leaned back in his chair and pushed his glasses up atop the crown of his head. "Libby is . . . a difficult girl. I tried to reach her. I know I'm an old man and all, but I've been doing this a long time." Kropp displayed his bachelor's and master's degrees, both in psychology, on the back wall of his office. The dates on both confirmed his statement. "I can reach most kids. There are always a few, though, you can't." I learned you couldn't reach some men from *Cool Hand Luke*. Teenagers were the same, according to Kropp.

"Did anyone else try?" I said.

"Sure. I sent her to talk to a colleague . . . a woman. I thought it might have been easier. Same result."

"She didn't want to talk about herself?"

"She didn't want to talk about anything, really. Students have to see their counselors at least once a semester . . . more often if something dictates it. It's usually routine. Libby kept all her appointments. She was even on time for them. But I never got her to say very much."

"You know she hasn't been to school in a couple months?"

"I do." Kropp nodded. "As her counselor, I hear all of those things."

"You don't seem surprised," I said.

"I guess I'm not. Even though she didn't talk to me, I knew Libby had a difficult life. Sometimes, the things kids don't say can tell you a lot. I heard her mother was a wreck."

"Definitely."

"All things considered, Libby was pretty well-adjusted. A little withdrawn, maybe even reticent, but nothing abnormal."

"Until she disappeared."

Kropp shook his head. "I wish I had something to offer you there."

"Maybe you do," I said, leaning forward in the chair. "Did she have any close friends here? Someone who might take her in if the situation at home got too bad?"

"I don't think so, no. The impression I got is she didn't talk much to anyone."

"It's only an impression."

"One formed from talking to her teachers and a few other students," said Kropp.

"Fair enough."

"Like I said, I wish I had something to offer you. Libby is a good girl. She's bright. She has potential. Someone really needs to reach her. I wish it could have been me. Hell, I wish it could have been any adult who works in this building."

"Well, I don't know if I can reach her, either, but I'm going to keep trying to find her."

"Good luck." We shook hands again.

"I think I'm going to need it," I said.

CHAPTER 5

ON MY DRIVE BACK TO FEDERAL HILL, I CALLED
Sergeant Gonzalez of the Baltimore County Police. I dealt
with the BCPD less often than their city brethren, but
Gonzalez impressed me as a good cop and a good man.
"What happened this time?" he said in greeting.
"Can't I call to see how this day in the life of a dedicated
public servant is going?"
"No."
"OK, you have me there. I'm trying to find a girl."
"Aren't we all?" he said.
"This one is fifteen and might be missing."
"What's the name?"
"Parsons," I said. "Libby Parsons."
"Doesn't ring a bell."
"Her mother is a druggie and hasn't seen the girl in a
couple months. She hasn't been to school this quarter, either.
I don't know what's happened to her."
"The mother hire you?"
"The aunt," I said.
"I'll check around and see if anyone knows anything.
Might take me a day or so."

"You know how to reach me."

"To my eternal consternation," Gonzalez said, then hung up.

He and Rich always did this. It must be taught in every police academy in the state.

* * *

To MAKE sure I covered all the bases on detectives who might hang up on me, I called Paul King of the Baltimore Police Department. King worked vice, so he knew a lot about drugs, prostitutes, and other fun conversation starters. "I was wondering if you'd ever come back from vacation," he said.

"I was tempted not to."

"No doubt. What can I do you for?"

"A girl named Libby Parsons. She's fifteen and missing from her shitty mother and equally shitty home in the county."

"You talked to someone in the county already?" he said.

"Sure did."

"And you think this girl might make her way to Baltimore?"

"No one seems to know where she is," I said. "Bad things could happen to her anywhere, but I think she's more likely to get swept up into something really bad in the city."

"Better not let the mayor hear you talking shit. It'll wipe out all the new ads."

"If I could be so successful. Those ads are terrible." I felt the mayor was, also, but elected not to derail the conversation.

"What do you think this girl might get involved in?" King said.

"Don't know. Her mother is a druggie, so I would start there. It gets worse."

"Name's not familiar, but I'll see if she turns up."

"Thanks," I said.

"Don't mention it." King hung up.

Definitely an academy thing.

* * *

When I got home, I heard Gloria milling about upstairs. She called down, but I couldn't hear her past what sounded like her hair dryer. Why would she be using a dryer at this hour with dinner plans to consider? I walked upstairs and into my bedroom. Gloria stood there in a purple gown working on her hair. She smiled at me in the mirror as I gaped at her. The first time I saw Gloria, about two years ago, she wore a red gown similar to this one. She managed to look even better now. "What's the occasion?"

Gloria turned the blower off and ran a brush through her chestnut locks. "Davenport's dinner. Didn't I tell you?"

"I don't think you did," I said.

"Oh. Well, surprise!" She smiled a lopsided grin at me.

"What's the occasion?" I repeated without hot air competition.

"Melinda's return. He's celebrating a victory for the Nightlight Foundation with a dinner tonight."

"The victory was mine, mostly at his expense, and certainly without his cooperation."

"That version of the story isn't going to make the press," she said.

"It should. It's the truth."

"He wants you there."

"Fuck him," I said. "I don't care what he wants."

Gloria frowned at me. "OK, *I* want you there. I know you don't like Davenport, but he took a chance on me by letting me be a fundraiser and advocate for his charity. I like paying that back."

"Does Melinda want me there?"

"I'm sure she does," Gloria said.

I sighed. "Fine. I'll go but only for you and Melinda. Tell your buddy Davenport he shouldn't try to get too chummy with me."

"I'm sure he won't." Gloria inserted a pair of amethyst earrings.

"I don't even have a suit that's recently been dry cleaned."

"Yes, you do. I picked up your blue pinstriped Armani today."

"When did I take it to the cleaners?" I said with a grin, knowing Gloria must have taken it.

"Around the same time I told you about the ball tonight."

"Very well-timed on my part."

"Indeed. You going to get ready? We need to leave in about twenty minutes."

"OK. You drive, though. I'll probably need a few drinks to make it through the evening."

* * *

I'D STARTED my second drink when Melinda Davenport tapped me on the shoulder. Before my license got suspended, and I whiled away those thirty days vacationing in Hawaii, I rescued Melinda from her life as a prostitute. After a major falling-out with her father, Melinda hit the streets and became Ruby. There were layers of psychological damage requiring years to peel back and repair. I suspected—and still do—Davenport knew exactly what happened to his daughter but didn't care. He took the opportunity to establish the Nightlight Foundation and try to bring hope to desperate families or something similar. The foundation did good work, but ever since I met Melinda and her father, I couldn't get past the cynicism in its founding.

"It's great to see you here!" Melinda said as she wrapped me in a hug and squeezed. "Thanks for coming."

"I wouldn't miss this," I said. Melinda wore a dark red dress—a ruby-colored one, I noticed—and put a white bow in her hair. She'd always been attractive, but her time off the streets helped her. She filled the dress out more than she might have six weeks ago. Her skin and eyes bore a glow undiminished by the seedy neighborhoods of Baltimore.

"How do I look?" she said.

"Like the belle of the ball."

"I know you and my father don't see eye-to-eye. I'm glad you put that aside for tonight."

"For tonight," I agreed.

"C.T., he's trying. He really is. I don't know that we'll ever have a normal relationship, but at least now we have the chance to have one again. He's hired me to work at his company, he's paying for me to go to therapy . . . it's good."

"Is this the part where I point out those are things he damn well should be doing?"

"You're probably right. We're in a pretty good place right now, though."

"Melinda, I'm very glad for you," I said. "Really, I am. You look great, and it sounds like you're getting your life in order. You know I'll always help you however I can." She smiled and nodded. "I'll put on a happy face and smile for the people and the cameras tonight. Only, don't expect me to send your father a Christmas card."

"For what it's worth, I don't think he's sending you one, either."

"It's just as well," I said.

A few minutes later, we took our seats, and the soirée began. Gloria and I sat with a few of the Nightlight Foundation's larger investors. They all knew Gloria and were very eager to meet the boyfriend she told them so much about. They found my career far more interesting than I did. "Have you ever shot anyone?" a middle-aged woman whose name I didn't care to catch asked me.

"Yes," I said.

"Oh." It shut her down. I understand people feel they need to ask the question for whatever ridiculous reasons. Maybe they never expect an answer in the affirmative. Gloria squeezed my hand under the table. The wait staff brought out salads packed with bright greens and reds. After the appetizer round, Vincent Davenport got to the podium. He turned what started as a small Baltimore bakery into a regional empire and national business. It made him a power broker in the city and a person whose bad side was best avoided.

I didn't care.

Davenport thanked everyone for coming and promised to introduce the star of the evening after dinner. He also assured us the Foundation's work would continue even after Melinda's rescue. "I want other families to experience what I did," he said. I liked the sentiment; I hoped he meant it.

After dinner—this time, with no chance to choose beforehand, I got stuck eating mediocre steak—Davenport took the podium again. The wait staff cleared everyone's dinner plates and served coffee as he talked. Davenport called Melinda up to the front. She received a well-deserved standing ovation from the crowd. Melinda and Davenport hugged, and the sincerity of it surprised me. Maybe Davenport really was committed to making his life work with his daughter again. If so, good for him.

"This happy reunion was made possible because of the tireless efforts of one person," Davenport said. "He's here tonight and I hope he'll join us up here. Please welcome my daughter's hero, local private investigator C.T. Ferguson." Applause rang throughout the room. I hadn't expected a summons to the podium. I looked at Gloria. She smiled at me and waved me onwards. I stood, buttoned my suit jacket, and joined the Davenports. Melinda and I hugged while a bunch of people took pictures. Davenport shook my hand and wore a genuine look of gratitude. Maybe he meant it. Maybe he was a good actor.

Either way, this turned out to be great press for me.

I don't like whoring myself to the media. When one has a free detective business, however, such whoring proves inevitable. This time, at least, Davenport had pimped me out. I was off the hook for this one.

We posed for a few pictures. I declined to make a speech or take questions. This evening should be Melinda's, and I would do my part to make sure it remained hers.

* * *

THE NEXT MORNING, I struggled to get up at 9:00 AM after a restless night. Readjusting to eastern time is not an immediate process. I'd set my alarm for 8:30, but it just didn't happen. A few snoozes later, I crawled from bed feeling semizombified. Gloria capitalized on me getting up by sprawling out and taking up most of the mattress. I smiled at her and at the way the sheet pulled up to reveal most of her shapely leg before I headed downstairs.

First order of business: make coffee. My grocery situation forced me to stop at the store last night, so some basics were on hand. A few minutes later, I flipped a pair of omelets, sprinkled pepper jack cheese and Old Bay seasoning on each, and let them finish cooking. Gloria would have joined me by now on most mornings, but she must have been sleeping off the time zone differential as well. When the omelets cooked through, I plated mine and left Gloria's in the skillet on an unused burner.

When I finished my breakfast and downed a second cup of coffee, I called the agency for child welfare in Baltimore County, then the city version of the same organization. Neither would release such information to a mere private investigator over the phone. More in-person talking would be in order. I felt like hacking their systems just to spite them but decided to go along to get along here. After brushing my teeth and putting on some clean clothes, I left the still-sleeping Gloria in bed and embarked on my day.

* * *

I WENT to Baltimore Child Protective Services first. Their records showed no Libby Parsons nor Libby Anyone. Next, I drove into Essex to visit the Baltimore County CPS. I walked into the building and received a visitor's pass from a security guard who asked his questions in a monotone and barely looked at me the entire time. And people wonder why social engineering works. I took my badge, asked him where I should report, and couldn't understand a syllable of what he mumbled at me. I figured pressing him would be useless, so I entered the building proper. How hard could it be to find one room?

It turned out to be a minor ordeal. Logical numbering broke down in various places throughout the halls. I have a master's degree and needed a map. I wondered how people without much education could come in here and avail themselves of Baltimore County government services. After a few minutes of wandering, I found the main room for CPS, opened the door, and walked inside.

A short hallway led to an open reception area. Past it, the corridor continued, lined with doors on either side. All were currently closed. The middle-aged lady with graying hair behind the desk took a swig from a coffee mug easily doubling as a bludgeon. She looked up at me and offered a smile I barely noticed. "Yes, sir?"

"I called earlier," I said, showing her my badge and ID. "I'm looking for any information I can find on Libby Parsons."

The secretary picked up the phone and pressed a speed dial button. After a moment, she said, "the man who asked about the Parsons girl is here . . . I'll tell him." She hung up. "Please have a seat, sir. The case agent will be with you shortly."

I sat in an uncomfortable guest chair and wondered when "case agent" became such a popular term. The magazines on the end table did a great job appealing to young children and twenty-year-old girls. I flipped through news headlines on my phone while I waited. A few minutes later, a woman who looked young enough to have earned her degree the previous week came out to greet me. "Mr. Ferguson?" she said. I stood. "I'm Jaime Lombard, the case agent."

"Nice to meet you," I said. Jaime Lombard might have reached 5'3" and weighed 100 pounds if she carried a brick in her purse. She looked lean and lithe as she led me down the hallway. I pegged her as a distance runner. We walked about halfway and then turned into an office on the left side. I sat in another uncomfortable guest chair. Jaime's didn't look any more comfortable than mine, but at least it sported arms.

Her desk was a rat's nest of folders, papers, and coffee cups. The cups had formed ring stains on some of the documents. I hoped they weren't official. "You're here about Libby Parsons?" Jaime said.

"Yes."

"Might I ask the nature of your inquiry?"

"You might, but you don't need to be so official." I flashed my best winning smile. She gave me a tentative one in return. I would need to improve her reaction before I left. "Her aunt hired me to try and find her." I showed Jaime my badge and ID.

"Libby's aunt thinks she's missing?"

"Isn't she?"

"Libby . . . has been a difficult child to deal with."

"So she has been in CPS?"

"For a while now, yes. You met her mother?"

"I did," I said. "She's a memorable lady."

"She certainly is."

"How did Libby end up in CPS?"

"She came in herself," Jaime told me.

"Really?"

"It's something we never see, but I can hardly blame her. One home visit, and I was convinced she should be anywhere but her mother's house."

"And the father's family wouldn't get involved?"

"I got the impression that the mother soured them on anything involving Libby. It's wrong, and it's unfortunate, but on some level, I understand."

"You said Libby has been difficult to deal with. What do

you mean?"

Jaime sighed. She looked at her overcrowded desk with resentment in her eyes. "She came in here on her own because she knew her home situation was a disaster. The problem is that she got used to dealing with her mother. She treats all of the foster families as if they're the same as Karla. It's not fair to them, and it's made her challenging to work with."

"You've been her case agent the whole time?" I asked.

"Yes."

"How long has she been in CPS?"

"About a year now," Jaime said.

I hadn't expected the duration. Madeline made it sound like the situation at Karla's house reached critical mass recently. I was now forced to wonder how involved Madeline had been with her sister and her niece. I couldn't blame her for wanting to scale back her involvement, of course. What took her so long to get involved if she were so concerned?

"From what you're saying, I gather she's been placed with a few different families."

"She has," Jaime confirmed with a nod. "Children who are difficult to place rarely stick with the first couple families we put them with. It's a sad reality."

"Do you know where she is now?"

"I know which family she's staying with, yes."

"Could you call them?" I said.

"You're concerned she's no longer there?"

"Her aunt is concerned, yes."

"OK, give me a moment."

Jaime punched up something on her computer and then left the room. I don't know why she needed privacy simply to call the family who may or may not have been housing Libby Parsons, but she did. I sat in the guest chair and admired the chaos of Jaime's desk. I kept mine clean—a lot of this was through not working hard, but I also hated the clutter of a busy desk. A minute later, Jaime came back into her office. Some of the color had drained from her face. She walked past me and plopped into her chair.

"She's gone," Jaime said.

CHAPTER 6

"Tell me what happened," I said.

Jaime sat at her desk. She stared in the direction of her monitor, but her eyes didn't focus on anything. I let her sit this way for a minute before waving my hand in front of her face. "Jaime?"

"Huh?" She shook her head. "Sorry. It's just . . . I've never lost a child before."

"And I'll do my damnedest to make sure you haven't lost her for long. To do it, I need to know more." I gave Jaime a moment to collect herself. "Tell me what happened."

"The family she was with . . . they tried to get through to her. They did their best. They've fostered kids before . . . even tough ones. They couldn't get through to Libby, couldn't get her to listen or respect them. That's become the common theme with her. She simply doesn't listen or doesn't seem to care. Then she's gone." Jaime paused and shook her head. "Now she's *really* gone."

"How long?"

"Over a week."

I did my best to hide my reaction. The timeframe meant

Libby could be anywhere in the world of her own free will or not. Or she could be dead. I'm sure Jaime understood the calculus, and I figured doing the math to be the source of her anxiety. I felt bad for Libby, her family, and Jaime, but I needed to press on. "It means there's still time to find her. Jaime, I need to know the family she was placed with. Probably the ones before them, too."

"Why?"

"I'll need to talk with as many as possible. There might be things in common . . . patterns which could emerge. Something I uncover could help me find her."

"I'm not sure I should give that to you."

I offered a gentle smile. "Jaime, I'm going to level with you. My background is in hacking. You can give me the information, or I can find it. I'll get it either way. If you give it to me, it'll take me less time to track down the families, and I'll have more to look for Libby."

Jaime stared at me for a few seconds, as if I'd told her my background was in cannibalism. She finally nodded and worked on her computer. About a minute later, her printer whirred to life and she handed me a warm document fresh off the laser press. "Those are the last three families we placed her with," she said. "You can see she didn't last too long with any of them. I'm not sure how useful any of that will be."

"It's more useful than not having it," I said. "I'll do my best to find her."

"Please keep me updated."

"I will."

"Thanks." Jaime gave me a weak smile. "Good luck."

"Now I know I'm going to need it."

* * *

I DIDN'T GET an answer from any of the numbers Jaime gave me. I left messages with all of them and hoped they would call me back. In the meantime, I popped in to a couple of homeless shelters to see if anyone there knew Libby. First, I checked the shelter closest to Karla's palatial mobile home. I showed Libby's picture Madeline sent me. No one there knew her. Next, I doubled back and found the closest temporary refuge to the Baltimore County offices. Another swing and miss. I stopped at another shelter and made it oh-for-three. I decided to stop before achieving the dreaded golden sombrero.

While smarting from my hat trick, I got a return call from the second-to-last family who took Libby in. They lived about fifteen minutes from where I happened to be and were willing to meet me at their home, so I drove there. I zipped around the Beltway, got off at Belair Road, and ended up parking in front of an upper middle-class house in Perry Hall. The residences all looked less than ten years old. Each had at least a one-car garage. The Sanders enjoyed room for two cars, a brick front, and a wraparound porch with a swing. Perry Hall sat nestled in a nice part of Baltimore County, with plenty of civilization nearby to keep anyone entertained. I wondered what compelled Libby to leave this house as I walked up the steps to the front door.

I rang the bell, and a large dog barked. Footsteps approached, and a man shushed the dog. He opened the door enough to peek out at me while keeping the dog at bay. "You're the investigator who called?"

"Yes, I am." I showed him my badge and ID.

"Come in. Come in. Don't mind Mercury. He doesn't bite. He's just loud."

Mercury was a gray-muzzled chocolate Labrador. He barked at me while also wagging his tail and trying to shove his snout into my crotch. Dogs are famous for their mixed messages. The pooch followed us into the living room. New furniture probably purchased along with the house greeted me. I noticed barely a speck of dust. Even the magazines were neat and straight atop the coffee table. Off-white walls yielded to gray carpet, and the furniture was differing shades of dark brown. I noticed crucifixes above both doorways in the living room.

"I'm Derek Sanders," the fortyish man who answered the door said. He extended his hand and I shook it. "My wife, Debbie."

"Hello," Debbie said from the sofa. She looked about the same age as Derek.

"Thanks for seeing me," I said.

"You're here about Libby?" Derek sat beside his wife.

"Yes." I took the loveseat opposite the sofa. Mercury, who quickly lost interest in my crotch, flopped down beside the couch. "Her aunt came to me recently. She's concerned about Libby."

"So are we," said Debbie. "That poor girl has problems."

"You've heard about her mother."

"Yes." Debbie shook her head. "I've never met that woman, and I hate her. God forgive me. Giving birth to someone might make you a mother, but it doesn't make you a mom."

"Has something happened to Libby?" Derek said.

"She's missing," I said. "She disappeared from the next house they put her in."

"The poor girl. We'll keep praying for her."

I thought about pointing out the lack of effectiveness this strategy displayed so far but bit my tongue. "I'm trying to get some insights into Libby," I said. "My hope is I can learn about her, maybe find some patterns to the way she acts and use the information to find her."

"Do you think it'll work?" Debbie said.

"Honestly? No, but it's better than the alternative."

"We'll tell you what we can. Libby seemed nice enough at first. A little distant and awkward, I guess, but it's a tough situation to be in when you're a kid. Especially a teenager. She didn't talk much at first, but we didn't think a lot of it."

"Have you taken in foster children before?" I said.

"Quite a few. We have a couple now, in fact. They're in school."

"Have you had any problems like Libby before?"

"Not really," Derek said, "at least, not to such a degree. When you get kids who are a little older, they're often withdrawn, a little distrustful. They're not usually outright resentful, though. Deep down, they want to be part of a loving family and a home, and they hope you're going to give it to them."

"Libby was resentful?"

"Yes. Not right away, but it didn't take very long. We fostered another child at the same time—Madison, and we still have her. Libby accused us of favoring Madison because she'd been here longer . . . or she looked more like us . . . or whatever reason she made up in the moment."

"Madison got to do some things Libby didn't," Debbie added. "She's also a year older and more mature. That makes a difference. Libby didn't see it that way. We were mean to her, we were holding her back, we didn't really want her here . . . you name it, she accused us of it at one point or another."

"It never got any better?" I asked.

"She had her good days here and there. In general, though, she didn't want to be here. She didn't respect us . . .

she even came out and told us that." Debbie smirked. "At least she was honest about it."

"Cold comfort, I imagine."

"Definitely."

"Is there anything she liked to do when she was here?" I said. "Maybe when she would storm off after an argument? Do you know of any places she liked to go?"

"Libby enjoyed parties," Derek said. "I think she enjoyed them too much. She was very trusting of kids her age, even older kids. Some she talked about were inappropriate for a girl her age, but she went anyway. We couldn't stop her."

"Inappropriate how?"

"Teenagers shouldn't have alcohol at a get-together. It leads to all sorts of bad things."

"So I should troll the high schools and ask who's having the cool parties this weekend?"

Debbie chuckled at me. "I don't think you'd get many responses."

"I hope not. Is there anything else she liked to do, or places she would go?"

"White Marsh Mall. All the kids go there."

I knew the mall. It was sprawling enough to miss someone even if you were looking for them. "Any particular store?"

"Clothes stores, I guess," Derek said. "Libby liked clothes. We figured it was because her mother would never buy her any."

I nodded. "Did Libby have any friends?"

"No one she was close to. She came here from the other side of the county. She might still have some friends over there."

"I've reached out to the last few families she's stayed with."

"God bless you, Mr. Ferguson," Debbie said. "You're doing good work."

I didn't put much stock in the blessings, but with the daunting task before me, I figured they couldn't hurt.

* * *

As I DROVE HOME, the last family Libby stayed with returned my call. I turned around and headed back into the county. They lived in Kingsville, which was a few miles past Perry Hall. If I charged by the mile—or at all—Madeline's bill would fund a nice steak. I got there in about fifteen minutes. Their house looked smaller than mine and sat nestled in a community of similar-looking homes. Parts of Baltimore looked like this, too, with those houses being built either in the 1800s or just after World War II. I placed the Venturas' home as being built in the 1960s.

I walked up a short walkway and a couple of steps. The doorbell dinged inside the house. No dog came running this time. A minute later, a short, paunchy man opened the door. "You're the detective?" he said.

"I am," I said, showing him my badge and ID. He bade me come inside, and I followed him into the living room. We passed an antique dining room table and a modern curio cabinet. The living room continued the modern motif. The furniture was dark and boxy in a way the designer probably intended as cutting edge but ended up looking cheap.

Once we were all situated on the discount-store furniture, the introductions began. "I'm Carl Ventura," the man said. His jowls shook when he talked. I pegged him for mid-forties, but his girth added a few years to his appearance and docked a few from his life expectancy. His wife had a medium build and carried it well. She looked a few years younger. "My wife, Margie." They both sported identical shades of blond hair. I wondered about the color code on the bottle.

"Thanks for getting back to me," I said.

The topic shifted to Libby quickly. "A difficult girl," Margie said. "I think she wanted to do the right things, but she didn't know how. Does that make sense?"

"Sort of," I said.

"I guess . . . she never had much of an example. She wanted to be a good kid. I believe that." Margie Ventura shook her head. "The damage was already done, though. Have you heard about Libby's mother?"

"Heard about her and met her."

"What was it like?" said Carl.

"A singular experience," I said, "and I hope it remains so."

"We tried to keep Libby in line," Margie said. "We tried being lenient with her and giving her space. We tried being strict with her. In the end, I think she just didn't know how to be a kid. It was like something in her experiences with her mom made her want to skip all the kid stuff and go on to being an adult."

The Sanders hadn't said anything along those lines. "What do you mean?"

"Well, she ran away a lot," Carl said. "She usually hung out with older kids—in some cases, eighteen and older."

"You think she was doing anything illegal?"

"I'm sure they were drinking and smoking. Most kids are resourceful enough to get alcohol or tobacco . . . or stronger stuff. Beyond that, I don't know."

"Where would she tend to go?"

"You think you could find her at one of her old haunts?"

"I think those are the only places I could look."

"It was a bunch of places," Margie said. She paused. "Although . . . she did end up in Cecil County a few times."

"Cecil County?" I said. It was a good forty-five minutes from Kingsville and across a choice of toll bridges over the Susquehanna River. Libby couldn't have ended up there by accident.

"Yeah. I guess she knew someone up there."

"It's kind of far away to know someone. Do you recall what part of Cecil County?"

"Port Deposit, I think."

"Did you pick her up from someone's house?"

"We did," Carl said. "A boy named Conrad. Hard to forget a name like Conrad. He was eighteen if he was a day. He might have been even older."

"You never saw his parents?"

"Conveniently enough, they were never around. They lived in a pretty big house. New construction."

"You think Libby is up there?" Margie said.

"It's worth looking into," I said. "Libby's case worker seemed surprised to find out she was gone. Did you report her missing?"

Carl nodded. "We called every time something happened with the girl. Even the times we found her again pretty quickly."

"Have you fostered any children since Libby?"

"She was enough for a while," Margie said. "We had a lot to deal with when it came to her. The county can't promise us a nice, sedate child unless we take an infant, and we don't want to do that."

"Will you keep us posted?" Carl said. "We feel responsible for Libby."

"It wasn't your fault," I said. "The family she stayed with before you reported a lot of the same things."

"I know. I guess we hoped we could turn her around. We took on a couple of challenging kids before and were always able to get them back on the right path. Something about Libby, though . . . we just couldn't reach her."

"Not everyone wants to be reached," I said. The Wisdom of Kropp.

CHAPTER 7

A FIRST NAME LIKE CONRAD AND A CITY—PORT DEPOSIT
in this case—is plenty of information for someone like me. In
under a minute, I learned the family in question via basic
research on my phone. The Milburns had some explaining to
do. Considering the role their son might have played in
Libby's disappearance, they held little incentive to talk to me
or anyone else. Instead, I took time in a coffee shop to do a bit
more research. Conrad's father, Conrad Sr., worked from
home as some sort of management consultant and life coach.
He would no doubt be an interesting fellow. Conrad's mother
Autumn stopped working years ago to raise the family's children. A housing boom swept through Cecil County a decade
or more ago, and the Milburns capitalized, turning a century-
old house into a large, modern one.

The drive through Harford County proved to be scenic. I
elected to take a back way across the Conowingo Dam,
featuring the hidden benefit of avoiding tolls on Route 40 or
I-95. Cellular signal faded in and out as I drove narrow roads
and what must have been horse or cow paths in the county's
recent past. Eventually, I made it to Rock Run Estates, which
sounded hoity-toity and looked nice but not high-level. I

consider myself an expert in all things hoity-toity, so I am qualified to make this judgment.

The Milburns lived at the end of their street, their house nestled at the top of a long and winding driveway lined by trees. My parents owned a long and winding driveway, too, theirs being superior on both counts. Still, I wondered what drove rich older people to have driveways like this. I snaked the Audi up there and parked it beside a pair of twin black Mercedes E-class sedans. I wondered which one young Conrad would inherit, or if he would be gifted with a new model so as not to appear a pauper to his friends—or more importantly, his parents' friends.

As I sat in the car a moment, I pondered how I would introduce myself to the Milburns. They could dismiss a private investigator. However, I carried a badge in an impressive, official-looking bifold. A quick flash of it, coupled with an introduction of myself as "Detective Ferguson" would give them a much harder time dismissing me. I practiced this bit of subterfuge once before. Rich found out, but under the circumstances, he didn't get upset.

Detective Ferguson, however, would not drive an Audi S4. I reversed my way back down the driveway, leaving the car about a half-block away in front of another house. I returned up the driveway on foot and rang the bell. A man of about fifty with every hair on his head and face perfectly coiffed answered the door. Someone coined the word *punchable* for fellows like this. "Yes?" he said.

I flashed the badge. "Detective Ferguson from Baltimore." Technically, I told the truth. If he inferred I worked in the BPD, so much the better.

"What can I do for you, Detective?"

"Are you Conrad Milburn?"

"Yes." The man shifted his weight from foot to foot. He did it often enough it threatened to make me uncomfortable. "I'm looking for a missing girl and was told she knew your son."

"Conrad didn't tell me one of his friends went missing."

I shrugged. "I didn't tell my parents everything when I was his age."

"Yes, well . . ." Milburn trailed off. I figured he wanted to make a crack about the way a typical detective would be dressed. My clothes, however, were at least the equal of his. If anything damaged the illusion of me as a proper detective, it was my wardrobe budget.

"May I come in?"

"Hm?" Milburn frowned and shook his head. I'd rattled him. "Yes, sure. Come on in. My son just got home a few minutes ago."

Milburn led me into the sitting room. His wife Autumn lounged on a white leather couch. She wore designer yoga pants and a Hilfiger T-shirt. The Milburns even loafed around in style. I felt no need to upgrade my Under Armour and Nike athletic wear, however. "I'll get our son," Conrad said. He walked past his wife, who sat up and studied me through weary eyes.

"Detective Ferguson, ma'am." I flashed the badge again. She didn't seem awake enough to focus on it, but why take any chances?

"What brings you up here?" Autumn Milburn said as she sat up on the sofa.

I sat in a matching white leather recliner. My body sank into it, and I felt luxury envelop me. A few minutes of sitting here, and I might be asleep, too. The elder and junior Conrads made sure I stayed awake by coming down the stairs. I tried to get a read on their expressions. The younger one looked annoyed, but he was at an age where his face might've frozen in the expression. The elder Milburn wore a small smile I took for satisfaction, but I couldn't place why he would feel this way.

"What's this all about?" the younger Milburn said as he joined his parents—sitting between them, of course—on the sofa.

"I'm looking into the disappearance of a girl named Libby Parsons," I said.

"I don't know who she is." Conrad Junior made it a point to look at anything in the room but me.

I grinned. "Conrad, I hope you're a better liar when you tell your teachers why you didn't do your homework." His mother wanted to say something, but I cut her off. "Let's start again. I'm Detective Ferguson from Baltimore. I'm looking into the disappearance of Libby Parsons." The lesser Conrad sat there and didn't say anything. His parents stared at him. "This is the part where you answer me," I said.

"Libby wasn't from Baltimore," Conrad said after a moment.

"I'm aware. However, we think she disappeared from Baltimore, so here I am. Now, with the geography lesson over, why don't you tell me how you knew her?"

"Who told you I knew her?"

I didn't say anything.

A minute of silence spurred Conrad to talk. "I don't know. Some friends would bring her around. She'd always manage to get a ride up here somehow."

"And what would she do up here?"

"You know . . . hang out."

"Your generation has done a lot of work to muddy the phrase, Conrad. Even more than mine. Still, I think it meant something different when I was eighteen." No objection or correction; Conrad must have been eighteen. "What exactly would Libby do in her excursions up here?"

"She came to parties."

"You have a lot of parties?" Both of Conrad's parents glared at him now. I wondered if they knew. They didn't strike me as the oblivious types, even though Margie Ventura recently told me she never saw them. Maybe they were aware of the festivities but didn't know there was a missing teenage girl who used to be involved.

Conrad shrugged. "Yeah, I guess."

"So you're the man."

"I guess."

"Is there drinking at these parties?" I said.

"Of course not," the elder Milburn answered. "My son isn't of drinking age yet."

"It's a good thing no one ever sampled booze before they turned twenty-one," I said.

"Yeah, OK, we had some booze," the son said.

"Conrad!" his mother said. I couldn't read her tone. I didn't hear any surprise in it. Was she upset he admitted to having underage drinkers at their house? If I really were a cop, I might know the legal liabilities involved.

"It's OK, ma'am. I'm not here to hassle Conrad for buying alcohol before his twenty-first birthday. What I'm after is more information on Libby. I want insight into her, maybe where she might have gone."

"I got nothing."

"When was the last time you saw her?"

"I dunno . . . about a month ago, I guess."

"Where did you see her?" I asked.

"Here."

"At a party."

"Yeah," he said.

"She's not eighteen yet. She's not even sixteen. Was she the youngest person at some of these parties?"

"I dunno. I didn't check IDs at the door."

"But you know how old your friends are."

"Sure," he admitted.

"They all at least sixteen?"

"Yeah."

"I wonder what happened to Libby at your parties, Conrad," I said.

"I dunno."

"Why did you allow her to come?"

"What do you mean?"

"She wasn't from around here, and she wasn't rich, so I'm going to guess she wasn't among your friends. Someone brought her here. It means someone had a reason for bringing her. I'm wondering what the reason was."

"I'm sure it was nothing sinister, Detective," Conrad Senior said.

"The girl is missing," I said. "I'm not ruling anything out at this point."

"This is a long way to come from Baltimore, isn't it?" The small smile returned to the elder Milburn's face.

"I get reimbursed for my gas."

Milburn chuckled. "What I mean is you've come here by yourself. If you're concerned something happened to the girl here, why not come with a county sheriff's deputy?"

"I can come back with one if you prefer," I said. "Can't guarantee they'll be willing to overlook the teenaged drinking, though."

"Conrad needs to tend to his schoolwork now, Detective."

"All right." I took another look at the younger Conrad. He again made a point of looking at anything in the room but my face. "I'm sure we'll talk again . . . maybe when you have less homework."

"I'll walk you out." I stood and let Conrad Milburn lead me back toward the front of the house. He opened the front door for me. Then he said, "Don't come back here and waste our time again."

"Mr. Milburn, I'll do whatever I have to do to find out what happened to Libby."

"I know people," Milburn said, narrowing his eyes at me.

"Did you just threaten me?"

"See you don't show yourself around here again."

"Did you say the same to Libby Parsons, too?" I asked.

Milburn slammed the door in my face.

CHAPTER 8

No sooner did I trudge back to Baltimore and pull onto the parking pad behind my house than my phone rang. It was King. "Turns out your girl is in the system," he said.

"For what?"

"Someone who looks an awful lot like her was busted for turning tricks a few months ago."

"You don't know if it was her?"

"She used a fake name, and we didn't get a hit on the prints."

"Figures," I said.

"It's not all. The same girl who looks a lot like the one you're trying to find got popped for meth."

"Hooking and drugs? So she was already into the double whammy."

"Sometimes it's pot, sometimes it's meth, but this shit happens to stupid young girls all the time."

I doubted all of them were stupid, but I didn't want to debate King while he fed me information. "You know the meth dealer?"

"I was hoping you'd ask," King said. "Real peach of a guy who goes by Blade."

"Am I looking for Wesley Snipes?" I asked.

"If he's playing a methed-out white guy, sure. This prick loves to beat women and kids. Be a real shame if his face ran into your fist a bunch of times."

"What if he tripped and fell down the stairs at least twice?"

"It'd break my heart."

"I'll do my best to leave you crestfallen, then."

"I knew I liked you for some reason," King said and hung up.

I looked forward to meeting Blade. I also looked forward to dinner. Blade would still be an asshole in about an hour.

* * *

GLORIA and I ordered Chinese delivery for dinner. I told her about the families I met, and we speculated over what might have happened to poor Libby Parsons. Gloria felt the case worker was negligent; I thought the accusation implied a deliberate lack of action and couldn't agree. There'd been some kind of communication breakdown between Jaime Lombard and the Venturas, and both bore some responsibility for it. Pointing fingers did not help me find Libby, however.

After dinner, I drove to my office. I try to do as little work as possible out of my house to enforce the separation between home and business, especially with Gloria around more these days. At the office, I got to work on figuring out who Blade was, other than a fellow with an unimaginative street name.

Accessing the BPD's network has always been easy for me. It probably would have been regardless, but in my cousin Rich's last days as a uniformed officer, he unwittingly gave me a look at his computer's IP and MAC addresses. Using these, I learned a lot about the BPD's network and have been able to tap into its resources ever since. This time, I used it to search for drug arrests and the name "Blade."

I got one result.

His birth certificate listed the miscreant as Bernard Jones, Jr. If my choices were Bernard, Bernie, and Blade, I think I would have opted to name myself after a knife, too. I sympathized and empathized with people who went by their initials or some invented nickname to escape the birth names inflicted on them by their parents. Bernie—the name I decided to call Mr. Jones when I met him—got himself popped for drugs twice with the second for operating a meth lab. He made bail, and now the system awaited his trial. Meanwhile, he was no doubt back to making meth and poisoning people again.

I found a couple of addresses for Bernie but didn't put much stock into them. He wouldn't use an address where the police once found him. I didn't ascribe a great deal of intelligence to Mr. Jones, but any criminal could figure out something so basic. I tried looking for Blade's known associates to see if he might be with any of them, but the BPD had none on record for him. Being tired and lacking any better options for the nonce, I called Mouse.

Mouse is a professional informant who has earned his nickname. He would distribute information to whomever paid him the most for it—within a few ethical lines he drew for himself. His profession forced him to walk a tightrope at times, but nothing ever stuck to Mouse. "You're keeping late hours," he said in greeting.

"With good reason," I said. "I'm trying to find a guy named Blade. Got popped for having a meth lab a few months back."

"If you're looking to score meth, I know a few people who can hook you up."

"Very comforting, Mouse," I said. "I'll keep it in mind if I ever want to lose my teeth. I need this guy for something he might be able to tell me."

"And he goes by Blade?" Mouse said.

"I already made a Wesley Snipes joke."

"I figured as much. OK . . . I'll call you when I have something."

"Thanks, Mouse," I said.

We hung up. I didn't have much else to do until Mouse called me, so I went back home.

* * *

MY PHONE RINGING and vibrating on the nightstand woke me. A quick glance at the screen showed me it just turned 6:00. Caller ID reported the offender to my (and Gloria's) slumber as Mouse. I answered the phone in a sleepy mumble.

"Sounds like I woke you," he said.

"Of course you woke me. We all can't keep your hours, Mouse."

"Information waits for no man."

"Why don't you put your slogan on a T-shirt?" I said. "Maybe I'll buy one at a more reasonable hour."

"I found your boy Blade."

"I never doubted your abilities. Only your phone tact."

"And I never doubt your ability to pay me," he said. "Don't we have a great relationship?" I hated the chipper tone of Mouse's voice. In a couple more hours, I might have appreciated it.

"Just tell me where to meet you," I grumbled.

"How about your office? I always wanted to see the place."

"Sure it's not too high-class for you?"

"They rented to you, so I figure it's safe," he said.

"Touché. Give me about forty-five minutes?"

"Jesus, make me wait. Fine. Forty-five it is." Mouse hung up. I set the phone down on the bed and peeked at Gloria. She stirred when it rang but now, barely two minutes later and in the face of a conversation, she'd fallen back asleep. Gloria possessed many talents I admired, but I always envied her ability to doze back off quickly no matter what. If the United States ever got invaded during the night, I didn't doubt Gloria's ability to sleep through the bombing runs. Shock and awe had nothing on my girlfriend.

I got out of bed, brushed my teeth, threw on yesterday's clothes, and went downstairs. I scarfed down a banana in the kitchen before heading out the door.

* * *

Forty minutes later, blessed vanilla latte in hand, I walked up to my office and unlocked it. I sat behind the desk, sipped my latte, and ate a pumpkin muffin. I was rarely early; I might as well savor it when it happened. The other denizens of my floor who keep respectable hours had not yet arrived, so I heard the elevator ding from down the hall. One set of light footsteps moved down the hall. Either Mouse or a woman in cross-trainers would walk through my door in a moment.

The informant stood maybe five-seven and weighed 140 pounds only with the aid of steel-toed shoes. He bore a thin, wispy mustache, brown hair, small eyes, and always dressed in gray. In a crowded room, he was the guy your eyes would pass over, and it worked to his advantage. Mouse glanced around, nodded at what he saw, skittered into my inner office, and sat in one of the guest chairs.

"Not bad," he said.

"I would hire a secretary, but then I'd feel compelled to work more."

"We can't have that."

"You found Blade?" I said, getting down to business at this beastly hour.

"Yeah. I figure you saw his police report." I nodded when Mouse paused. "Those addresses weren't worth shit. I knew they wouldn't be. Your boy's got a bit of a reputation, though, as someone who's handy with a knife. He's known for more than just being a small-time meth guy."

"Everyone needs a hobby," I said.

"I heard he's not to be taken lightly."

I smirked. "Mouse, it almost sounds like you're concerned."

"Well, if this bastard stabs you, I lose out on a good meal ticket."

"I get the feeling you do all right for yourself."

"It's a living," he said.

"So what do you have?"

He fished a folded piece of paper out of his right front pocket and slid it across the desk. "This is where he's holing up."

"He with anyone?" I asked.

"One other person. I didn't get the name. The other guy is into meth, too."

I took two folded hundreds out of my wallet and slid them across the desk. He pocketed the bills without pausing to look at or count them. "Pleasure doing business with you, as always," he said.

"Likewise," I said.

Mouse showed himself out. I unfolded the paper and looked at it. I recognized the street as being in Gardenville in northeast Baltimore. A couple of my cases took me into the area. I looked at my watch: six-fifty. I could get to Gardenville easily via the highway and Moravia Road. Should I expect a pair of methheads to be awake this early? If they were making meth, they probably did the bulk of their work at night and in the wee hours of the morning. No, I could drive to Gardenville later. I decided to go back home and catch up on my sleep.

* * *

I WOKE up a few minutes after nine, ran about four miles, showered, and ate a proper breakfast with Gloria. This, of course, meant I cooked the meal. I trusted Gloria to operate the coffee maker, the toaster, and nothing else. Sometimes, blackened bread forced me to consider revoking her toaster privileges. I scrambled some eggs and fried strips of turkey bacon while Gloria worked on a pair of wheat bagels—after I verified the darkness settings. I didn't want the smoke alarm to tell us the bagels were extra crispy.

"Did Mouse come through?" she said as we ate.

"I have an address," I said. "I'm going to check it out later today."

Gloria looked at her plate for a few seconds. "Do you think the girl is still alive?"

"I don't know."

"I want her to be."

"So do I." Even though the odds were against her remaining among the living, I wished the same for Libby.

"I know you're not a big Vincent Davenport fan," Gloria said, "but his charity does a lot of good work."

"I would never dispute it."

"When I hear about a girl like this, I wonder if Nightlight could have helped her or her family." Gloria pursed her lips and held her fork tightly.

"Working with this charity has really gotten to you," I said after watching her for a moment.

She nodded. "It has. It feels good to make a difference. I used to think it was crap when you told me, but it's true."

"I hope I'm in time to make a difference for Libby," I said.

"Me, too." Gloria let out a breath and went back to eating. She'd been a hedonist when we met. I still harbored those same tendencies in me then. We enjoyed a relationship devoted to fun for a while. Then I began to extract more meaning and satisfaction from my job, rather than seeing it as something my parents cornered me into doing. This rubbed off on Gloria, and over time, she kicked off a lot of her pleasure-seeking and replaced it with a genuine concern for people.

I smiled at Gloria and squeezed her hand. I would never be comfortable viewing myself as an inspiration, but I loved the changes Gloria made in her life. She squeezed my hand, too. We didn't need any words.

WHEN A MORE RESPECTABLE hour for methheads and potential dealers to be awake rolled around, I got into the Caprice and drove to Gardenville. I found their house easily enough. It sat on a street called Evanshire Avenue, across from a large field and a block from Hazelwood Elementary School. I wondered if Blade and his friend set up shop here because of the proximity to the school.

I parked the Caprice two houses down in front of a home

with no cars in the driveway, no lights on inside, and a yard which looked like it hadn't been maintained since the summer. Blade could have been sleeping in the tall grass and overgrown shrubbery, and I never would have noticed. I kept an eye on the building in question while also reading the news on my phone and sipping from a bottle of water.

After about a half-hour, someone came out the front door. I looked at Blade's picture. The fellow who exited must have been his roommate. He was short and dumpy, with stringy black hair even my barber couldn't have done much with. After checking the mailbox, the guy puttered around on the small porch before going back inside. Ten minutes later, he came out, dressed in a shabby, ill-fitting track suit. He closed the door behind himself and headed up the street, toward Gardenville Avenue, and made a right. I gave him five minutes, then got out of the Caprice.

I walked up to the corner and peered up Gardenville Avenue. The other guy was gone. I moved back to the house. Through the front window, I saw a light on farther inside. Nothing I heard or smelled struck me as unusual. I didn't even know if Blade was in there, let alone awake. If he were inside, vertical or not, the odds he would want to talk to me would be slim. I'd dealt with worse than a guy who carried a knife and gave himself a lame nickname.

Three stone steps led me to the porch. It held a small card table and a pair of weathered lawn chairs on it. An ash tray full of cigarette butts sat in the center of the table. I opened the storm door and looked at the lock and deadbolt. They were Schlages, and the scuffing and wear made them look old. I figured I could get past them both in about two minutes if Blade didn't answer. I used the knocker and rapped hard on the drab red wooden door.

After thirty seconds of hearing nothing, I did it again.

Another thirty second passed, so I rapped again, harder this time. Finally, I heard some unintelligible grunts coming from somewhere in the house. Over a minute passed before Bernard Jones, Jr., AKA Blade, opened the door. He was about my height, six-two, but slender and wiry, a physique aided by his meth habit. When his mouth opened, I noticed a few missing teeth and breath rancid enough to make a bloodhound faint. "Who are you?" he said.

I flashed the badge again. For sure, Blade saw a few up close in his day, but I hoped to catch him tired or annoyed—or both. He didn't pay it much mind, instead looking past me to the cars on the street. His bleary eyes focused on the Caprice two houses down. "The hell they send you in that old thing for?"

"No way to speak about a classic, Bernie," I said. "Can I come in?"

He frowned but backed up and let me inside. I almost wished he hadn't. The run-down interior—filled with old and smelly carpet, mismatched paint, and furniture for which immolation would have been a mercy—made me long for the porch again. "Name's Blade. I don't answer to Bernie."

"Wesley Snipes was Blade," I said. "You're not Wesley Snipes. You're Bernie."

"Did you come here to bust my balls?" He left the living room and retrieved a pack of cigarettes from the dining room table. I didn't follow him.

"No, I came to ask about a girl. Libby Parsons."

"Don't know her," he said right away.

"Sure you do."

"Oh, yeah? How do you know, smart guy?"

"Because most people will think about a name for a few seconds when they hear it. Only liars have an immediate denial ready."

"Yeah, well . . . I said I don't know her."

"And I've said you're a liar," I told him. "How do you propose we resolve this?"

"I don't know, but you ain't a cop." Bernie took a large hunting knife out of the back of his pants. He still stood at least twelve feet away. "So now what?"

"Now I stop pretending to be a cop." I drew the 9MM from under my coat. "Looks like you brought a knife to a gunfight, Bernie."

"You need a gun?"

"You need a knife?"

"Toss them down?" he proposed.

"You first," I said.

"Why?"

"Because you're a fucking criminal is why. Toss your knife into the kitchen, and I'll reholster my gun."

"You could just get it again."

"I'm not throwing it anywhere you could get your hands on it."

Bernie stood there and thought about it for a minute or so. I figured the fog of waking up had something to do with it, coupled with the fact his bulb didn't burn very brightly on a good day. After what passed for careful contemplation in the mind of Bernie, he gave the knife an overhand toss and I heard it land somewhere in the kitchen. I put my gun back in the holster and clasped it shut. "OK," I said. "Now we can talk about Libby."

Talking was not on Bernie's agenda, however. He let out a yell and charged. I ducked his wild haymaker while half-turning and shoved him in the back. I couldn't get much behind it, but he still went face-first into the wall. He pushed off of it and turned to me again. I presented my side to him and assumed a defensive stance. "Last chance to tell me about Libby," I said.

"Fuck off," Bernie said. He advanced once more with a couple more wild punches. He didn't use his hips enough. I blocked each, but it didn't deter him. Unless Bernie took a lot of exercise for a meth user, he would wear himself out with these haymakers before long. After another flurry or two, the punches slowed, and I heard my adversary breathing heavily. I blocked one more punch, then leaned back and planted a side kick into Bernie's stomach. He folded in half over my foot; without lowering it, I booted him in the face, which dropped him to the carpet.

"All I want is information about Libby," I said. "Make it easy on yourself."

Bernie rolled over to his stomach, wobbled to his feet, and glared at me. "I lied," he said.

"So you want to tell me you knew Libby?"

"No." He reached under the leg of his track suit and took out a smaller knife. I owned one like it. A three-inch blade, solid steel, very sharp. "I carry more than one pig-sticker, and you ain't got time to get your gun now." He came at me again. It was a while since I practiced defense against someone wielding a knife. I've never cared for it. One lucky swing, and the encounter can be over. I didn't plan on giving this asshole the opportunity to get lucky.

I grabbed his wrist with my left hand, his elbow with my right, and spun him away from me. Bernie staggered toward the dining room but recovered without falling over. He twirled the knife in his hand. "The hell with Wesley Snipes," he said. "You're gonna see why they call me Blade."

He stabbed at me again. As before, I grabbed his wrist, but this time I backed him into the closest wall. He tried to jab and slash me anyway but couldn't move the blade enough. I slid my grip closer to his palm and brought my right elbow down hard onto his wrist. Bernie maintained his grip on the handle. I did it again, harder this time. I heard something crack inside his wrist, and the knife fell from a hand which could no longer hold it. While Bernie winced, I used my right elbow to clobber him in the jaw. His head bounced off the drywall, and he sagged to the floor.

I slapped him across the face. "Don't pass out on me, Bernie," I said, "not until we talk about Libby."

"What about her?" Bernie's voice grew quiet. He clutched his wrist, tried to flex it, and obviously restrained himself from crying out.

"She's missing. I'm trying to find her. Sources say she would hang out with you."

"So? Nothing wrong with that."

"There is if you had sex with her," I said.

This time, Bernie grimaced, and not because of his wrist. "No, man, it wasn't like that. Libby wanted to get away. Bad shit at home, she said. She hung with us. I only gave her some meth."

"She hang out with anyone else?"

"Yeah," he said.

"Who?"

"I don't know, man. They were dudes who were around, you know. Looking for meth and shit. She let some of them fuck her." I shook my head. "They gave her some cash."

"Because money makes it OK to have sex with a fifteen-year-old girl?"

"She asked for it."

"She's a minor, you asshole," I said, punching him in the face to accentuate my point. "She's a girl who needed a friend, not a meth junkie and a bunch of guys violating her."

"People don't always get what they want."

For this comment, I gave Bernie a quick kick to the solar plexus. He gasped for a few seconds while I smiled in satisfaction. When he recovered his wind, I said, "You have any idea where she might be now?"

"No. None."

"Don't lie to me, Bernie. There are other bones in your wrist I could break."

"I ain't seen her!" he said, clutching his lower arm and staring at me with wide eyes. "It's been a while. She just stopped coming around."

"You know any other places she liked to go?"

"I heard her mention Cecil County. Some town up there. Port Something-or-other."

"Port Deposit."

"Yeah."

Maybe I needed to make another trip over the Susquehanna. "Thanks, Bernie," I said. "I hope your information helped." I started for the door.

"What am I supposed to do about my wrist?"

I turned around. "Honestly, I don't give a shit." I walked out.

CHAPTER 9

BERNIE DIDN'T SPILL MUCH NEW INFO, THOUGH HE confirmed my suspicion Libby Parsons had been taken advantage of sexually. While I could have lived without the affirmation, I needed to hope the knowledge would help me somewhere down the line. The way Bernie told it, trading sex for money (or meth) had been no big deal for Libby. It made me wonder if she toiled under a pimp. Libby impressed me as a very streetwise girl, but girls who got busted for turning tricks usually became involved with pimps.

My main problem was being no closer to finding Libby. Gloria asked me if I thought the girl would still be alive. She'd been on the streets and mostly off the grid for at least a month. Despite the streetwise impression she gave me, Libby remained a young girl in an environment not known for nurturing. The logical part of me said she was dead. Then the hopeful part of me buoyed by Madeline Eager's genuine concern for her niece told me Libby could still be alive.

On a lark, I called Melinda. She and I worked hard to get her off the streets and out of the life, but I couldn't think of anyone else who might be able to give me insights into Libby. Melinda was reluctant at first, which I understood, but said she would meet me at my office in an hour. I agreed. It wouldn't take me an hour to get there from Gardenville, but lacking anything else to do, I drove back into Canton.

I parked in the lot, went into the lobby, and took the elevator to the sixteenth floor. It stopped at my floor, I got out and made the usual right turn. I saw the unusual sight of three men standing in the hallway near the outer door to my office. They all stared at me. Behind me, the elevator doors closed, and it moved to another floor.

"Welcome back," the one closest to me said. All of them were about six feet tall and heavy. One classed up the joint by wearing a tie in the pattern of the confederate flag. I hoped I got the chance to choke him with it. The one who talked wore a denim jacket. The third man dressed casually for the occasion in a T-shirt and sweatpants.

"I already have a case," I said as I slowly walked forward and sized up the trio. "I usually don't take more than one at a time."

"We'd like you to drop the one you have." The same guy talked. He must have been the spokesman.

"And if I don't?"

"Then we persuade you."

"I'm difficult to persuade," I said.

All three of them smiled. "We're prepared."

I kept walking and made sure to look relaxed. If I tensed up and appeared ready to fight, they would, too. For now, they looked confident, stemming from their sizable numerical advantage. I needed to reduce it. My training both here and in Hong Kong always emphasized reducing superior numbers as quickly as possible. "I don't think there's any need for violence," I said. The gap between me and the spokesman closed to three paces. "I'm a reasonable man. You all seem reasonable."

"Exactly what we like to hear," he said.

I doubted his words. "Why don't we go into my office and chat?" I came to within one step of the talker. His posture didn't change. His advantage was three to one, and it was good enough for him. Instead of taking the last step up to him, I planted my left foot and booted him as hard as I could between the legs. His eyes threatened to pop out of his head as his upper body lurched forward. I grabbed him by his ratty hair and smashed him face-first into a doorknob on the right side of the hallway. The art agency owner would just have to forgive me.

As Denim Jacket slid down the door to the floor, the other two spread out and advanced. They were tensed and ready for a fight now. "Is it still too late to go inside and talk?" I asked. Captain Sweatpants moved in from my left. He tossed a couple of punches I blocked. Confederate Tie tried to get behind me. I stepped to the right and cut him off. From my left, Sweatpants struck at me again. I avoided it and gave him a hard shove into his friend. Confederate Tie stumbled backwards and fell over.

As my casually-dressed foe turned around, I cracked him in the face with my left elbow. Before he spun away, I drove my right knee up into his stomach. He doubled over, and I kicked him square in the side of the head, dropping him in the center of the hallway.

Confederate Tie smiled.

I wondered why until I felt my arms grabbed from behind. Either a fourth enforcer snuck up here, or Denim Jacket recovered enough to get back into the scrum. I pushed off with my legs and drove us rearward into the wall as the tie-clad assailant advanced. He stepped over his fallen comrade in the sweats. I snapped my head back and struck the man holding me flush in the face. He didn't let go.

Confederate Tie waded up and wound up for a big punch. I exhaled and clenched my abs, and it still hurt when his fist smashed into me. I couldn't let him do it again. He brought his other arm back.

I kicked him in the thigh. It wasn't hard, but it stopped him. I did it again. Then I pushed backward again, driving the man holding me into the wall. Tie Guy took a small step and readied another punch. I kicked him in the stomach. Then, instead of just putting my foot down, I drove it heel-first onto the foot of the man holding me. His grip loosened. I smashed my head into his face again. His grip slackened some more.

It proved enough for me to wrestle my left arm free. Tie Guy recovered and glared at me. He brought his fist back. I spun and felt the punch rock the man with his arms around me. He grunted in my ear and threatened to fall. I shook him free and spun again. Confederate Tie was ready, throwing a few quick punches. I blocked them all and countered with a short right to the nose. It didn't break, but the blow staggered him. I boxed his ears a couple of times, kneed him hard in the stomach, and gave him my best side kick flush in the face. The last one put him down.

The first foe I'd tangled with, the one who grabbed me from behind, got to his feet. His face was a mask of mixed anger and pain. First, the kick to the balls, then the face to the doorknob, then the various blows I hit him with while he pinned my arms, then the hard kidney punch from his friend. He'd be peeing blood for a week after this. "Last chance to walk away," I said.

"Fuck you," he said.

"Eloquent. Whatever they're paying you, it's not worth this."

"I finish my jobs." Denim Jacket came at me and tried to

grab me in a bear hug. He was consistent, at least. I ducked under the attempt and elbowed him in the back as he passed. This got him to cry out as he staggered forward. I must have hit the same spot his friend did.

"Walk away," I said again.

His answer came in the form of another punch. The blows he already took slowed him. I blunted his punch with ease. The next one came in even slower and weaker. I blocked his third one with force, sending his arm out wide, then followed with a couple of hard jabs to the stomach. He had no defense. I kept them coming. I finished him off with a hard right elbow followed by a strong heel kick. He staggered backwards and crumpled to the floor. I heard him struggle for breath.

Then his cheeks puffed out and he vomited blood into the hallway.

The elevator dinged behind me. Melinda stepped out, looked in our direction, and gasped. "You're early," I gave her the best smile I could summon under the circumstances. She started to talk, then only pointed behind me. "They were trying to convince me to stop searching for the girl." I looked back at all three splayed on the ground in varying stages of consciousness and injury. The guy I tangled with last vomited again. "They were unsuccessful."

"Is that guy going to be OK?" Melinda said.

"His friends can call nine-one-one if he's not. Let's find somewhere else to talk."

We got into the elevator and left the trio in the hallway. I shuddered to think of the cleaning bill I would get from the building management.

CHAPTER 10

WE WALKED A FEW BLOCKS TO PASTA MISTA OF CANTON.
The dining room was about half-full. I asked for as isolated a
table as we could have. The hostess smiled as she escorted us
to a cozy corner removed enough from nearby diners so we
shouldn't be overheard. My scuffles with Bernie and then the
three goons in the hallway made me hungry. The hour crept
past lunchtime. A late lunch/early dinner needed a good
word like "brunch." "Linner" simply didn't have any ring to
it, and "dunch" sounded like an insult.

Melinda shrugged out of her coat. She looked good. She'd
always been pretty with the potential for more, even though
years on the streets dulled the potential. Now with her life in
order, Melinda realized her full beauty. Her red hair regained
the luster her life under night lights sapped from it. She'd
gained a few pounds and judging by the way she filled out
her sweater and jeans, those pounds went to the exact right
places. Melinda wore little makeup and didn't really need to,
but the coloring in her face improved since she rebuilt her
life. If I didn't know she'd spent five years as a prostitute, I
never could've discerned it.

Melinda smiled at me. She must've known I'd been

checking her out. Women tended to have a sense for this, and women with Melinda's rough background probably honed the sense to a keen sharpness. A waitress who might've been pretty but looked plain compared to Melinda dropped off two waters and walked away while we examined the menus. When the waitress came back two minutes later, Melinda and I had decided to split an *Insalata Caprese* appetizer and a thin crust buffalo chicken pizza. Melinda kept her voice low. "Did you know those guys in the hallway?"

"I know their type," I said. "They usually get by on intimidation. If it doesn't work, they're used to ending a fight with one punch or two."

"Goons. Thugs."

"Guys who don't have any otherwise useful skills, so they hire on for what they're good at."

"I've seen a few in my day." Melinda flashed a self-deprecating smile.

"I've tangled with a few in my day, too," I said. "This was the first time I made one puke, though."

"That was gross," Melinda said, frowning. "I wish you didn't have to do things like that for your job."

I shrugged. "It's ugly sometimes, but I do good work at other times. I've come to like the job over the last couple years."

"They were trying to keep you from looking for that girl?"

"Yes."

"Do you know who sent them?" she asked.

"I have a couple ideas."

"What are you going to do about it?"

"I haven't decided yet," I said.

"You could call Rollins."

"If I need to, I will. He has a job, and it doesn't include *pro bono* help for me."

The waitress dropped off our appetizer. Slices of tomato alternated with fresh mozzarella on a platter, drizzled with olive oil and Italian spices. Melinda scooped a couple of mozzarella and tomato pairs onto her small plate, and I did the same. She placed her napkin in her lap and arranged her silverware exactly as Miss Manners would have suggested. Melinda's proper upbringing came out at times like these.

"Thanks for taking me here," Melinda said as we enjoyed the caprese. The fresh mozzarella really made the dish.

"I was overdue for lunch, anyway," I said.

"Do you think I might be able to help you find this girl?"

"Libby Parsons. I don't know. I'm kind of grasping at straws. No one has seen her for a while."

"My father's foundation might be able to help."

I pursed my lips and shook my head. "I'd rather keep your father out of it, at least for now."

"You don't trust him?"

"Not in the least. And I don't want to owe him anything."

"He's not as bad as you think."

I smiled. "Let's focus on Libby."

"All right. How can I help?"

"I'm kind of hesitant to ask you, honestly."

"That's sweet of you," she said, giving me a grin. "It is. I'm getting a handle on everything, though. Something like this could be good for me."

"As long as you're sure."

She nodded. "Hit me with your best shot."

"All right. Libby isn't yet sixteen. I know for a fact she's been away from the last foster family she stayed with for a couple months. During this time, she's fallen in with a meth dealer, traded sex for money and drugs, and probably got popped for turning tricks. The kicker is I don't know if she's even alive at this point."

"What does your gut tell you?"

I took another bite of the caprese and thought about it. "She's dead," I said after some honest thought and reflection.

"I hope she's not."

The waitress brought out pizza on a short tower, along with a metal serving spatula and two plates. She asked if we needed anything else. I ordered an unsweetened tea, Melinda a diet soda. The server returned with them in a moment. We waited for her to walk away again before resuming the conversation. I cast my eyes around the restaurant. No one sat any closer to us than before. "I'm going to operate under the assumption she's not until I learn otherwise." I used the spatula to deposit a slice on each of our plates, then added hot peppers to mine.

"The buffalo sauce won't be hot enough for you?" Melinda said.

"Probably not." The pizza itself radiated steam, however, so I let it cool.

"What if you discover the girl is dead?"

"Then I'll figure out who did it and make sure they pay for it," I said.

"I guess you want me to tell you how plausible her story is?"

"I already know parts of it are true. The meth dealer confessed some of it to me."

Melinda grimaced. "Under duress, I hope."

"You could say so."

"It's a story I've heard before, more than once."

"Does it ever end well?"

After taking a bite of the pizza, Melinda sucked air into her mouth and put the slice back down. After a moment, she said, "Not often."

"I'd guessed as much," I said. "OK, Libby is on the streets, in the county or the city. It probably doesn't matter which. She's going to need a place to sleep and eat. How would she get them?"

"You said she'd probably been busted for turning tricks?"

"A girl who looks like her has been."

"That's the obvious way to get what she needs. There are some other things she might try. The meth dealer could have had her selling some product for him."

"Do drug dealers often find places for their young charges to stay?" I said.

"I was never into drugs."

"Good. I didn't think you were, but you probably knew some girls who were."

"Yeah," Melinda said, looking down.

I filled the conversational gap by trying the pizza. It cooled to the point I could eat it. The buffalo sauce packed a good tangy heat. "We don't have to do this if it's dredging up too many bad memories."

She shook her head. "I'm OK. I want to help." Melinda took a deep breath.

"Who's helping you?"

"I have a therapist."

"Is it going well?" I said.

"Yeah." Melinda smiled. "I didn't want to do it at first. My father insisted, after everything that happened seven years ago. I'm glad he did."

"Good. I'm glad you're getting some expert care."

"You ever see a therapist?"

I nodded. "After my sister died. My parents insisted."

"Did it help?"

"Not really," I said. "I went a few times, thought the shrink was full of shit, and stopped going. I got back on track."

Melinda nibbled at some pizza. I gave her time. A few months ago, she'd been a hooker on the streets of Baltimore, turning tricks in seedy motels. Now she left the old life behind, reconciled with her father, and held a real job. She'd come a long way. I felt bad making her sift through her past, but I needed any insight I could gain into Libby's disappearance.

After a couple minutes of crust and contemplation, Melinda said, "Do you think Libby made her way into Baltimore?"

"It's likely," I said.

"So you want to know who might put an underage girl to work."

"Does it happen a lot?"

"More than you want to know."

I shook my head. "Who looks for the young girls?"

"I heard a few guys do," she said. "I ran into some underage girls here and there."

"You remember the names?"

She thought about it for a moment. "Ratbone was the one I heard about the most. My guess is he could be your guy."

I pondered whether a nickname of Ratbone was any better than Blade. Then I chided myself for thinking about such drivel. "Anyone else?"

"Weasel Boy is another," Melinda said after considering my question.

"Where do they get these street handles?"

"I stopped wondering."

At least she provided me two leads. "Can you think of anyone else?"

"Not offhand. I'll see if I can remember more later."

"OK. I have two to look into in the meantime."

"Be careful, C.T.," she said. "These guys are no pushovers. They're a lot harder than Shade was."

"I'll be careful."

"You going to look for them tonight?"

"Maybe," I said. "There's someone I want to talk to first."

"Gloria?"

"No," I said. "A pimp."

* * *

BEFORE I COULD CALL my favorite prostitute manager, I got a call from Mouse. "Working overtime?" I said.

"Only for you," said Mouse. "I think I have some more information."

"About the meth dealer? I already talked to him."

"No, about the girl you're looking for."

"I never told you about her," I said, frowning.

"I'm in the information business, C.T. People tell me things all the time."

"What kinds of things?"

"In her case, someone else she might have been with."

"How long ago?"

"I don't know," Mouse said.

"Here I thought you were in the information business," I said.

"Go find the guy and ask him."

"OK . . . what's he called."

"He goes by Donatello," Mouse said.

The name gave me pause. "Is he a Ninja Turtle?"

"No."

"Dead Italian sculptor?"

"He's a street artist."

I expected Mouse to elaborate. He must have figured I

knew what being a street artist meant. It could have been someone who drew roads for all I knew. "What the hell is a street artist?"

"Someone who lives on the street and draws for money."

"So this guy is homeless?"

"I don't know," he said. "Homeless implies you never have a steady place to sleep." I trusted Mouse's take there. "This Donatello could live somewhere and maybe prefers doing what he does to having a real job."

"I guess anything's possible. What do you know about this kid?"

"He's seventeen. Tall, mixed race, pretty slender, always wears a Tigers cap. He's usually seen around Fells Point, maybe into Little Italy and Harbor East."

"He might find someone to commission a real painting down there," I said.

"There's one other thing about him."

"What?"

"He's missing," Mouse said. "No one's seen him for weeks."

CHAPTER 11

Now I NEEDED TO MAKE A DECISION. I COULD EITHER talk to my contact in the pimping world, Romeo, and see if he could point me to either of the two fellows who may have worked as Libby's pimp, or I could try to find the missing Donatello. My first thought was to call Leonardo and the gang. If only things were so simple. If Donatello was also missing, I wondered if he found himself caught up in whatever ensnared Libby. Mouse said the boy was seventeen. Someone somewhere should have been worried about him.

I considered going to my office but didn't know if those three goons would still be littering the hallway. Even if they weren't, building management might be nosing around, and I preferred to avoid them at the moment. I headed home. My office there had been partially disassembled and moved for the proper one, but I could still do what I needed. I checked every couple minutes to make sure no one followed me, took a circuitous route, and pulled onto the parking pad behind my house.

Gloria greeted me as I entered the house. It amazed me how much I grew used to her being there and how much I missed her when she was gone. We chatted for a bit as I went into the remains of my office. "Now you think another kid might be missing?" she said.

"It's possible. Finding him would be a good thing unto itself, and I might be able to use him to find Libby."

"Who is he?"

"He goes by Donatello," I said. "I don't know his real name yet. He's some kind of street artist." I logged into my computer and set about getting onto the BPD's network.

"Donatello," Gloria said. "That name sounds familiar."

"You've probably heard it mentioned along with Michelangelo, Raphael, and Leonardo."

"Italian Renaissance painters?"

"The Ninja Turtles."

"Oh. I don't think I ever knew their names. They were silly."

"You just crushed my childhood with a single word," I said.

"Really?"

I grinned. "No. I was more into superheroes."

"Good luck finding that boy. I'll let you do your research." Gloria kissed me and walked out of the room. I watched her leave as I always did. The view would never get old.

After appreciating Gloria's sashay down the hallway, I got to work. Donatello fancied himself a street artist. Not everyone received such people with open arms and good cheer, meaning he might have been arrested for something like vagrancy at some point. I didn't expect the *nom de l'art* to be on his birth certificate, but he might've provided it to the cops, especially if he felt the charge was bullshit. I searched arrest records for Donatello and found nothing.

I broadened my inquiry, going back two years and searching for boys aged fifteen to seventeen who had been picked up for vagrancy and similar charges. It scored me a lot of hits. I would need a team to sift through them in time. Lacking such help, I devised a better way. I dumped the results into an Access database, which played well enough with the BPD's system. I made the assumption someone in Donatello's profession would have an artistic background. A query for art schools and schools known for their art programs turned the long list into a more manageable set of twenty-two names.

Now, I needed to make more assumptions. I presumed Donatello was something close to the lad's real name. Maybe he had been born Donald, or something else more boring also starting with D. My list of twenty-two names contained two starting with D: David and Donnell. I could make a further assumption Donnell Becker had become Donatello, but I had to eliminate David as a possibility. A quick call to his house, wherein I posed as a school administrator, found him to be home and not living on the streets or drawing on them or whatever a street artist did.

I called the phone number listed for Donnell, wondering as it rang if he just gave the cops a number to give them one. The man who answered turned out to be Donnell's uncle and legal guardian, and he confessed to being quite worried about his nephew. He agreed to meet me at the Starbucks on St. Paul Street, not far from Johns Hopkins University. We agreed on a half-hour. I did a little more research, then headed to my car.

* * *

JOHNS HOPKINS HAS AN IMPRESSIVE CAMPUS. I visited it when deciding which college to attend—eventually choosing Loyola—and went there a few times during my undergrad and graduate years. Beating the Blue Jays in lacrosse always felt great. The Starbucks on St. Paul offered a great view of a field open to the east, with buildings in the other three directions. It also sat less than a mile from the site of the former Memorial Stadium. Since the Orioles left it in 1991 and the Ravens in 1997, Memorial Stadium was razed in favor of senior apartments. A new baseball field had been constructed on the site in the last few years. I was too young to get attached to the old place, but I still liked the history it represented.

I got in line and ordered a sugar-free vanilla latte. Maybe it constituted a concession to turning thirty, but I'd been trying to limit my sugar intake. After getting my drink, I took a seat at a quiet table. The Hopkins crowd must have been busy studying tonight. A few minutes later, a middle-aged black man came in, ordered a beverage, and scanned the tables where only one other person sat. I raised my hand and waved; he came over and sat down without introduction or invitation. "You're the one who called me?" he said.

"I am."

"I'm Barry Sims." He extended a calloused hand and I shook it.

"How long has Donnell been with you?"

"I guess about three years."

I expected some elaboration there and didn't get any, so I rolled with it. "How did you come to be his guardian?"

"His mother, Tamika, is my sister. His father split when Donnell was a baby. My sister had him young. When he got older, she got hooked on crack."

"Where is she now?" I said.

"Hospital out of state. She was traveling somewhere, got all messed up, and never recovered."

"I'm sorry."

Sims shrugged. I could see the world-weariness in his gestures. Here was a man who had taken on too much. His hands painted him as a hard worker in a blue-collar job. His left showed no signs of ever having a wedding ring on its fourth finger. "Shit happens," he said.

"Is Tamika your only sibling?"

"Yep. It was either Donnell goes with me or into the foster system. I didn't want to see it happen to the boy. I've done the best I could with him."

"I'm not trying to say otherwise."

Sims sipped his coffee. My comment seemed to placate him. "You think you might know where Donnell is?"

"Maybe," I said. "I've heard he's working as a street artist in the Fells Point area."

"The hell is a street artist?"

"As far as I can gather, it's someone who's homeless and tries to make some kind of living as an illustrator."

"Donnell always had a talent for it." Sims shook his head. "Don't know why he'd want to be homeless, though. My house had plenty of room for him. I wasn't too strict with him."

"What happened before he left?"

It took Sims a minute to answer the question. He pondered it over a couple sips of his coffee and an equal number of sighs. I wondered if he'd talked to anyone about this before. "He just got hard to reach. I guess that's the best way of putting it." Emotion bled through Sims' voice in periodic cracks. "I never had no illusions I was the boy's father and neither did he, but he always listened to me. He knew I wanted what was best for him." Now I knew what drove Sims' emotion: the sense he failed. He'd been Donnell's last chance, and now his nephew lived on the streets. A situation like this would be tough for a no-nonsense blue-collar man to take.

"Did he ever mention a friend . . . a girl named Libby Parsons?"

"He talked about a couple girls here and there. Were they dating?"

"I don't know," I said. It seemed like a nice detail to acquire.

"Is the girl missing, too?"

I nodded. "Her aunt hired me to try and find her. Along the way, I stumbled upon Donnell. I'm hoping to find her by finding him."

"I wish I could tell you more. Donnell and me didn't talk much about his personal life. I told him he could come to me about anything. He just didn't want to share some things, and then he got . . ."

"Harder to reach."

"Yeah."

"Libby's guardians said the same thing about her."

"Guardians?" Sims asked.

"She was in the foster system. Her mother is a junkie and doesn't seem to notice or care her daughter is gone."

"I'm sorry to hear."

"Do you have a recent picture of Donnell?" I said.

"I'm sure I have one at home."

"Good. Can you send it to me?" I slid him a business card.

"I will."

"Thanks. I'll let you know if I find your nephew."

"Will you tell him to come home?"

"I'll tell him you want him to," I offered.

"I guess I'll take it," Sims said.

* * *

DONATELLO WOULD BE hard to find. For now, I decided to focus on someone who might be easier to locate: whoever served as Libby's pimp. Over a year ago, I worked a case bringing me into contact with a pimp named Romeo. Since then, I've used him as a contact whenever questions arose about the world of prostitution. This has happened far more often than I might've expected.

Romeo agreed to meet me in a half-hour. He eschewed Crazy John's, our usual meeting spot, much to my delight. Instead, he wanted to meet at Johnny Rocket's in the Light Street Pavilion in Harborplace. I drove down St. Paul Street, stayed on it as it became Light Street, and went past the Harbor back into Federal Hill. I parked on my own pad and walked across Federal Hill Park to the Harbor. It was one of my favorite walks in all of Baltimore. I entered the Light Street Pavilion three minutes late and got to Johnny Rockets two minutes after.

As I expected, Romeo and Tank were already there. They were both black men looking to be in their early thirties. Tank had the most apt nickname in the city. He stood about six-seven and was built like an M1 Abrams battlewagon. How he missed out on a football lineman's career to be a bodyguard for a pimp would remain a mystery to me. As he always does, Tank dominated the bench he sat on. Romeo, tall but about half the size of his bodyguard, occupied the opposite side. If I wanted to sit, I would have to share the bench with him. Having no other seating options, I plopped down next to Romeo. He frowned.

"You could always share with Tank," I suggested.

"Shit," said Romeo, "the skinniest girl I got ain't fitting there."

"Tank," I said with a nod. He bobbed his head in return. He didn't say much, and with Romeo around, he rarely needed to.

"We're hungry," Romeo said. "You're buying." He stood. I took out my platinum AmEx and handed it to him. He eyed it and smiled.

"I'll chase you down," I said.

"You want anything?"

"I'll take a chocolate shake." So much for watching my sugar.

Romeo stood in line to order at the counter. I didn't say anything, and Tank joined me in appreciating the silence. We watched a few people walk by. A minute later, Romeo came back. He dropped my card and a receipt onto the table in front of me. I glanced at the receipt before putting it in my pocket. I didn't know Johnny Rockets could be so expensive.

"What do you get out of this early dinner?" Romeo said.

"You mean besides your charming company?" I said.

"You ain't the type to make a social call."

"I'm looking for a girl. It's been a circuitous route so far." I told him about Libby's age, home situation, and the likelihood she turned tricks in exchange for money or meth.

"Pretty fucked up," Romeo said.

"Honestly, I don't think the girl is alive, but I owe it to her aunt to find out."

"You think someone was pimping her out?"

"I think it's possible. I got two names: Ratbone and Weasel Boy."

Romeo looked at Tank and both shook their heads. "Those are some assholes," Romeo said. "I know what I do ain't legit, but I got rules, you know? I got standards . . . lines I won't cross. Those two don't have no lines."

"Which one is more likely to send an underage girl out there and give her meth?"

"Pick one," said Tank.

A Johnny Rockets staffer dropped off our food. Romeo and Tank each got a double cheeseburger and fries. Tank's order included onion rings and a shake. I swirled mine around in the cup some before taking a drink. Acceptable.

"It sounds like getting either of them off the streets would be a public service," I said.

"It would," said Romeo. He took a large bite of his cheeseburger while pondering something. "Tank, didn't Ratbone get popped a couple months back?"

Tank shrugged and eventually said something sounding like, "I think so" around a mouthful of food. His eating habits reminded me of Joey Trovato's.

"Depending on when this shit went down, I think Weasel Boy is probably your guy," Romeo said.

"You know where to find him?"

"His girls usually stick near Hopkins."

"The hospital?"

Romeo shook his head. "The college."

"I was near there earlier today," I said.

"They ain't out and about all the time. Sometimes, they get called to dorm rooms or parties."

"Low-end call girls?"

"More or less," he said.

"Who would call for a girl who isn't even sixteen?"

"The same kind of sick asshole who'd put her out there."

I took another drink of my shake. "Anything else I should know about Weasel Boy?"

"Yeah." Romeo chuckled. "He's pretty easy to spot, as far as pimps go around here."

"Why?" I asked.

"He's white."

*　*　*

AFTER BIDDING ADIEU to Romeo and Tank, I walked back
to my house, climbed into the Audi, and drove once more to
the Hopkins area. After a few minutes of frequent turns onto
one-way streets, I saw a woman whose attire didn't match the
chill in the air. I snagged the first spot I saw on the street. I
got out and leaned against the driver's side door as the girl
approached. She might have been eighteen. Flipping a coin
would be how I would guess.

I smiled at her as she approached. She showed me one
which almost seemed sincere but couldn't overcome the
world weariness already written on her young face. In
another reality, I would have said she was cute, maybe even
pretty, but the uncertainty of her age combined with the
certainty of what she did for a living removed any chance.
"Hey, cutie," she said. Despite the winter chill in the air, she
wore a tiny skirt revealing a lot of her bare legs and a coat
unbuttoned enough to make guessing her cup size academic.

"Hey, yourself," I said, realizing I possessed no knack for
chatting up a prostitute. This struck me as a good social skill
to lack.

"You looking to have some fun?"

"Pretty much always."

"You work at the college?"

"Sometimes. I'm a man of many parts."

Behind me, I heard two sets of footsteps. The girl glanced
over my shoulder. The almost-happiness on her face
vanished. "So where you wanna go?" she said.

"I don't know. I hadn't really thought about it yet."

"Well, you better get to thinking, man," someone from my

six o'clock said. I turned. The girl lined herself up behind me. Two white men approached. One, decked out in a gray fur coat, looked to be almost my height and of average build. A larger man probably six-four and close to three hundred pounds walked beside him.

"Who are you?" I said, playing ignorant.

"I'm the man telling you to decide." Weasel Boy did his best to sound black, but in the end, he couldn't even mimic Eminem.

"Then who's he?"

Weasel Boy smiled. I noticed two gold teeth. "He's the one who makes sure you decide quick. You wasting our time." He snapped his fingers and the larger man advanced.

"Get in the car," I whispered to the girl behind me. She didn't move. Her indecision could complicate things. I took a step to the left. She moved with me. This definitely complicated things.

The enforcer tried to grab my collar. I snagged his pinky and bent until it snapped. He pulled his hand back as if he burned it on a stove. It left him wide open. I planted a hard kick in his ample belly, which rocked him and bent him forward. Another hard kick took him in the solar plexus. He folded over and gasped for air. I drove my knee up into his face. His head snapped up, and he toppled over. I watched his skull bounce off the sidewalk. He didn't get up.

I looked at Weasel Boy, who stared down at his fallen goon in horror. "I think we need to have a conversation," I said.

Instead of staying to chat, he darted into the street and took off. "Get in the car," I said again to the girl as I ran after him. I'm not the fastest runner out there. I'm not going to win any 5K or 10K races. Weasel Boy shared my lack of blazing speed. However, I run about twenty miles in a typical week.

Weasel Boy did not. He slowed after about a hundred yards. I caught up to him, grabbed him by the rear collar of his stupid fur coat, and whipped him into a parked truck. He rebounded off of it and sagged forward. "Stay awake," I said, squatting to slap him hard across the face.

"Ow," he said. Panic filled his eyes but the impact with the truck tempered his ability to run. "What the hell, man?"

"I'll do worse if you don't answer my questions."

"You a cop?" I shook my head but didn't say anything. "What do you want to know?"

"Libby Parsons," I said.

"I . . . I don't know who she is."

I slapped him again, even harder. "Next time, I'm punching you in the nose. Maybe tasting your own blood will compel you to tell the truth."

"OK, OK, OK," he said, raising his hands to shield his face. "I know Libby."

"You pimped her out."

"She did some work for me."

"You know where she is now?"

"Hell, no," he said.

"Don't lie to me."

"I'm not! I'm not. I ain't seen her in a month at least."

"Where did you see her?" I said.

"Around here, you know? She was doing some work for me."

"And you paid her in meth."

"Some of the girls like that shit. Besides, it gives me a bigger cut."

I fought down the urge to put Weasel Boy's head through the side window of the truck. "Did you know how old she was?"

"I don't check IDs, man. If there's grass on the field, someone will want to play ball."

I shuddered. Putting his head through something hard and fragile grew more tempting by the second. Fragility optional. "What else can you tell me about Libby? Why did she stop working for you?"

"Just never came back. Shit happens sometimes. Girls move on, get strung out, whatever. It's the life. It's Baltimore."

"Was she strung out when you saw her last?"

"I don't know. I . . . I guess so."

"Any idea where she would go?" I said.

"No, man. No clue."

"All right." I stood, backed up a step, and held out my hand. Weasel Boy grinned, took my hand, and pulled himself up. Before he could thank me, I kneed him hard in the groin and slugged him in the stomach. I grabbed him by his hair and slammed his head into the side window of the truck. The glass cracked but didn't completely break. Weasel Boy's dome bounced off it, and he slumped to the street. Blood ran from his forehead and face.

"She was fifteen, you asshole," I said to his unconscious form as I walked back toward the Audi.

CHAPTER 12

AFTER ALERTING THE POLICE AND PARAMEDICS TO Weasel Boy's condition and location, I drove away with the maybe-eighteen prostitute in my passenger's seat. She looked at me with an expression I couldn't read. "Who are you?" she said.

"Someone who's trying to find a missing girl," I said.

"You think Weasel Boy knows her?"

"He did. If he'd seen her recently, I think he would've told me back there."

She fell silent. "Can I help?"

"Maybe. Have you seen a girl named Libby around?"

"I saw her a couple times. Can't say I knew her. She's the missing girl?"

I nodded and tried a hunch. Why the hell not? "You know anyone named Donatello?"

"The artist?"

"Yes," I said. "Not the Renaissance sculptor, though."

My comment drew a smile. "He's a sweet boy." She paused. "Do you think he knows where Libby is?"

"It's what I'm hoping. I have a general idea of where

Donatello is supposed to be. Could you recommend a way to find him?"

"He lingers around MICA," she said.

"Really?"

"Yeah. Something about not getting in. I don't know the story. But I've heard he's there some nights."

"Thanks." I'd driven back toward Federal Hill out of habit, but I had no idea where my young passenger needed to get out. I pulled over on Light Street. "What are you going to do?"

"What do you mean?" she said, avoiding my eyes.

"I mean, your pimp and his goon are bleeding on the street. They're headed to jail. Even if they get out tomorrow, you can't go back to them." She nodded. "Are you even eighteen?"

"In a few months." She sat up straighter and stuck her chest out. I didn't fall for it. "I look it, though, don't I?"

She did, but I decided not to encourage her. "You're still young. You seem like a smart girl. You're too good for this life."

"What else am I going to do?"

"What about your parents?"

"That's . . . a long story."

"It often is." I took out my smartphone to look up an address, then wrote it on the back of an old receipt. If it were from CVS, I could've added turn-by-turn directions. "This is the address for a foundation," I said, giving her the piece of paper. "Someone is supposed to be there around the clock."

"Will they help me?"

"They'll take care of you," I said. "You have cab or Uber money?"

She shook her head. "Weasel Boy said I hadn't earned my keep yet."

"The hell with him. He's got a concussion and maybe worse." I took a twenty and a business card out of my wallet and gave them to her. "Go to the Nightlight Foundation now. Tell them I sent you."

"Thanks," she said, giving me a sincere smile. "I don't even know your name."

"C.T. It's on the card."

"Nice to meet you, C.T." We shook hands. "I'm Katie."

"Good luck, Katie."

"What are you going to do?"

"I'm going to try and find Donatello," I said.

* * *

THE MARYLAND INSTITUTE COLLEGE OF ART isn't exactly next door to Little Italy, where I'd heard Donatello spent a bunch of his time. Walking between them would cover a distance of about two miles, definitely doable for a healthy teenage boy. I headed back up Light Street, took Calvert Street north, then cruised Mount Royal Avenue west to MICA. I didn't expect Donatello to be lurking in the doorways and, in fact, did not find him there. I started canvassing the streets.

People often complain about the number of one-way streets in Baltimore. You get used to them after a while. I've always liked the way they simplify traffic flow. I drove a slow circle of Mount Royal, Dolphin, John, and Lafayette. When this combo didn't turn up anything, I made a circuit of Mount Royal to Dolphin to John to Lanvale to Park to McMechen. On my second loop of the wider circumference, I saw a couple teenagers congregated near Mount Royal Elementary. The light hit them enough for me to get a good look at them. I called up the picture Barry Sims had sent me. One of the two boys was Donnell.

I pulled to the curb and got out of the Audi. They heard the car door slam and eyed me warily as I approached. Potential energy coursed through them: they could either bolt across the lot or charge me, depending on how the next several seconds went. I aimed for humility. This is not in my wheelhouse, so I did my best. "Donnell," I said, spreading my hands, "I need your help." I hoped this also showed them I was not a threat.

"Run, Donnell," the other teenager said. He charged me while Donnell took off. I ran after him, shoving the other boy aside as I did. Donnell had a head start on me and was the quicker runner. However, as the distance mounted, his lead ebbed. He was a sprinter. I didn't do a lot of top-speed effort, but I could dial it up when I needed to. I hung back a few paces as Donnell slowed.

"Donnell, stop," I said, grabbing his jacket at the collar and shoulder. He slowed and tried to shake and shimmy out of it; it presented me an opportunity to grab his upper arm. "Stop. You're not going to outrun me. I could do this for miles. How about you?"

Donnell turned around, breathing hard. "I don't know you, man. What do you want?"

"You go by Donatello, don't you?"

"You chased me down over my name?"

"No, but I want to be sure I have the right man."

"Yeah, I go by Donatello. What about it?"

"I need your help," I said.

"You a cop?"

"You see many cops drive Audis?"

He stood there catching his breath and shook his head.

Donnell looked past me, across the lot. "Guess not. What you need?"

"Libby Parsons."

His eyes shot to me and focused on my face. "Libby? Is she in trouble?"

"I think we need to talk."

* * *

WE SAT on a curb in the parking lot of Mount Royal Elementary. Donnell's friend left after his attempt to stop me proved futile. "What's happening with Libby?" Donnell said.

"I was hoping you could tell me."

"You looking for her?"

"Her aunt is worried about her. How much do you know about Libby?"

Donnell shrugged. "Only what she's told me."

"Her mother is a walking disaster," I said. Donnell's lack of reaction meant this did not surprise him. Good. "She apparently fled a bad situation and landed in a worse one. You aware she resorted to turning tricks at one point?"

"No." Donnell shook his head. "I mean . . . I had an idea. She started dressing a lot differently. Pretty soon, she looked like she was strung out sometimes."

"Her pimp paid her in meth on occasion."

"That's pretty messed up."

"About as messed up as letting a fifteen-year-old girl work as a prostitute."

"You seen this pimp?"

"I talked to him earlier," I said. "He might be awake by now."

"You beat his ass?" Donnell smiled.

"Someone needed to." We hit a lull in the conversation.

Donnell stared into the distance, like he expected someone to be coming. "How did you know Libby?" I said.

"Seen her around," he said. "We both hung out in the same areas."

"How often would you run into her?"

"A few times a week, usually." He smiled again, this time wistfully. "My boy said she liked me. I don't know . . . maybe she did."

"Have you seen her recently?"

"Not for a few weeks."

"Is this normal?"

"No. Even when she was . . . working for that dude, I'd see her at least once a week."

"Have you talked to anyone about her?"

Donnell looked at me. "Man, who am I gonna talk to? I live on the street. Libby lived on the street. Yeah, we're sad stories and all that shit, but no one actually does anything about it."

"I'm trying to do something about it," I said.

"Because someone asked you to."

"Right. Someone was concerned enough to look for a person they care about. Sometimes, it's all it takes. One person can start something."

He looked away again. "Maybe."

"What about your uncle?" I said.

"What about him?"

"I talked to him. He wants you to come home."

"Ain't nothing for me there," he muttered.

"There's an uncle who misses you."

Donnell fell silent. I waited him out. After a couple minutes, he said, "Is Libby still alive?"

"I don't know."

"What do you think?"

I took a deep breath before answering. "I think no one's seen her for weeks. I think the streets are a tough place to survive if you're an adult, let alone a teenage girl. Drugs make it even harder."

"So you think she's dead."

"If I'm forced to guess . . . I would say she is."

"So why you looking so hard?"

"Because there's a chance she might be alive," I said. "I've talked to people who cared about her. Her life mattered. Maybe it still does. Someone needs to find her if she's still out there."

"Big if."

"They usually are."

"Can I help?"

"You can tell me where she might have gone."

"I wish I knew," he said. "Even when I saw her pretty often, I never knew where she spent her nights."

"Do you have a recent picture of her?"

"Yeah. I'll text it to you." I gave Donnell my number. I wondered how he afforded a cell phone. He could have made enough as a street artist to afford a no-contract model. A decent smartphone made a respectable computer, and Donnell could use one to do a lot. He texted me the photo. Libby's smile stopped short of her eyes. She stared past the camera, looking for something she may have never found. She wore clothes I wouldn't want any teenage girl to wear.

"Did you talk to Libby on the days you didn't see her?" I said.

"Yeah," Donnell said, "sometimes we'd send messages back and forth."

I used a basic program I'd written for my phone to see if Donnell's Bluetooth was on. It was. He put his phone back into his pocket, but I connected to it and dumped his contacts and text history. Bluetooth represented an easy attack vector for any device supporting it. The whole process barely took ten seconds. I would go over the data dump at home. If Libby's cell were still in use, I might be able to use it to find her.

"You need anything else?" Donnell said.

"Not right now," I said. "Keep my number, though. If you think of something, hear from Libby, hear about her, whatever . . . let me know."

"I will, man. Good luck."

"I've been wished it a lot," I said.

WHEN I GOT HOME, I uploaded the contacts and text data I jacked from Donnell's phone to my computer. Sure enough, he had an entry for Libby. It contained four numbers. I presumed all were burners. The list gave no indication which numbers, if any, were still valid or which got added most recently. I turned to Donnell's text history.

His last text exchange with Libby occurred almost two months ago. After then, he sent a few texts which never got returned before giving up five weeks ago. I conducted some research on the last number he used for Libby. It belonged to a no-contract phone on the Virgin Mobile network. The account showed as active, meaning someone either funded the account in advance or made a payment within the last month. No cell towers reported anything approaching recent contact, however. When I called, it went right to an anonymous voice mail.

I didn't have Libby's cell. I might be able to clone her SIM card, but it would take time and maybe yield nothing. Instead, I poked around on Virgin Mobile to see if I could learn anything else about Libby's telephone life. I hunted, pecked, and hacked my way into a record of the texts and calls sent and received by her phone. Providers were required to store this data in case the government came along and demanded it. Sometimes, government regulations work out in your favor.

Any number Libby called or texted—or one reaching out to her—more than once went into a spreadsheet. When I finished compiling the list, I eliminated numbers like Madeline Eager's and Donnell's. Of the remaining ones, an initial search showed three belonged in Cecil County. None tried to contact Libby within the last few weeks. Here was another Cecil County connection, and the caller seemed to know when Libby wouldn't be reachable anymore, despite being a good distance away. This bore further investigating.

I remembered my conversations with the Milburn family. Maybe this time, going to the Cecil County Sheriff's Office first would be a good idea. I looked up the nearest location to Port Deposit. The sheriff's office had its headquarters in Elkton and a new community law enforcement center in Rising Sun. I put the address into my phone, got into the Audi, and headed for Cecil County again.

On the way, I called Rich, both to pass the time and because I hadn't heard much from him in a while. His phone went to voicemail, so I left a message telling him the high-level details of the case I caught and where it took me.

* * *

I ARRIVED at the Rising Sun Community Law Enforcement Center about forty-five minutes later. The building was new construction, probably less than a year old. The brick still displayed its red luster, and the glass still shone in the moonlight and headlights. I walked in and found a deputy at the front desk. His name badge said Johnson. He talked on the phone, and I looked around to avoid overhearing. When he hung up, I approached the desk. "Yes, sir?" Johnson said with a helpful smile.

"I'm looking for some information," I said, "and some help, I guess." I showed him my badge and ID.

"What can I do?"

"I'm trying to locate a missing girl. She lived in Baltimore County, spent a lot of time in the city, and I know she visited your county several times."

"You think she's still here?"

"I don't have a clue where she is," I said. "I'm turning over all the stones."

"I'll see what I can do. What's her name?"

"Libby Parsons." I spelled the names for him. "She's fifteen."

Johnson typed on a keyboard. "She's not in our system. Tell you what, though. There's a deputy downstairs who might be able to tell you more. He works a lot of cases like this with missing kids."

"Great. Who is he?"

"Deputy Connors." Johnson directed me downstairs, where I found a few desks and a half-dozen unoccupied holding cells. A tall, slender deputy sat at one of the desks. The nameplate read Connors.

"Deputy Johnson sent me down to see you," I said as I approached. I introduced myself, showed him my badge and ID, and told him why I'd come.

"Huh," he said, "the name sounds familiar."

"I've heard she spent some time up here."

"Did she disappear from here?" he asked.

"I'm not ruling anything out."

Connors pursed his lips. "Let me check something," he said, standing. I moved aside to let him pass, and he walked by. I heard something slide over leather. Before I could turn, something hard slammed into the back of my knee, sending me to the floor. I looked up and tried to muster a defense, but all I saw was a nightstick speeding toward my head.

CHAPTER 13

I NEVER LOST CONSCIOUSNESS, BUT I SPENT A FEW minutes wishing I had. When my faculties returned in full, I found myself inside one of the holding cells on an uncomfortable metal chair, my right wrist handcuffed to one of the bars. The door remained open. Connors sat on an identical chair a few feet in front of me. He wore a serious expression. I noticed the nightstick still in his hand. "I guess you really have heard of Libby," I said.

I regulated my breathing to keep my heart from racing. I felt it pumping in my chest. This crept back into Chinese prison territory. My mouth felt dry. Images of my jailers there, especially the sadistic Fan, flashed before my eyes. I fought down those memories and focused on the present. I occupied a cell in Cecil County, the prisoner of some dumb hick who took orders from a marginally smarter person.

"Can't have you nosing around," Connors said.

"Nosing around what?"

"Us."

"Who's us?"

Connors answered by getting out of his chair to surge forward, jamming the nightstick under my chin and bending

118 / TOM FOWLER

my neck back enough so my head touched the bars. This put me in a bind. I couldn't see Connors well, though I could infer where the body parts worth targeting were. The facts he stood over me, and I was tied to the metal meant I had no leverage. Any punch or kick I threw wouldn't have much behind it. It could inconvenience Connors enough for me to try something better, but I didn't want to take the chance now. I would need to wait for a better opening. Connors didn't strike me as a pro, so I figured he would give me a chance sooner or later. "Don't worry about who we are," Connors said, jamming the nightstick farther into my neck. "You can't touch us." He pulled the nightstick back and jabbed me in the stomach with it.

I took a minute to recover my breath. Then I said, "You're mighty tough when you have a nightstick and your opponent is handcuffed."

"Yeah?" Connors popped a stick of gum into his mouth. "What are you saying?"

"I'm saying put your toys away and take these cuffs off. Then we'll see who's tougher."

"You think you could take me?"

"You and any two of your asshole friends."

"Big talk for a man who's shackled to a chair," he said.

I rolled my eyes. "You're an amateur, Connors."

"Yeah? Why do you think so?"

"Because you're obviously keeping me here until someone else arrives. It means you're just a lackey. Lackeys don't scare me. I spent three weeks in a Chinese prison, Connors. I don't think you have what it takes to make me afraid."

Before my captor could answer, the radio on his chest crackled to life. Someone announced he was on his way down. Connors said, "Ten-four" into the radio and then looked at me. "We'll see how afraid you can get in a minute."

Another deputy walked through the door and into the room. He couldn't have been any taller than five-eight and was built like a bowling ball. He looked strong and solid despite his height. The new deputy stared at me the whole way as he walked into the cell. He kept staring at me as he entered and slugged me in the gut. I saw it coming and clenched my abs, but the punch still hurt. Breath eluded me for a few seconds.

"You been nosing around?" this deputy said. I looked at his name tag: Rakin.

"You been keeping a teenage girl prisoner?" I said.

Rakin and Connors looked at each other, then back at me. "This is gonna be fun," Rakin said. "Just not for you."

* * *

"WHAT DO YOU KNOW?" Rakin demanded. Connors sat in the chair. Rakin stood beside him. It made them about equal in height.

"I know you two are dumb assholes," I said.

Rakin shook his head. "We're taking it easy on you right now. Keep mouthing off, and it'll change."

"Libby Parsons is missing. I can deduce you two don't want me to find out much more."

"We don't."

"Your buddy there said I couldn't touch you."

"You can't," Rakin said with a confident smile.

"Then what does it matter what I know or find out?" I said.

"Gotta assess our threats."

"Am I a threat?"

"You could be."

"To what? To whom?"

"Never you mind," Rakin said. He started a slow walk toward me. "You're not a cop. You might know some cops, though. Means you might tell them."

I needed to act if they threatened me. Even partially immobilized, I liked my odds against a couple of overconfident blowhards. Their nightsticks made things more complicated. If I had to, I could use the chair I sat on for offense or defense. Rakin represented the bigger threat. Connors possessed more reach but not as much power. If I took Rakin out, Connors could lose his nerve.

Rakin's radio squawked. Someone was upstairs asking for him. "Can you stall them?" he said into the radio.

"It sounds urgent."

"All right," Rakin said. He looked at me. "I'll be up." He slapped me hard across the face. My cheek stung, but I didn't give him the satisfaction of showing any pain. He left the cell and walked out the door to go back upstairs. His departure left Connors alone with me. I wondered if he would have the nerve to try and rough me up while Rakin was gone. I figured he wouldn't. Rakin was the alpha on their team, and Connors would defer, even with Rakin out of the room.

"We're not going to let you talk," Connors said. He stayed in his chair.

"What are you going to do to stop me?"

He flashed me a grin. "Just wait and see." Definitely the beta.

I watched the door while putting together a plan for what I would do when Rakin came back. They didn't want me talking, but they also wanted to learn what I knew. Whoever they worked for would want to know what I knew. This meant they would need to keep me alive—at least for a while.

Rakin would take the lead. I would need to take him out. So far, I'd mouthed off but offered no real resistance. I hoped this gave me the element of surprise.

The next thing I knew, the door exploded into the room, falling off its hinges. Rakin rolled off it like the bowling ball he was and shook his head to clear cobwebs. Leon Sharpe strode in behind him. Connors frowned and inched out of the cell. Sharpe picked Rakin up by the back of the collar and dragged him along. When Connors approached, Sharpe put his other hand on the back of Rakin's pants and tossed him at the thinner man. He managed to get his hands up, but Rakin slammed into him, and both of them went down in a heap.

"C.T., you all right?" Sharpe said.

"I'm fine, Leon."

Rich followed. Behind Rich, Captain Casey Norton of the Maryland State Police walked in, leading the deputy from upstairs in handcuffs. "What are you all doing here?" I said.

Sharpe used his foot to push Rakin onto his back then stepped on the prone deputy's chest. "We're here to have a conversation," he said.

* * *

RICH UNLOCKED ME USING CONNORS' keys. We then herded my captors into the cell and cuffed them to the bars like Connors did to me. Sharpe pulled the door shut. We sat on the various edges of a nearby desk. "What are you guys doing here?" I said.

"Your voicemail to me," Rich said. "It's what sent us up here."

"I'm not used to such a rescue squad."

"Don't be," Sharpe said. "It so happens I assigned Rich to

a task force looking into a connection between Cecil County and rumors of pedophilia and child abduction."

"Wow," I said. "This is what I've stumbled onto?"

"Probably."

"Wouldn't it be a matter for the state, though?"

"It is," Norton said. "We're leading the task force, but I wanted opinions from other folks, too. Your cousin was a good fit."

"Even though Rich technically doesn't report to me," Sharpe added, "I knew he'd be excellent for this."

"And I might have suggested him," Norton said.

"OK, I get it," I said. "Rich is a rock star. Somehow, I wandered into the same thing you're investigating. Where do we stand?"

"We?" said Rich.

"Yes, we. After I got detained by the *Deliverance* cousins over there, you're cutting me in."

Rich looked at me. Sharpe nodded; Norton shrugged. "I hadn't learned much of a definitive nature yet," said Rich. "Tonight is basically a coup. Now I know the innuendo we thought existed really does, and some members of the county S-O are involved."

"I don't think they're at the top of the pyramid," I said.

"No?"

"The skinny one in there, Connors," I said, causing him to perk up. "He's a lackey. Definitely not management material. His friend Rakin is the alpha of their little pair, but he's not smart enough to be in charge of anything."

"Fuck you," Rakin said.

"Q-E-D," I said.

"We need to find out what they know," Rich said, lowering his voice.

"I doubt they'll tell us much," Sharpe said.

"Then we'll enjoy questioning them."

Sharpe grinned. "Normally, I wouldn't condone something like this, but these assholes let kids get raped and then probably fly the confederate flag on their pickup trucks. Fuck 'em." Sharpe unlocked and opened the cell door. He walked inside, pulled Rakin to his feet, and socked him in the midsection. The punch lifted the disgraced deputy off the floor before he crashed back onto the seat. The chair topped over and Rakin spilled awkwardly to the concrete, his handcuffed wrist preventing him from landing flat. Sharpe threw a punch like a steam piston. He was six-six, an easy 270 pounds, and knew how to use his hips to power a blow. I made a mental note never to be in a position where I had to fight him.

"You two need to start talking," Sharpe said.

Rakin coughed and struggled back onto his knees. He rearranged his chair and sat heavily in it. Sharpe stared at him. Rakin couldn't meet his gaze. The rest of us watched. I'd never seen this side of Sharpe, and I guessed the same for Rich and Norton. It was easy to look at Sharpe and see he carried the size and build to be a badass. I enjoyed seeing he possessed the demeanor for it as well.

"I'm normally a very calm man," Sharpe said. "I sit behind a desk most of the day. Sure, I get out in the field when I can, but most of my job happens in the office." He punched his fist into his palm and looked from Rakin to Connors. Connors' eyes threatened to pop from his head. I wondered how long it would take him to wet himself. "Any chance I get for exercise, I take it." Neither deputy said anything. This time, Sharpe lifted Connors out of the chair and jackhammered him in the stomach. Air evacuated his lungs with a huge groan as his chair toppled backwards and he fell along with it. As with Rakin, the handcuffs around his wrist prevented Connors from landing flat.

"I think we've seen enough to break Connors," I whispered to Rich and Norton.

"Really?" Rich said.

I nodded. "He's a lackey, not cut out for this. If he thinks Leon is going to hit him again, he'll piss all over the cell."

"It'd be funny," Norton said.

"You two want to give me some more exercise?" Sharpe said.

Rakin said nothing. Connors shook his head. "No, sir," came his raspy voice. Connors collected his chair and plopped down in it again. "No more exercise."

"Shut up, Connors," Rakin said. Sharpe slugged him again, sending him sprawling as far as his cuffed wrist would allow. He coughed and groaned.

Connors stared in horror. "It's true," he said. "There are people who like children."

Rakin tried to say something but couldn't put any words together past his wheezes and coughs.

"We need more, you skinny prick," Sharpe said.

"Sometimes, we helped."

"By 'we,' you mean deputies?" Connors nodded. "Sheriff know about this?"

"No, sir. He's not involved."

Sharpe leaned down and clamped his hands on the arms of Connors' chair. He got right in the deputy's face and stared. "Tell me again," he growled.

"The sheriff isn't involved. He doesn't know."

For a few seconds, Sharpe glowered at Connors. Then he nodded. "OK. I believe you."

Rakin's radio crackled to life. Someone summoned him upstairs. Sharpe grabbed the unit off Rakin's chest, pushed the button, and said, "Whoever you are, you'd better come down here."

Norton stood. Sharpe opened the cell, and they each unlocked one of the deputies. Rich and I tried to look busy. Another Cecil County deputy walked through the remains of the door, looking at the destruction with wide eyes. His hand rested on the butt of his holstered gun. Sharpe and Norton moved to the front. "Who the hell are you?" the newcomer said.

"Captain Casey Norton of the Maryland State Police. This is Captain Leon Sharpe, Baltimore Police."

"What are y'all doing all the way out here?"

"Looking into a ring of pedophiles," Norton said. "Who are you?"

"Deputy Hudson. I'm the shift commander."

"I think we need to talk," Sharpe said.

CHAPTER 14

Hudson herded us into an office about half the size of Sharpe's. He carried in another chair to accommodate four guests. I got the feeling a shift commander in Cecil County was not busy often and used his office to meet with people even less frequently. "OK, let's talk," Hudson said when we all arranged ourselves in the small space.

"I mentioned a ring of pedophiles," Norton said.

"Serious accusation. You have proof?" Hudson sounded defensive, but I would have too in his place. Any charge of pedophilia was serious. The mere assertion could taint lifes and ruin careers.

"We're working on it," Sharpe said. "Right now, I have a man liaising with some state cops." He nodded at Rich. "The task force is making progress."

"But you couldn't arrest anyone yet."

"Not yet. You know how these things go."

Hudson nodded, then looked at me. "How do you factor into all this?"

"I stumbled into it by accident," I said. "I'm trying to find a missing girl. She had some ties up here. I came to ask around and got accosted by Tweedledee and Tweedledum out there."

"We'll take care of them."

"I'm sure you will." I made a mental note to see if I could find out what fate befell Connors and Rakin. Deputies getting implicated in a pedophilia investigation would make the news.

"You don't trust me," Hudson said.

"Would you, in my place?" I said.

"Probably not. Look, whatever these guys are doing, I don't know about it. I'm sure the sheriff isn't aware."

"I wonder."

Hudson frowned. "What do you mean?"

"Connors and Rakin implied they were untouchable," I said. "They weren't worried about me sniffing around. It means they're part of something with somebody high up calling the shots."

"It's not the sheriff."

"You're convinced he's not involved," Rich said.

"I've known him since we were kids. One of the first cases he worked after he became a deputy was a bunch of kid touchers. If someone hadn't stopped him, I think those two guys would've been buried in buckets."

"People change," Rich said.

I disagreed, but Hudson answered for me. "Not to such a degree," he said. "It's not the sheriff."

"OK, let's accept your sheriff isn't the higher-up," I said. "Who else might be protecting men like Connors and Rakin?"

"Could be a lot of people. Might be someone under the sheriff. Could be some bigwig in the county."

"We'll find out who it is," Norton said. "In the meantime, I'd appreciate you keeping this as quiet as you can."

"I'll do my best," Hudson said, "but considering the circumstances, word's going to get out."

"Of course. But the less, the better."

"Like I said, I'll do my best."

"What about those two assholes?" Rich said, nodding toward the cells where Connors and Rakin sat and stewed.

"We'll deal with them."

"I mean, what can you tell us about them? Anything might tip us off to what they're involved in?"

"Something I won't read in their personnel files," Sharpe added.

"I don't think so." Hudson leaned back and stared at the ceiling. "They're not remarkable. I know you could interpret it a lot of ways. I probably mean it in all of them."

"So they're nothing special."

"For good or bad, no. Rakin's a bit of a hothead, I suppose."

"So I noticed," I said.

"Yeah. Sorry about that. Connors is . . ."

"Not management material," I said.

"Definitely not," Hudson said with a grin. "He does his job well enough, but we know he's not cut out for anything approaching leadership. So do his fellow deputies."

"They don't respect him?" Sharpe said.

Hudson thought for a moment. "They know he'll do a decent job, but they . . . understand his limitations."

"We're going to be poking around here a lot," Norton said. "After today, I'll need to talk to the sheriff."

"I'm sure he'll make time for you."

"I think it's best if we meet him alone," Norton said, looking at me.

I shrugged. They might not have pertinent information if not for me, but they also wouldn't have needed to reveal their task force so soon if I hadn't gotten imprisoned by Connors and Rakin. On the whole, I called it a wash. "Fine, but I'm staying involved. I have an interest in this, too."

"We'll keep you in the loop."

Like any good programmer, I planned to define the loop.

* * *

RICH, Sharpe, and Norton all left to talk to the sheriff. After the official party departed, I persuaded Hudson to let me talk to Connors and Rakin. It took a few minutes of chipping away, and I needed to overcome his objection to the whole thing being irregular. He put them in an interrogation room, cuffed to the table. I let them wait a few minutes and then walked in.

"The fuck are you doing here?" Rakin said. Connors studied the tabletop.

"Giving you two pieces of shit a chance to talk," I said. I sat in the open chair across from them.

"We're not saying nothing."

"Which means you must be saying something."

"What?"

"Double negative. Didn't you learn anything in school?" Rakin gaped cluelessly. "Don't answer."

"I'm not answering shit."

"You try to make it sound like you're untouchable."

Rakin flashed a wolfish grin. "We are."

I reached out and slapped Connors across the face. He recoiled and frowned as if I'd exposed his darkest secret. "I just touched Connors. Pretty sure I can touch you too."

"Now who's tough when someone's handcuffed?"

"I'll be glad to have Hudson uncuff you both," I said. "You two don't worry me." I looked at Connors, who busied himself looking at anything else. "But I'm pretty sure I worry at least one of you."

"Connors, don't you tell him anything!" Rakin said. If he could have reached across and grabbed Connors, he would have.

"What are the odds I could get him to talk?" I said, standing. Connors looked at me with wide eyes. "I don't hit as hard as Leon Sharpe, but I can make up the difference in volume."

"Please," Connors said.

"Hudson, you going to let this happen?" Rakin said. His raised voice betrayed some nervousness—probably over Connors and what he might say.

"I think he hates you almost as much as I do," I said. I grabbed Connor's hair and yanked his head back. His bottom lip quivered. How could anyone count on him in any kind of threatening situation?

Hudson opened the door. "You've gone far enough," he said. "You want to ask them questions, fine. Ask away. But no further. We're not the CIA."

"Pity," I said. I leaned a little closer to Connors. "One day soon, you'll be somewhere I can get to you," I said through clenched teeth. He shook his head. "Look over your shoulder."

"You're the one needs to look over your shoulder," Rakin said. I strode behind him, taking the long route around the table. He glared at me as I walked. I slapped him hard in the back of the head. His head snapped forward and nearly hit the table. Rakin grunted in pain, which made me happy.

"I want to press charges," Rakin said, shaking his head to clear the cobwebs. I'd given him a good shot.

"You're really pushing it," Hudson said.

Where was all this official concern when they used me for a punching bag? "Someone needs to," I said.

* * *

WHEN I GOT HOME, I told Gloria about my adventures in Cecil County.

"How repulsive," she said after I insisted I emerged no worse for wear. "Deputies shouldn't be involved in something like that."

"At least two are."

"You don't know who's protecting them?"

"No. Not yet, at least."

"What do you think is going to happen to them?"

"I hope they rot in prison for a while," I said.

Gloria pursed her lips. "Do you think they will?"

"Why not?"

"If someone is protecting them like you think," she said, "wouldn't they get released from jail pretty quickly?"

I hadn't thought about it. If those two were as untouchable as Rakin claimed, Gloria was right: they wouldn't spend a lot of time behind bars. I vowed to keep an eye on the situation. "Thanks," I said. "I didn't consider it."

"They'll make the news, though."

I nodded. "Accusations of being involved with a pedophile ring will make them look guilty to the public. I doubt they'll go back to their jobs anytime soon. Even if they're not in jail long, they'll be out on administrative leave, or whatever the sheriff's office up there calls it."

"It sounds better for everyone if they're taken off the job."

"No doubt."

"What are you going to do now?" Gloria said.

I pondered her question for a moment. Many detectives possessed a well-developed gut they would follow in situations like these. In any sense of the term, my gut was one of the least developed. I tended to pick at things until they came apart. Right now, I couldn't pick much at the Cecil County deputies. They were in jail where they belonged, and even if I got in to talk to them again, they wouldn't tell me anything. I needed to loop back to the original driver of the case: Libby Parsons. "I'm going to stick to Libby," I said. "The deputies basically confirmed she ended up in Cecil County at some point. I'm not going to find out much more about it right now. Maybe I can explore whatever situation drove her there."

"You're going to talk to her pimp?" said Gloria.

"I doubt he'd have much to say to me. He'll complain I put him in jail. I'll claim I put him in the ambulance, which he deserved, and the ambulance took him to jail." Gloria raised an eyebrow in my direction. "It's pedantic but true."

"Who are you going to talk to, then?"

"Weasel Boy stabled other girls. I'm going to find them."

"You've been talking to a lot of hookers recently," Gloria said. I knew she trusted me, but her point was valid.

"Professional hazard."

"Well, I guess they're better than people trying to kill you."

"I'm sure I'll run into them at some point, too."

"You're not giving me a good feeling here," said Gloria.

"Welcome to my world," I said.

HISTORY IS full of power vacuums. A leader gets deposed and someone else rises to fill the void. The results for the people are usually the same as they were before. Meet the new boss, same as the old boss. I had no idea how this principle applied to prostitutes and pimps, but I figured it was similar. One pimp is going to be very similar to the next one. I didn't know if anyone took over for Weasel Boy yet, but it wouldn't take me long to find out.

I parked near enough to the Hopkins campus so I could be conveniently located and still need to cover ground on foot. Spotting Weasel Boy's former girls wouldn't be enough —I needed to talk to them. I also hoped the ones I talked to didn't choose the same alternate compensation methods Libby had. If I were going to converse with prostitutes, I wanted them to be able to remember what happened a few months ago.

Streets near campus weren't crowded at this hour. I saw plenty of lights on in residence halls and houses. The buzz which would envelop me on the sidewalks of Fells Point or Federal Hill at this time was nowhere to be heard. I passed a few people, but they took no interest in me. I neared the end of my second sweep of the area when I finally spied something promising.

Weasel Boy's enforcer had tried to get me to make a quick decision, ending with his head bouncing off the pavement. I wondered if he got hauled off to jail with his boss, but he must've come to and gotten away before the cops rolled up. I saw him walking around with his hands stuffed in his pockets. He didn't look aggressive and didn't appear to be scanning around for anyone. By the time he noticed me, I'd closed to within a few paces of him. He stopped and glared.

"I'm not here for trouble," I said, putting my hands up. I wouldn't object if he decided to start something, of course. He worked for a terrible person, with full knowledge of what went on, and this made him a terrible person, too. If he thirsted for a rematch, I'd be happy to accommodate him.

"What do you want, then?" he said. He kept staring at me. I noticed discoloration and swelling around his eyes. The bruising wouldn't help his job prospects with whomever took over.

"The same thing I wanted the last time you saw me —information."

"You a cop?"

"No."

"You got money?"

"You charge the same rates as the girls?" I said.

"More."

"Then I want to know what I'm buying. I'm looking for one particular girl. No one's seen her for over a month. Her name is Libby."

He snorted. I realized I didn't know his name. "I never learned the girl's names. They come and go."

"You ever sample the merchandise?"

"Does it matter?" he said with a sneer.

I took it as a yes but didn't press the issue. Instead, I grabbed my phone and showed Weasel Boy's erstwhile enforcer a picture of Libby. "She look familiar?"

He squinted at the picture and shrugged. "I guess. I remember seeing her around."

"When was the last time you saw her?"

"I don't know. It's been a month or more."

"Anyone who might have seen her more recently?" I asked.

"You got money?"

I peeled a hundred from my money clip and handed it to him. "The girls make more than this," he grumbled.

"They're prettier than you," I said. "Probably chattier, too. You want more, you need to come up with better information."

"I could just take the rest of your bankroll."

"You're welcome to try. How did it work out for you the last time you assaulted me?"

He glared again. I shifted my weight and readied myself for an attack. Deliberation played out on his face. Eventually, he decided against it. I didn't relax until he unclenched his fists. Even though our first encounter was brief and favorable for yours truly, I preferred avoiding fights if I could help it.

"Some of the girls mighta seen her," he said.

"Anyone I should ask?"

"Katie."

"Already talked to her. She didn't know much."

"Try T.J."

"T.J.?" I said.

"Tami Jean, I think. Shit, I don't know. Half these girls are probably using stripper names."

"You were Weasel Boy's muscle, right?"

"Yeah, so?"

"So . . . shouldn't you have kept tabs on the girls, like Libby?"

"I can't be with them all the time. Don't want to, either."

I didn't have much argument with what he told me, at least in principle. When I tried to keep an eye on Melinda, I made sure to not be around when she took a john into a room.

"All right. Who's taking over for Weasel Boy?"

"Who said someone needs to?"

"I know he got arrested. And I know he's stupid, so he'll stay arrested."

"Maybe I'm gonna be the man."

I shook my head. "No, I don't think so."

"You don't think I could do it?" He balled his hands into fists again.

"I think you're better at being an enforcer than trying to manage a bunch of girls and keep tabs on them," I said in an effort to be diplomatic. "It's not an easy job, and you're a bigger target. I don't think you want it."

He frowned but unclenched his fists. "I guess you're right."

"I'll look for T.J. Can you describe her?"

"Tall, skinny, decent tits."

"Does she have hair?"

"Yeah. Yeah, blond."

"Anything she likes to wear or something to help me find her?"

"She'll be in a gray dress. Weasel Boy liked the girls to have something gray on. Said it was his color or some dumb shit. Some of the girls took it more seriously than others."

"All right, thanks." I half-turned to leave.

"That was good info," he said. "You got any more money?"

"Not for you," I said, "but you're welcome to try and make a withdrawal."

He walked away.

CHAPTER 15

AFTER A FEW MORE MINUTES OF WALKING AROUND, I found a girl who fit T.J.'s description. She had blonde hair, looked to be at last five-nine, and was slender to the point she needed to cram a week's worth of cheeseburgers into her next couple meals. Having no idea how old this girl was, I didn't verify the comment about her chest with more than a token glance. She smiled at me as I approached. The smile never reached her eyes. I wondered how many of her potential clients noticed and how many of them cared.

"You looking for a good time?" she said. The halfhearted smile found its match in enthusiasm which never entered her voice. It sounded like she recited lines she didn't like in a school play.

"Actually, I'm here for some information," I said.

Her eyes narrowed, and her lips turned to a sneer. "You a cop?"

"Do I really look like one?"

Her gaze raked me up and down. I still didn't know if this girl could vote, so I found it more than a little uncomfortable. "No, I guess not. Who are you?"

I showed her my badge and ID. "Libby's aunt hired me to try and find her. So far, I haven't had much luck."

"What happened to Libby?" The sneer yielded to a genuine look of concern. Maybe T.J. would have something useful to tell me.

"No one seems to know. I'm trying to find out."

"I liked Libby."

"I hope I can find more people who did."

T.J. frowned. "Tell you what. I'll find some other girls, and maybe we can help. You know where Zombie Coffee is?"

"I'll find it."

"Meet us there in a half-hour."

"I will."

"You got money?" She winced as she said it.

"If you need it."

Her expression didn't provide an answer. "A half-hour," she said.

* * *

THIRTY MINUTES LATER, I sat in the small Zombie Coffee shop. It offered a cheaper alternative to Starbucks with hours friendlier to college students cramming late at night. I had made a vanilla latte for myself and also bought four cups of coffee for T.J. and her crew. If she had a crew. If she showed up at all.

Five minutes later, three girls walked into the coffee shop. Like T.J., the other two wore mostly gray in the form of small dresses begging people to gape at them. All the girls could have been anywhere from sixteen to twenty. I wondered how many Weasel Boy kept in his stable and what percentage were underage. T.J. sat right across from me. The other two eyed me warily as they pulled out their chairs and thought for a few seconds before sitting.

"I'm not a cop," I said.

"Cops say that," one of them said.

I put my badge and ID on the table. Both of the other girls leaned over and scrutinized it. "You're a PI?" the non-trusting one said.

"I am."

"You ever shoot anyone?"

"Yes."

She smiled. "Wanna tell me about it sometime?"

"Right now, I'm here to get some information."

"This is Alex," T.J. said, nodding toward the talkative one. "That's Velvet."

I made no comments on their names. True to her *nom de rue*, Velvet garbed herself in a light jacket of her namesake material. Alex kept fixing me with what I could only presume was supposed to be a sexy look. Velvet sat there and sipped the coffee. She ripped open two sugar packets, added the contents, and tried the coffee again. Now she smiled at me.

"You're looking for Libby?" she said.

"Her aunt hired me," I said. "Libby's mother is a mess, as you could probably infer. Her aunt hasn't seen her or heard from her in several weeks."

"You think we know where she is?" Alex said.

"I'm trying to find someone who can point me in the right direction."

"You got money?"

T.J. frowned at Alex. I'd expected it, though. I peeled three hundreds off and set one in front of each girl. None moved to pick them up yet.

"I haven't seen her in at least a month," Alex said.

"Me, either," Velvet said.

"Girls come and go," T.J. said with a shrug. "Mostly, they go."

"What happens to them?" I said.

T.J. shrugged. "Whatever. We don't ask questions."

"What do you think happens?"

"Nothing good."

"Definitely nothing good," Alex added.

None of them elaborated. Velvet sipped her coffee and looked around at everyone. I kept digging. "You must have some theories."

"Weasel Boy is small time," Alex said after a moment of thought. "Some might want to move up to varsity."

Ambition is a good servant but a mad master, I thought. "What about the rest of them?"

"This ain't a nice city sometimes," Velvet said. "It's big enough to get swallowed up. Some of the girls can't avoid it. They get wrapped up in bad shit."

"I heard Weasel Boy pays some of the girls in meth."

"He offers it to all of us. It's probably cheaper than actually paying money. Some take it." She paused, looking down at her coffee cup. "They're usually the ones who disappear."

"Did Libby take meth a lot?"

"I saw her take it a few times," Alex said. "I always say no to that shit. This ain't a good life to be in, y'know? Don't need to make it worse by taking drugs."

"How was Libby when you saw her last?" I said.

"Not good," Velvet said. "Strung out, I guess. She started taking her pay in meth more often. She was looking pretty rough."

"Did you see any of the guys she went with?"

T.J. shook her head. "I didn't see her very often."

"There was that one guy," Alex said. She peered across the table at Velvet. "Who was he?"

"The old dude?"

"Yeah."

"I don't know his name or anything." Velvet shuddered. "He gave me the creeps, though. I didn't like him."

"What else can you tell me about him?" I said.

"I think he liked them young. We're all over eighteen, so he never asked for us. He wanted Libby and the other younger girls. I think she ended up being his favorite."

"What did he look like?"

Velvet shrugged. "I don't know. He was old."

"Old like fifty or old like seventy?"

"Probably around fifty," she said. I remembered thinking people in their fifties were old when I was eighteen. Anyone past sixty might as well have been a fossil. Ah, to be young.

"Gray hair," Alex said. "He wasn't bald or anything. Gray beard too."

"What else?" I said.

"Not much," said Alex. "Kind of average height. A little heavy, I guess, but not like totally fat or anything."

"Definitely creepy," Velvet said.

"How did he know you were all over eighteen?"

"Weasel Boy told him. He only steered this creep toward the young ones."

I hated Weasel Boy even more now. "You don't have any idea who this old man might be?"

"Never seen him except around here," Alex said. "He got real possessive of Libby. I remember that."

"Possessive, how?"

"Like, I saw Libby less and less. If I saw her, that grandpa was usually somewhere around."

"You think Libby was staying with him?"

"Maybe."

"I wouldn't put it past Weasel Boy," Velvet said. "If a guy

offered him a lot of money, he'd let Libby stay with someone a while."

"You've seen it happen before?" She stared down at the table. "All right."

"Weasel Boy is fucked up," T.J. said. "We're all glad he's gone."

"Would you know this older man if you saw him again?" I said. "Or saw a picture?"

"Definitely," Alex said. Velvet nodded.

"Thank you, girls. It's more than I had before."

"How you gonna find this creep?" Velvet said.

"I'll figure something out."

"Be careful. He was a perv, but I also got the feeling he could be dangerous. Just a vibe he gave off, you know?"

"I'll be on my guard," I said. The girls sipped their coffee. Alex held a cup in each hand. "What are you going to do with Weasel Boy gone?"

"Hope the next one is better, I guess," T.J. said.

I shook my head. "Get out of this life. Take this chance and go."

"Go where?" Velvet said. "This city don't have much to offer used-up whores."

"Have you heard of the Nightlight Foundation?"

"What's that?"

"It's a group setup to help families and missing children. They . . . have a soft spot for girls trying to get out of the life and get back to something normal."

"Is it free?" Alex said.

"It's a foundation. Of course it's free."

"People ain't that nice," Velvet said.

While I didn't think much of Vincent Davenport, the girls didn't need to know my personal take. He and Melinda might be able to help them. "Give them a chance. They do good work."

"We'll check them out," T.J. said. Alex and Velvet looked at her. She glared at them, and they nodded.

"Good. Don't wait for someone else to try and take over."

"What about you?"

"What about me?"

"How do we get a hold of you if we think of something else?"

I gave each of them a business card. "Call me if you have something else for me," I said. "Or if you need help."

They each took the business cards and stuffed them inside their bras. Alex drank from each coffee cup in turn. The girls all stood. "Thanks for your time," I said. "I hope I'm able to find Libby."

"I hope so too," Velvet said. "She's a good kid. She didn't deserve that jerk."

"No one does."

Alex and Velvet started toward the door. I noticed T.J. looking down at the hundred she had yet to pick up. "I don't want to take it," she said. "But . . ."

"Take it," I said. "You earned it . . . all of you. Honest pay for honest work."

She smiled at me, then turned away. She caught up with Alex and Velvet, and the three young women left the coffee shop.

I downed the rest of my latte. I had a creep to find.

CHAPTER 16

I DISCOVERED A PROBLEM. IT WAS SOMETHING I ALREADY knew, but now I saw it manifest itself in this case. The world does not lack for creeps. Pedophiles, a subset of creeps, also existed in unfortunately large numbers. I couldn't even do much research on them without sickening myself.

Were Alex and Velvet right? Did a certain man favor Libby, even to the point she stayed with him? I wondered how willing Libby and the other girls were with this arrangement. They couldn't have been getting rich off it. What if this older man showered them with gifts? Would they be more willing to go with some pervert if he bought them a few nice things along the way? I could ask Melinda, but I didn't want to involve her more than necessary. She needed to get over the last five years, not serve as my oracle for all things prostitution.

Instead, I held my nose and looked into area pedophiles. Alex and Velvet said Libby went with a man fairly recently. It seemed reasonable to presume this man had been in the system for pedophilia already but now walked free. The BPD's network allowed me to search the entire state, so I did.

A few seconds later, the visages of several disreputable gentlemen darkened my screen. With the system yielding results, I could filter them. The girls told me the man who may have taken Libby had been white and somewhere around fifty. I eliminated all non-white suspects, any still in prison, those under thirty, and those over seventy. This cast a bit of a wide net, but I'd rather get too many fish than too few. I sifted through my list of names and tried to find similarities beyond race and gender.

It took me a few minutes of sorting to uncover a connection. Four of the men saw their convictions overturned in Cecil County. Were the deputies protecting someone? I researched the cases of all four men; each had his conviction tossed out by Judge Clement Wilson. At some point, I would need to talk to the judge. I wanted to drive up there and confront him right away but thought better of it. If he were in league with those fond of underage girls, he could tip them off. Instead, I looked over the files of each of the four bastards some more, then called Casey Norton.

Norton arranged to meet me at the Daily Grind in Fells Point. Like most people in this circumstance, he'd been waiting a few minutes when I arrived. He sipped a drink and nodded as I walked in. I got in line, ordered a vanilla latte, and joined him a couple minutes later.

"Any progress?" Norton said.

"Maybe," I said. "What'd you learn from the sheriff?"

"Not much, really. He doesn't know what's going on. We believe him."

"Did anyone rake him over the coals for letting it happen? A 'lack of institutional control,' or whatever you folks call it?"

"We wanted to," he said. "Leon didn't. Ultimately, we need the sheriff to work with us. Going in there and berating him would most likely cause him to shut down."

"You think he'll be useful?"

Norton shrugged. "We're optimistic. We think there are more people involved than only Rakin and Connors. They'll probably go quiet for a while and wait for this to blow over, but they'll stick their heads up again. It's where we hope the sheriff comes in."

"I hope it works," I said.

"Me, too." He paused. "You must have some other reason for wanting to talk this morning."

I sipped my latte. The vanilla flavor was a little subtler than Starbucks'. Overall, I preferred it. "I do. You'll find four names in your inbox. Each belongs to a man indicted for pedophilia. Each had his eventual conviction overturned. Three guesses which jurisdiction it happened in."

"Good grief." Norton shook his head. "The more I learn about this case, the angrier I get."

"I know what you mean. One other interesting thing—the same judge overturned all their convictions."

"Really?" he said. I nodded. "He must be a part of it."

"Doesn't mean he's involved," I said, "but it does make you wonder."

"You going to talk to the judge?"

"Not yet. If he *is* involved, I don't want to spook him. I might check his docket, though . . . learn if he has any pedophilia cases coming up soon. It'll be interesting to see how one would turn out."

"I think we can predict the outcome," Norton grumbled into his cup.

"What I'd like to do is talk to these four assholes," I said.

"You think it's a good idea? What if they're tight with the sympathetic judge?"

I frowned; I hadn't thought about this angle. My goal of not alerting Judge Wilson would unravel if one of these scum happened to be his friend. "OK . . . not a good idea."

"They might be worth watching, though. You could get something on them."

"I don't relish the idea of following any of these people around."

"I wouldn't, either, yet you can't flash your ID to the judge and expect much in return."

His comment gave me an idea. "No, I suppose I can't," I said.

Norton stared at me. "What do you have in mind?"

"I think I might need to talk to the judge after all, but not in my official capacity."

"Why the hell would he talk to you otherwise?" he asked.

"I . . . might have a press card," I said.

"What?"

"A judge can't resist the First Amendment."

"If you do this—and I hope you don't—be careful. Judges are good at setting and avoiding traps."

I took a long pull of my latte. "If it comes down to semantics, I like my chances."

Norton rolled his eyes. "Maybe you should flash your badge and take your chances."

"This attitude won't get you quoted in my story," I said.

* * *

ON AN EARLIER CASE, my friend Joey Trovato made my very believable press ID so I could use the reporter angle. His work was successful; my attempt to put it into action was not.

I've used it here and there over the last couple years. Judge Wilson would likely be friendlier to a reporter than criminals, though he was also more likely to scrutinize the credential.

I took off my gun and holster. Not having the pistol on my hip was heavier than feeling its familiar weight at my side. I'd been assaulted a couple times already, and here I was about to ride headlong into the lion's den unarmed. I decided to drive the Caprice—it fit the role of reporter's car more than the Audi—and to keep a gun in my glove compartment.

I took breakfast alone. Gloria stayed asleep. While I ate, I poked around the Cecil County government network. They possessed some idea when it came to security, at least, but I happened upon a server running an outdated version of its file transfer protocol software. One FTP exploit later, I gained access. A couple minutes after, I found what I wanted. Judge Wilson looked forward to a boring docket today, but this allowed him plenty of time to meet with a reporter. On his docket for tomorrow, however, was a man on trial for pedophilia.

Gloria slept in beauty like the night as I got dressed and headed back downstairs. I sympathized—when the hell did I get comfortable leaving the house at eight?—but I had work to do. I put my 9MM in the glove compartment of the Caprice and set off for Cecil County. In the mornings, more traffic comes into Baltimore than leaves it, so I enjoyed a smooth ride heading north through the Fort McHenry Tunnel, past White Marsh, into Harford County, and across the Susquehanna River. Judge Wilson held court in Port Deposit within a modern courthouse looking out of place amid the quaint, century-old Victorians and buildings surrounding it. I parked and entered.

When you walk into a Baltimore court, you're greeted with metal detectors framed by armed guards. Cecil County dialed back the security. They employed guards, too, but their metal detectors appeared more subtle and less like science-fiction contraptions. I showed my press pass and corresponding fake ID, received a cursory pat-down from a muscular but uninterested guard, and passed through the metal detectors without alarm. I found Wilson's courtroom down the hall and settled in to the benches in the back.

The judge presided over a case involving criminal negligence behind the wheel. I tried to pay attention, but the lawyers were too boring, droning on in their opening arguments. Some jurors struggled not to nod off. I felt their pain. The prosecutor pounded his fist into his palm at various points to emphasize the dangers of negligent driving. The defense attorney impressed me by not looking smarmy, but she sounded like a lady accustomed to helping guilty people wriggle off the hook.

After two hours feeling like fifty, opening arguments concluded. Judge Wilson decided to take a break and lunch, calling for a recess until one o'clock. I liked the hours he enforced. The jurors seemed relieved to be going anywhere else as they filed out of the courtroom. Wilson left the bench and went out a back door. I approached it and got intercepted by a bailiff. I showed him my press credentials. He did not appear impressed.

"You want to see the judge?" he said. He was tall, white, buzz-cutted, and imposing, but whatever intimidation factor he carried fled when he opened his mouth and sounded like a yokel.

I bit down a sarcastic reply and nodded. "I'm working on a story and I think he'd have some good information."

"You call ahead?"

"Didn't know I needed to."

The bailiff frowned. "Wait here. I'll talk to him." He

went through the door. I stood there until he returned a couple minutes later. "The judge says he has some time for you," he said.

"Great. Thanks." I walked through to the end of a short corridor. I took out my phone, set it to record, and slipped it back into my pocket.

"Come in," the judge said when I knocked.

I walked in. Judge Wilson stood from behind his desk and came around to greet me. He showed a warm face and smile with hair and a beard like Kenny Rogers—or at least as I remembered the crooner from my youth. I guessed him for fifty or so, but the hair and beard added a few years. The judge shook my hand. "Pleased to meet you," he said, looking at my press pass, "Mr. Fitzroy."

"Please, Judge, call me Trent," I said.

"Well, Trent, I'll be glad to, but only if you call me Clem." His accent sounded the same as the bailiff's—and like Rakin's and Connors'. It made it hard for me to take him seriously. Everyone up here must have been used to hearing it.

"Fair enough."

"What can I do for you, Trent?"

"I'm working on a story." To complete the image, I took out a notebook and a pen.

"What paper you with?"

"*City Paper* in Baltimore."

"Long way to come," he said with a smile. It was another failing to rise to the eyes.

"Clem," I said, "I've been doing some research. It started as something else, and then I found this interesting. It's about four men accused of being pedophiles."

Judge Wilson frowned. "A charge I take very seriously. I don't like it when people do . . . such things to children."

"I don't think anyone does. Except men like those, I guess."

"Disgusting," he said, shaking his head.

"What I'm wondering is why this quartet didn't get convicted."

The judge pondered his answer over a sigh and a long look around his office. "Legal questions of this nature are hard to answer directly, Trent. They often make sense only to other lawyers."

"Try me."

"Do you have the men's names?"

"Vincent Brown, Aaron Jameson, LaQuan Wilson, and Timmy Youngblood."

"In alphabetical order, too. I'm impressed." A brief and isolated smile flashed across the judge's face.

"My reporter's sense of organization."

"What else do your reporter's senses tell you?"

"I'm not sure," I said. "I mean, you must've had reasons for letting these men go free. I wonder what the families of the victims think about those reasons."

"It's something I can't worry about. As a human being, I care, but my duty is to the law."

"Isn't the law established for the betterment of society?" I said. And for book publishers; Wilson's office could have doubled as a small library.

"Did you go to college, Trent?"

"Yes, sir."

"You graduate?"

"With a master's, yes."

"Good," the judge said, "you're educated, then. You learn a lot about the law in law school, and you even learn about it in regular college. Was it established to better society? I think so. Is this how we use it?" He shrugged. "I'm not so sure."

"Well, if you're not sure, how can you be confident in your rulings which overturn another judge and jury?"

"I have precedent to guide me. And each case has to meet standards of proof and evidence. Not all of them pass muster."

"So these four men all experienced convictions which didn't pass muster?"

"For one reason or another, yes."

"This must frustrate you," I said.

"What do you mean?"

"You said your duty is to the law. I think part of you also feels some duty to society, too. Why else be a judge? I think it would be vexing when the system you expect to send these men to jail lets you down." Score another mark against it.

Wilson nodded. "It is. It's a system people have come to expect will protect them. They expect it to put bad people in jail. For the most part, it does. Sometimes, it fails. Depending on how it fails, I have to let it happen. Yes, it's frustrating."

"I'm sure it is."

"For those men, their cases all contained problems with evidence. The system loves to put pedophiles away, Trent. It's a disgusting crime to everyone except the people who carry it out. To them, it's something natural. They feel persecuted, railroaded by a system which doesn't seem setup to protect them. You've seen what even an accusation can do to people's careers . . . to their lives." I nodded. "I have to make sure I'm protecting people from society putting one over on them, regardless of what they're accused of. You say the law is supposed to be for the betterment of society. It has to protect everyone equally, even those accused of unpopular crimes. Maybe especially people like them.

"I've seen a lot of terrible criminals and worse crimes. I was a prosecutor before I moved behind the bench. The court of public opinion can be stronger than the ones we build in our cities. It's beyond my control. What I *can* control is what happens in these walls. Police have jobs to do. So do prosecutors. They have rules they need to operate in. Part of my job is enforcing those rules. It's not always popular. Victims' families never understand. They say they want justice. What they really want is revenge."

I understood his last statements all too well. My sister's killer would rot in jail, though I started out determined to put him in a pine box. "Isn't revenge a part of justice?"

"Historically, yes," he said. "I'd like to think we're a little more advanced now."

"Maybe not all of us are."

Judge Wilson looked at his watch—the universal sign a polite exit would be forthcoming. "Trent, I've enjoyed talking to you, but I have to get some lunch if I'm going to be ready to go again by one."

"I understand."

"You got what you needed?"

"I think so, yes." I jotted a couple things down to maintain the appearance. "Thanks for your time." I stood. Wilson stood. We shook hands.

"Good luck with the story."

"So far, I've needed it," I said and left to scrub my hands.

NEXT MORNING, I did the whole thing again: got up early, ate alone, and drove to Cecil County at an hour I once considered unfit. Judge Wilson's calendar told me his session would begin at 9:30. It didn't give me much of a reprieve.

I got to the courthouse just before 9:15 and took a seat three minutes later. Many more people filled the benches today, and still more filed in as the witching hour approached. I sat in the back because I didn't want Wilson to spot me easily. I kept hoping for a tall fellow in a ten-gallon hat to plop down in front of me, but it never happened. Even so, the volume of people would make it difficult to pick me out.

A bailiff closed the courtroom doors at 9:31. Two guards led a handcuffed prisoner in through a side entrance. He was a slender white man whom I pegged for forty-five. His shaggy hair, creepy eyes, and thin mouth pegged him as a kid toucher. I knew two seconds after looking at him he was guilty. Now, we'd see if Judge Wilson's technicalities played out yet again. I understood his points about evidence, but five slimy men skating on horrible charges made for an interesting pattern.

The scumbag exchanged whispers with his lawyer, a frumpy woman whose expression revealed how little she wanted to do with him. She looked less confident than her client. I wondered if she reconsidered her career choice. Everyone is entitled to a competent defense, but defending certain people would give me chronic insomnia. The prosecutor, a graying man in a nice suit, also looked confident. I wondered how many times Judge Wilson trampled all over his certainty.

A couple minutes later, the bailiff announced Wilson. Everyone stood as he strode into the room and took his seat at the bench. He gave the courtroom a cursory glance—not taking note of me in the process—before looking at the prosecution and defense tables. "Be seated," Judge Wilson said, banging his gavel once.

"Before we go any further," the judge said, "I have to say something. Mr. Burns, your office has prepared a strong case." The prosecutor nodded. "Before I send someone to jail, I have to review his or her case. It's more than just what you presented in this courtroom. Defendants have certain rights and protections because the state brings a lot of power against them." I knew Burns didn't need this Legal 101 lecture, but he sat there and took it. I noticed color leave his face, however. He must've suspected where this was going.

"You did a lot very well, Mr. Burns, you and whoever else worked with you. The defendant is accused of a heinous crime, one society tends not to forgive. Above any sentence I hand down, the court of public opinion has tried these men, found them guilty upon accusation, and refused parole regardless of trial results. Now, it's not the job of this court to try and correct every problem of society, but it is our job to make sure everything is right before a man goes to jail for a long time."

Burns looked down at the table. He did a good job keeping his composure. I don't think I could have. "Mr. McHugh," Judge Wilson said, addressing the prisoner, "you are accused of something terrible. Mr. Burns and his office mounted a strong case against you. A jury of your peers would likely find you guilty." McHugh's shoulder's slumped. I wondered how often people at both the prosecution and defense tables looked defeated. In this legal zero-sum game, one of them would win. I harbored a feeling which one would, and it nauseated me.

"Miss Murray," Wilson said. The defense lawyer looked up. "You have a job few would envy. You've done it well. Everyone is entitled to a competent defense, and you've provided this and more for Mr. McHugh. I'm sure it hasn't always been easy. There are questions for any court above pure guilt or innocence, however. There is due process. There are the rights of the accused. There are laws and procedures when the state brings a case against a person.

"Mr. Burns, I found a few instances where your office

didn't follow all those laws and procedures." Judge Wilson held up a few sheets of paper and set them down again. "You and the sheriff's office both made some mistakes along the way. I've detailed them in this report. While I'm sure you all find the crime Mr. McHugh has been accused of abhorrent, there can be no excuses for shortcuts in the law." The judge looked at the defense table. "Mr. McHugh. You might very well be guilty as the jury determined. I hope you're not. If you are, I hope this has served as an impetus to examine your life and the choices you make. There is no room in society for the things you're accused of." McHugh, for his part, nodded.

"The only just and legal decision I can reach is for the defendant to be freed." This caused a minor ruckus in the courtroom. I heard voices raised in protest and a few in support. The former outnumbered the latter, which briefly reaffirmed my flagging faith in humanity. Judge Wilson rapped his gavel. "There will be order in this courtroom, or I'll have it cleared." He banged it a few more times before everyone quieted. "Mr. McHugh, a bailiff will lead you out. You're free to go. I hope neither I nor any of my colleagues have to see you again." Wilson banged his gavel a final time.

"All rise," the bailiff said. We did. Another bailiff led McHugh from the courtroom. I saw a few people fix him with murderous glares as he left. They must have been the victim's family. I kept track of them as everyone filed out.

CHAPTER 17

ON THE COURTHOUSE STEPS, I CAUGHT UP TO THEM. They stood fuming as the bailiff ushered McHugh away. If looks could have killed, this family would have fired death rays from their eyes. "Excuse me," I said as I approached. All three of them turned to look at me. It took their expressions a moment to soften.

"We're not talking to reporters," the woman said. The two men with her nodded.

"I'm not a reporter." I took out my real ID. "I'm a private investigator. I think there's something bigger at play here than just this case, and I'd like your input."

"What do you mean?"

"I mean this is the fifth man freed under similar circumstances. I mean there could be sheriff's deputies enabling all of this."

"Holy shit," she said.

"Yeah," I said. "Do you have a few minutes?"

"Let's talk."

* * *

WE ENDED up in a Waffle House. I'd seen them farther south, but they must have spread to northern Maryland. The restaurant was about half full, but we managed to get a table as far from the door as possible. Sherry and Troy Hampton, mother and father of the victim, perched across from me. Bill Hampton, Troy's brother, sat beside me. The small booth didn't afford a lot of room on either side. Thankfully, Bill was the more slender of the brothers.

"What did you mean about the deputies?" Troy said after we'd all been served mediocre coffee.

"I'm looking for a girl who's gone missing," I said. "She's not from around here, but a few people from this area were involved somehow. When I asked questions at the sheriff's office, a couple of deputies tossed me into a cell. They didn't exactly announce their role in . . . whatever's going on, but they didn't hide it, either. They made themselves out to be untouchable."

"What do you think they meant by it?" Sherry said.

"I'm not sure. Someone I trust talked to the sheriff and is convinced he's not involved. I guess they think they have protection from someone even higher. It didn't stop them from getting arrested."

"You said this piece of shit is the fifth man to get off the hook," Bill said from my left. As I started to answer, our waitress came back. My three tablemates all ordered some variety of hash browns, doing things like smothering, chunking, and covering them. I opted to stick with the coffee. If a place can't elevate their java above average, I'm not going to trust them to fix me any food. I'd rather be spared the inevitable disappointment.

When the server left, I said, "It's an interesting pattern. All the men have been accused of some crime against children. All have come before Judge Wilson. Each time, he's found something wrong with the cases."

"So Wilson's involved, too?" Sherry said.

"I don't know. He's also sent quite a few people to jail for doing things like this. It's not like he dismisses every case before him."

"You think he has a soft spot for . . . these people?" Troy said.

"I don't know. Maybe he's simply a stickler for the prosecution doing things the right way."

"We're not a liberal county. That shit doesn't play up here."

"I'm still working on everything," I said. "If the judge has a role in it, I haven't figured it out yet. His behavior is . . . interesting, but it doesn't mean he's part of some conspiracy."

"What *are* you saying?" Sherry said.

"I'm saying don't talk to the judge about it. If he *is* involved in something, we don't want him to know we know."

"How many more monsters have to go free before you figure it out?" She posed a fair question.

"I hope the answer is none. I'm not the only one working on this. Other people from law enforcement are looking into it, too. We'll get it sorted out. And when we do, I'll make sure you know about it."

"I want to know if Wilson is involved," Sherry said. "Or the sheriff or McHugh."

"We'll have something for them," Bill said.

"I'm sure you will," I said.

* * *

I'D BARELY CROSSED the Susquehanna on my way back

home when my phone rang. I didn't recognize the number. "This the detective?" said a voice I couldn't place.

"Who's this?"

"Donnell."

"Donnell, what can I do for you?"

"I'm not sure. It could be nothing."

"Tell me."

"I got a message from Libby last night."

I fell silent for a few seconds. "Did you see her?"

"No, but I'm jacked 'cause I ain't heard from her for a while."

"I'm on my way toward Baltimore. Give me about forty minutes, and I'll meet you."

I stepped on the accelerator. The Audi's supercharged engine responded with a whine and a roar. I would make it in under forty minutes.

* * *

I MET Donnell in the school parking lot where we chatted a few nights before. He wore sunglasses despite the mostly cloudy sky. When he walked toward me to shake my hand, I noticed the unsteadiness in his gait. When we were close enough to shake hands, the fumes from his breath confirmed it for me. "You're drunk," I said.

He nodded. "Big party last night."

"You sure you heard from Libby?"

"Hey, man, I might be drunk now. I wasn't then. She messaged me on WhatsApp."

"Or someone with her phone did." Donnell shrugged. "What did she say?"

He called it up on his phone. "'Going to a house party tonight. Will I see you there?'"

"Nothing else?" I said.

"Nope."

"What did you say?"

"Asked her where it was."

Conversations with drunk people frustrate me. You have to extract information from them like yanking impacted teeth. "Come on, Donnell. Engage with me here. Libby is missing, and you're giving me a sentence fragment at a time. You're not much help to me or her if you're in the tank. Talk to me."

Donnell took a deep breath and shook his head to dispel the lingering fog. "Sorry. Ain't been hung over in a long time."

"Considering your age, I was hoping you'd never been."

He chuckled. "Shit. I've done most of my growing up on the streets. People ain't handing out money and jobs."

"Focus, Donnell. Libby messaged you about a house party. You asked her where it was. What then?"

"I didn't hear back from her. Tried a few more times and got nothing."

"What did you do then?" I said.

"I know how to find shit out. I asked around, learned where the party was. I showed up. Lots of people. Plenty of booze, some weed, meth, all kinds of shit. Didn't see Libby, though."

"How long were you at the place?"

He frowned. "A few hours. Got there around nine, I think. I didn't leave until after two."

"Would you have noticed Libby if she walked in?" I said.

"You mean, was I too drunk?"

"Yes."

"No way," he said. "I'm an artist. I notice things. I was

sauced, yeah, but I knew what was going on. She wasn't around, man."

I nodded and sighed. "You think it was really her?"

"I don't know."

"You haven't heard from her in weeks. No one has. Then she messages you out of the blue and invites you to some house party where she doesn't even show up. It sounds weird."

"It does."

"Did you ask if anyone else saw her?"

"Yeah," he said with a nod. "No one saw a girl looks like her."

"Who did you talk to?"

"I don't know, man. People at the party."

I took a slow breath. "What kind of crowd was it? Young, old, black, white . . .?"

Donnell thought about it for a moment. "Pretty mixed, I guess. A few people my age, college folks, and some older people there."

"How much older?"

"Old, man. Older than you and me put together."

I was about to ask Donnell how old he thought me to be but reconsidered it. "So these are middle-aged people?"

"At least."

"All men?"

"Now that I think about it, yeah."

"Try to remember, Donnell. Did you see those older men trying to pick up younger girls . . . girls who may not be legal?"

The outline of Donnell's eyes closed behind his sunglasses. "Yeah." he said. "I thought it was kinda creepy, you know? I was just glad none of those dudes was hitting on me."

"Did any of these old guys leave with a young girl?"

"I think all of them did."

Had Libby been to a party like this in the past? Maybe it explained a lot. She could have left with an older man and been off the grid ever since. A few thoughts came to me, none good where her survival was concerned. "Donnell, we need to find this house. Can you show it to me?"

"Shit, man. I don't remember where it was. I was lucky I could see the sidewalk when I left."

"Think back to when you got there. Do you remember anything?"

He fell silent for a minute. "Pretty big house. White. On a small street somewhere but . . . I don't remember where."

"How did you get there?" I said. "Bus?"

"Slugged my way."

"How long did it take?"

"I don't know," he said, frowning. "Twenty minutes . . . maybe more. Drove through some shitty neighborhoods to get there."

Sadly, none of this narrowed it down for me. Baltimore could boast of some wonderful neighborhoods, but it also had —to use Donnell's term—shitty ones as well. Driving through any such neighborhoods could take you pretty much anywhere in or near the city. This gave me an idea. "Were you still in the city?" I said.

Donnell nodded. "Yeah, but I don't think by much."

The added information still gave me long odds to find the house, but I was nowhere if I didn't try. "All right. Thanks for calling me."

"You gonna find the place?"

"I'm sure going to do my best."

"Take me with you when you go."

"No way," I said. "It could be dangerous."

"I might remember something."

While Donnell made a point, I couldn't expose him to any unnecessary risks. "Look, I know you want to help find Libby. You already did. I didn't know anything about this house party before you called. This is my job. Let me do what I do."

"All right." Donnell held out his fist. I bumped it, and then I left.

WHEN I WAS Donnell's age, I owned a car and an insatiable curiosity about the city of Baltimore. My friends—usually Joey Trovato and Vinny Serrano—and I would drive around, listen to music, and get denied entry into bars. I learned a lot about the streets and neighborhoods, and I also caught on where parties were. When you're rich and bored, finding these events (or getting invited to them) is easy. Someone in Donnell's circumstances would need to work harder.

How could I track down a house party from the night before with precious little information past a generic description? The first consideration was who would allow their place to be used for a raucous gathering. Every kid knows someone who has Those Parents who would do something like this—Conrad's folks struck me as the type—but I placed long odds on Donnell knowing someone fitting the bill. He said he needed to ask around about the party. He knew someone who knew someone who had an in. He probably accomplished it with a lot of texting and messaging apps.

I already possessed Donnell's cell number. A minute later, this info gave me his carrier. A couple minutes after, I scrolled through his text history. The person who gave him the party location appeared as "Getty" in Donnell's contacts.

I soon knew Getty was really James Paul Grove. I found his mobile number which provided me his location—a small coffee shop in northeast Baltimore. I got into the Audi and headed over there.

* * *

THE GRANDE BEAN sat nestled into a small storefront on Belair Road. This area experienced a lot of turnover, especially in small businesses. I wondered what this coffee shop used to be. The layout seemed odd—very wide but not deep. It only took me a few steps to get to the counter. I only saw one employee: a tall, pudgy white kid who looked to be about Donnell's age. Under his apron, he wore a nice shirt and pressed slacks. Maybe they called him Getty for more than just his initials.

One other patron sat inside the coffee shop. I ordered a vanilla latte and nursed it at the long counter as I waited for the other man to leave. A few minutes later, he accommodated me. I summoned Getty. When he stood across from me, I showed him a picture of Libby on my phone. He didn't give a reaction.

"Who's she?" he said.

"Someone who may have been at your house party last night, Getty," I said.

He frowned, then glanced behind him toward the back of the shop.

"I'd catch you," I said. "You don't look like much of a runner."

"You a cop?"

I shook my head. "Private investigator trying to find a missing girl."

"I ain't seen her."

"Rumor has it she was at your big party last night."

"They're not my parties."

"You're just the man who sets them up."

"No," he said. "I drum up interest. I invite people."

"Define 'people.'"

"Human beings?"

I scowled at him. "This isn't the time or place for you to be a smartass, Getty. An underage girl is missing, and from where I sit, you're complicit. I may not be a cop, but I know a few, and I guarantee they take shit like this seriously. So you have a choice: answer my questions or answer theirs."

The chubby idiot actually thought about it for a moment. "I invite people my age," he said. "Fifteen to eighteen, mostly."

"Girls?"

"I'm encouraged to invite girls."

"Encouraged by whom?" I said. More and more I dreaded talking to young people.

Now Getty shook his head. "I can't give him up."

I took the lid off my latte. Steam rose from it, carrying the subtle aroma of vanilla. "This is pretty hot," I said.

Getty shrugged. "Supposed to be. So?"

"So . . . I'm going to throw this drink in your face and beat your ass if you don't answer me. Who encourages you to invite girls?"

Worry spread over Getty's face. I didn't know if he was concerned about my threat or about the person he didn't want to give up. I hoped for the former. He looked at me. I gripped my cup harder and cocked my elbow.

"He's a realtor," Getty said. I waited, but he didn't elaborate.

"This realtor have a name?" I said. "Maybe an office?"

"I don't know his name."

"What do you call him?"

"Party Man."

Of course. "Does Party Man have a phone?"

"I text him, mostly."

"In other words, yes. Give me his number." He did. I figured it was a prepaid cell and couldn't be traced, but there was always the hope a criminal is stupid. I took out my phone and opened an encrypted tunnel to my server at home using a secure shell. "Do you have some reason to text him today?"

"He's supposed to pay me for the party."

It meant people were paying Party Man. I got a sick feeling what they offered money for, and it disgusted me. "Good. Text him."

"It's too early."

"Text him, or I'll break your fingers and do it myself." Getty took out his phone. "I want to see your messages, too. No tipping this asshole off."

Getty complied, asking when they could meet. I ran a cell tracing program on my server and accessed it via my phone. A minute later, Party Man replied. I registered a general location. If accurate, his office wasn't far from here.

"He said he's busy," Getty said.

"Text him again. Tell him you're bored at work and wondering." He did. Another response came a minute later. My location radius narrowed.

"He doesn't seem happy," said Getty. I heard worry in the young man's voice.

"One more. Tell him thanks and to contact you later." Getty complied. His phone chirped as another response came. My location radius narrowed again, this time to about 100 meters. "Good. Let me see your phone."

"I did what you asked."

I held out my hand. "Your phone, Getty. Now."

He handed it over. It was an Android model, several years old. Most importantly, it looked like it lacked modern features like water resistance. I yanked out the battery and dropped the phone in my latte.

"Hey!"

"The price of doing dirty business," I said. "I suggest you make this your last transaction with Party Man. I'm shutting him down. If you're still involved, you'll fall along with him." I left Getty to think about the warning. Once outside, I threw his battery on top of the building. Even if his phone survived the latte bath, he wouldn't drag himself up there to get the battery.

* * *

I MOVED the Audi in case Getty got any ideas. He didn't seem smart enough to have many of his own, but I decided not to risk him having a moment of revelation. I'd been hard on him, but he deserved it. I parked a block away from where the office in question should have been. Businesses clustered together on both sides of Belair Road here, broken only by cross streets and shared driveways. I walked a couple of blocks in each direction, going down intersecting roads, too, and discovered only one realtor: Doug Mann. I groaned at the bad Party Man pun as I strode to his office. A light shone through the sidewalk window, so I opened the door.

A small front office with an empty desk yielded to a larger back office. A blond man with a jowly face looked up as I entered. He summoned a smile, dragged his girth out of his well-used office chair, and came around his desk to meet me. "Doug Mann," he said, holding out his hand.

I shook his hand and vowed to use hand sanitizer later. "Doug, I'm looking for a house," I said.

"Well, I'm the Mann to see." He gave me an empty smile, like a comedian who has tired of his own joke after a long career.

"It's what I hear," I deadpanned.

He sat behind his messy desk and beckoned me to take a guest chair. Piles of random papers, manila folders, and real estate magazines littered the surface. The concept of the paperless office clearly eluded him. "What kind of house are you in the market for?" he said once we were both settled.

"I'm looking to upsize," I said. "There are a lot of houses around here bigger than mine."

"This is a good area for large houses. They built a lot after both World Wars. You don't mind a house with a little age, do you?"

"As long as it's got a lot of room inside."

"Plenty of those around here. What area are you looking at?"

"Something in this vicinity. I want to be in the city but close to the county."

"Work?"

"And friends," I said. "I'm popular."

"You want something like a Victorian, then."

I nodded. "It needs to have lots of space inside." I studied Mann for a reaction. "I love throwing parties."

He averted his eyes, acting like he peered at something on his monitor. "Well, I have a few I could show you. Did you want to look today?"

"I do."

"OK, let me get a list of some properties nearby." Mann busied himself with something on his computer. I looked around his office. His bookshelves were packed with volumes on real estate, health, and self-help. I hoped Mann were more successful at the real estate than the other two. A college degree from some school I'd never heard of hung on the wall behind his desk. Many colleges courted me, so I felt confident dismissing one I couldn't recall.

"OK, I think I found a few places to look at," Mann said. His printer whirred to life.

"You know if any of them threw parties recently?" I said.

Color left Mann's ample cheeks, but he stayed on script. "I'm afraid I wouldn't know what the sellers might have done before listing their home," he said.

"Oh, come on. I hear you're the party man . . . Party Man."

Mann stared at me, and his face went white. "I . . . I don't know what you mean."

"Spare us both the time of lying," I said. "You put together a house party not far from here a couple nights ago. I want to see where it was, and I want to know who you invited. And if you're not 'the Mann'"—I added very necessary air quotes—"then I want to know who is."

"Who are you?"

"A private investigator trying to find a missing girl who might have been there."

"You're not a cop?" He tried to show me a feral grin. I wasn't impressed.

"Don't get any ideas, asshole. I have a gun under this jacket. If you reach for something, I draw it, and I'm pretty sure I'm faster than you. You don't look like a runner, and I could take you in a fight. So why don't you sit there and tell me what I want to know?"

Instead of doing the smart thing, Mann stood and walked slowly around the desk. I remained sitting. He tried his best to look menacing, and I tried my best not to laugh. Mann stood about my height but carried an extra hundred or more pounds on his frame. He could possess some latent athleticism, so I didn't want to take him too lightly. "I don't like people coming into my office and making threats." He glowered down at me.

"And I don't like people who let bad things happen to underage girls," I said. "Guess we're at an impasse."

"I could make you disappear."

I couldn't fight the urge to laugh anymore, and it spilled out of me. Mann threw a punch to try and capitalize, but I was ready, blocking it aside. He tried again. This time, I caught his wrist, gave him a good shove to help his momentum spin him around, stood, and cinched in the hammerlock. Mann grunted and tried to escape. "Only makes it hurt more," I said. I tightened the hold to emphasize my point.

"What do you want?" Mann said.

"I told you. I want to see the house where you threw a party. I want to know who you invited. And you're going to tell me who's in charge if it's not you."

"You're asking for a lot."

"You're not very cooperative for a man in a hammerlock. I learned a lot of holds in Hong Kong, Dougie. Can I call you Dougie? This one might hurt, but I could break all the bones in your arm in a few seconds. I'm normally not violent unless I need to be, but when you let who knows what happen to young girls, I make exceptions." I ratcheted up the hold. A little more pressure, and bad things would happen. Mann winced. "You going to cooperate?"

He nodded. I kept the hammerlock on a second more then let him go. He rubbed his arm and glowered at me in a useless fit of pique. "The house, Dougie," I said. "Let's go."

"Fine." Mann grabbed his keys.

"No phone calls, either," I said. "You call any of your

buddies, and they'll be taking you to the ER when they get there. Now give me your keys."

"What?"

"Your keys, asshole. Hand them over. We're taking your car, and I'm driving. Now let's go."

Mann thought about it for a couple seconds but handed me his keys. "Good decision," I said.

CHAPTER 18

Mann directed me to the house. It was a white
Victorian on a street of them. A few smaller homes broke the
monotony, and different shutter colors tried to scream indi-
viduality amid a sea of sameness. This one's claim to distinc-
tion were blue shutters and a dark green door. "This is the
place?" I said.

"It's where I had the party," Mann said.

"Why here?"

"It's been on the market a year. Barely a bite. Two houses
across the street are for sale. The neighbor on the right is
deaf, and the one on the left is out of town a lot."

"You've done your research."

"I have to in my line of work."

"Better stick to selling houses full time, Dougie."

We got out of the car. I kept Mann's keys and snickered at
him when he held his hand out for them. "This is the house,
like we agreed," Mann said.

"Take me inside," I said. "I want to see the scene of the
crime."

"I sent a cleaning crew in here the next day."

"I'm sure the eventual buyer will appreciate it. Now let's go in."

Mann grumbled but cooperated. He retrieved a key from the lockbox and opened the door. I insisted he go in first. He didn't scare me in a fight, but I also didn't want to give him a free shot with my back turned. The foyer opened to a staged house. It featured cherry hardwood floors, a new paint job, and furniture so neutral and inoffensive no one would ever buy it. If I stared, I could almost see my reflection in the floors. Mann's cleaning crew did a good job. I still wanted to nose around, but my hopes of finding something usable took a beating.

"I don't need to be here while you look around," Mann said.

"You're right," I said, "you don't." I walked farther into the house.

"My keys?"

"Fuck off, Dougie. You can walk back to your office. You could use the exercise."

"Give me my keys."

"I'll drop them off."

Mann stalked close to try his angry and intimidating look again. It worked just as well as the first time. "I'll report my car stolen," he said.

"Oh, *please* call the police. It'll be epic."

"I want my car," he said.

"And I want to find a missing girl. To get the car back, do more than show me a house you had professionally cleaned."

I watched as Mann shook his head and turned. The only way the ensuing punch could've been more obvious would be with an engraved invitation. I blocked it with my left forearm, swung my right arm around, and clubbed Mann in the left ear with the bottom of my fist. He ducked, winced, and staggered to the side. I took a step forward. Mann held up his hands. "OK . . . OK," he said. "I'll go."

"Good. Get out."

"You'll drop my keys off?"

"I'll toss them down a sewer grate if you don't get out of here."

Mann glared at me some more before he left. Once the door closed, I looked around. His cleaning crew did a hell of a job. If they didn't conduct business with an asshole like Mann, I'd want to hire them. Then I thought of other people who might do business with Mann. I let him leave with his cell phone. He could have been calling some people much scarier than himself to pay me a visit. I quickened my searching, which only made not finding a damn thing go by a little faster. To feel like I accomplished something, I took pictures of the rooms as I entered them.

I went downstairs and started toward the front door. Mann's goons, if he contacted them, would come in this way. Even if I left beforehand, I had no intention of driving Mann's car and being visible on the street. I headed for the back door and left. A three-foot chain-link fence enclosed the small backyard. I hopped the low barrier, went down a grassy alley, and headed away from the place. I used my GPS to worm my way back to my car. Before I got there, I wiped my prints off Mann's keys and dropped them down a sewer grate.

I'm a man of my word.

* * *

WITH THE HOUSE BEING SPOTLESS, I didn't have anything to go on. Hell, I didn't even know if Libby went there. All I counted on were the hazy memories of a street artist who was blotto at the time. I sat in my car and plotted the next move.

What if Libby were there? As easy as it was to assume she wasn't, I couldn't. My GPS found a Kinko's nearby. I used my phone to send a picture of Libby to their print shop. Fifteen minutes later, I carried a hundred five-by-seven pictures of Libby.

I drove by Mann's office. He hadn't returned yet. I headed in the opposite direction and canvassed businesses and passersby. Because I didn't know if Libby had been there recently, I asked the folks I encountered if they remembered seeing her anytime in the last two months. A few people scrutinized the picture, but no one remembered seeing her at any point. The back side of the picture featured Sergeant Gonzalez's desk number at the BCPD.

A couple hours later, I'd given away all of my cards. I walked back toward my car. As I drew closer, I saw a couple likely-looking goons skulk from Mann's office. I stood in the shadows of the closest building. Mann stormed out behind them. He pointed and gestured as he talked, and I could see his red face even from where I stood. The large men listened to Mann's tirade. After a minute, one of them stepped forward and cocked his fist. Mann backed off and cowered faster than I thought him capable. The men left a moment later. I waited until they drove away, and then I left, too.

On the drive back home, my phone rang. "C.T., it's Leon Sharpe." This couldn't be good if Sharpe called me rather than delegating it to a secretary or underling.

"What's up, Leon?"

"Remember those two asshole deputies in Cecil County?"

"Rakin and Connors? How could I forget?"

"They've been released," Sharpe said. "Casey Norton just called me with the news."

"What the hell?" I said. "How could those two assholes get out so soon?"

"Judge's orders?"

"Which judge?" I had a feeling I knew.

"Clem Wilson."

Of course. Wilson's involvement got less and less coincidental as events played out. I might need to talk to him again, and not as an intrepid reporter. "I'm not surprised," I said.

"Is the judge involved?" Sharpe said.

"Depends. What's your opinion on coincidences?"

"Not very favorable."

"Then he's probably in it up to his shaggy gray eyebrows," I said.

*　*　*

I PONDERED what to do about the judge as I drove home. How involved was he? So far, he let a few "alleged" kid touchers go and released a pair of asshole deputies. It fell short of being a smoking gun. Leon Sharpe didn't believe in coincidences, however, and neither did I. Wilson was no doubt a part of the problem, but to what degree? Whose pocket was he in? Or was he the ringleader of this whole sordid mess? As I drove, I called Rich. "I already know," he said.

"Good news travels fast," I said.

"Casey Norton called me."

"He must have lost my number. Leon told me."

"I would have called you," Rich said.

"Uh-huh. After clearing it with your buddy Norton first. What do you make of all this?"

"I'm getting interested in the judge," Rich said. "I don't

see any good reason to let those two assholes go, but he did anyway."

"It's a pattern of behavior."

"So I've heard." Rich paused. "It doesn't mean he's connected to them, though."

"You just said you were interested in him," I said.

"Yes, but we have to be careful going after someone like him. He could just be a shitty judge."

"Or he could be in on everything."

"He could."

"Are you trying to discourage me from going after him?" I said.

"Of course. He's a judge. You can't simply walk into his house, beat him up, and expect a police department to make a charge stick."

"What if I beat him up somewhere else?"

"You know what I mean, C.T. We have to have everything in order if we're going after a judge. And because he's a few counties away, we need Casey Norton backing us."

"Fine," I said. "You get Norton on board. I'm going to keep pulling threads until someone's sweater unravels."

"Make sure it's not yours," Rich said.

"I will," I said and hung up.

For the rest of the drive home, I tried to convince myself Rich was a ninny and I should go after Judge Wilson with both my barrels of dubious legality. The more I thought about it, though, the more I saw he was right. Judges know piles of lawyers and cops. Taking one down isn't like busting some random person. I would need to keep working and building a case, circling around the judge while waiting to drag him down.

I hoped I didn't have to wait long. For Libby's sake, mostly, but also for my own.

* * *

GLORIA HAD ALREADY SET the table when I got home, and I found her in the kitchen. She tossed a salad full of vibrant greens and reds in a large bowl. Veal parmesan paired with whole wheat pasta steamed on plates nearby. "I've been busy," she said, smiling,

I lifted the lid of the trash can. It was empty. "Busy hiding the evidence," I said. We kissed.

"Just because I took the trash out?"

"Yes . . . and I know your aptitude in this room."

"Guilty as charged."

We carried our food to the table and sat. Gloria took in the salad, and I poured us two tall glasses of iced tea. I served us both some salad, cracked some pepper atop it, and looked at Gloria. "Thanks for dinner," I said.

"You're welcome. You've been burning the candle at both ends on this case. I thought you could use a nice dinner you didn't have to cook or pick up."

I nodded around a bite of my salad. I did the same when I worked Melinda and Samantha's cases at the same time. I needed something nice and simple after this one. "It's turning into a lot more than I first thought," I said.

"What do you mean?"

I caught Gloria up on everything from the past couple days. "Wow," she said. "You think the judge is involved?"

"Somehow," I said. "I'm still figuring out how much. Maybe I need to talk to Connors and Rakin again."

"Be careful. They're dangerous men."

"I'm not handcuffed to iron bars this time," I said.

"I'm serious. They're tangled in this to some degree. This whole case is dangerous."

"Most are."

Gloria nibbled at her salad. "This one is getting to you, though."

"Yeah, I guess it is. I just hate seeing kids victimized like this by adults who don't give a shit." A memory from high school flashed in my head. I ignored it for now. "They just move on to the next kid and ruin another life. I hate it. I hate *them*."

We ate for a few minutes in silence. Whoever cooked the veal parmesan did a damn good job. The meat barely needed chewing. The sauce was robust with a hint of heat. "Do you think Libby is still alive?" Gloria said.

I thought about it for a moment over a mouthful of veal parm. Summoning my optimism failed. "No."

"Why not?"

"It's been too long with no real sign of her," I said. "Statistically, she's almost certain to be dead at this point. When you factor in deputies and a judge subverting justice to some degree, I think it makes her odds even worse."

Gloria nodded. "So you're speaking for her at this point."

"I guess. Someone has to. Her aunt cares about her. Some of her foster parents did, too. I don't think her mother remembers she had a child most days." I paused for another bite of food. "If I'm not trying to track her down, who would be?"

"Probably no one," said Gloria.

"Because it's what the people she got caught up with do. They make kids disappear, and people stop looking. Even parents realize it's hopeless at some point."

"I hope she beat the odds," Gloria said after a moment.

"So do I," I said.

My phone ringing and vibrating on the nightstand roused

me from a deep sleep. Its display told me it was 2:45. We'd been asleep for three hours. "I think we found the girl you're looking for," Paul King said after I mumbled a greeting

Considering the department King worked in and the time he called, I again failed to summon any optimism. The news helped me shake off my tiredness, however. "I take it she wasn't alive?"

"Unfortunately, no. Found her wrapped in a comforter in an alley. Looks like she's been dead a while."

"Where are you now?" I said.

"Where we found the body. We're almost done here, though. Meet me at the morgue in about twenty."

"All right."

King hung up. I did the same. I looked at Gloria and saw she was awake. She frowned. "They found her body, didn't they?"

I nodded. "Yeah. I'm going to meet King at the morgue."

"I'm starting to hate the people who did this, too," she said.

I kissed Gloria on the forehead. Then I got dressed.

CHAPTER 19

THERE IS AN UNFORTUNATE DEARTH OF ALL-NIGHT
coffee shops in Baltimore. Armed with three hot beverages of
indeterminate freshness from 7-Eleven, I walked into the city
morgue. Dr. Gary Hunt and Paul King stood waiting for me.
I handed a cup to each of them; both nodded silent thanks.
The ventilation system kept the air neutral. Our drinks
created a pleasing aroma which trailed us as we adjourned to
an office.

"Got a call about an hour ago," King said. "Local working
girl called it in. She's been around the block enough to know
we're not going to hassle her about hooking when there's a
body in an alley."

"Can I see the pictures?" I said.

King shrugged. "Sure." He brought them up on a
computer. Like most alleys in Baltimore, trash lined the sides.
Lying amid the usual detritus was a rolled-up comforter,
green on the inside and blue on the outside. Successive
photos established the area and showed the face when the
comforter had been pulled back.

Based on the pictures I'd seen, it looked like Libby
Parsons.

"We think it's your girl," Dr. Hunt said.

I nodded. "Probably is. How long ago did she die?"

"My initial guess is about a day."

"She wasn't killed in the alley, then?"

"Doesn't seem like it," King said.

"She'd been dead several hours when someone discovered her," Hunt said. "Based on lividity, she was moved at some point."

I scrolled through the photos. Libby lived a tough life, but this was not the way for anyone to go out. I'm no doctor or forensics expert, but obvious bruising around her neck indicated strangulation. Libby's eyes were open, staring into the distance in the unsettling way dead people do. I wondered who she saw at the end. Did she know her killer? Did she trust him? "I think it's her," I said with a sigh.

Hunt gathered some papers. "Hard to confirm without someone to ID the body."

"There's her aunt."

"Not the mother?"

"I don't know the mother remembers she even has a child. Or . . . had."

"We'll need the aunt, then," King said.

I nodded. "It's early. How about I bring her by at a more respectable hour?"

"Fine," Hunt said. "I'll be here for a while still. By then, I should be able to tell you more about what happened to this girl before she died."

"All right. Thanks, Doctor."

We left the office. Hunt resumed his duties, and Paul King walked out with me. "This ties into the thing Rich is working on?"

"Sure seems to be," I said. "There are a few connections."

"Rich is working some heavy shit. Be careful. This may not be your garden-variety girl getting killed."

"Sounds dangerously close to you giving a damn about me."

"You buy me lunch at The Abbey. It's worth something."

"Usually at least twenty bucks if you're drinking on the job."

"Next time, I'm getting the most expensive burger they have," said King.

* * *

I DROVE HOME. Gloria remained in bed. I checked on her and realized it would be futile to try and go back to sleep. The case burned in my veins. A few hours remained before I felt comfortable calling Madeline Eager. She may want to know right away. I sensed her concern for Libby every time we spoke. In this instance, there was nothing she could do. There were no forms to sign in a hospital. Identifying the body would be a formality. No reason to rush it. In the meantime, I wanted to find out more about who killed Libby.

Judge Wilson may not have been the killer, but too many factors pointed to his involvement in some capacity. I dug deep on the judge and his family history. It took a while, but I discovered Wilson's father, Clem the Elder, had been arrested for child molestation. The charges were dropped, but the allegation hounded Wilson for the rest of his days. The judge acknowledged this in public only once, claiming the whole situation filled him with a profound sense of fairness toward those accused of horrible crimes. I didn't buy it.

Those more sensitive than I would say the elder Wilson's proclivities—and maybe his direct actions—shaped his son. I didn't buy the opposite psychobabble, either. The judge was his own man and made his own choices. And I intended to nail him to the wall for them.

I expanded my searches. Judge Wilson led a pretty boring life. He'd been married and divorced with no children. His ex-wife moved out of the state. I made a mental note to track her down. Wilson maintained a solid if undistinguished career as a lawyer and a judge. The only professional controversy I could find was the fact accused pedophiles tended to get easy treatment in Wilson's courtroom. Someone else would need to make the connection. Maybe I could feed a reporter a good story. Jessica Webber and I hadn't collaborated in a while.

After some more searching turned up nothing of interest, I called Madeline Eager. She picked up right way. "Madeline, this is C.T. Ferguson."

"It's a little early, Mr. Ferguson."

"It is."

"Do you have news?"

"I do," I said. I took a breath to ready myself. Doctors and cops are used to dropping these bombs on people; I'm not. "I'm afraid it's not good."

Madeline sighed into the phone. "Where should I meet you?" she said.

"At my office. I'll drive us from there."

"All right. I'll see you in a half-hour."

We hung up. I put on some more professional clothes, then headed to my office to deliver the bad news.

* * *

"You're positive it's Libby?" Madeline Eager said as we drove to the morgue.

"Pretty sure," I said. "They need someone to make a definitive ID, though. You're the only choice."

"I wonder if I should tell Karla."

"Up to you."

She turned beseeching eyes to me. "What would you do?"

I pondered her question. If Madeline caught Karla during a rare lucid moment, she might remember having a daughter and might even feel a sense of loss at the girl's passing. Catching her during a drugged-out moment would lead down a dark and unknown road. Would she even remember it later when the pot and meth wore off? I couldn't feel confident. However, I also knew what it felt like to be lied to about the death of a loved one. Karla Parsons, whatever her condition, should be spared a lie of omission. "I would tell her," I said.

"Why?"

"Because it's the right thing to do."

"She might not even know who Libby is . . . was. Hell, she might not even know who I am."

I shrugged. "What she does or doesn't do with the information isn't up to you. Libby was her daughter. She should know. She might even remember it in a moment of lucidity, and maybe it'll be the kick in the ass she needs to turn her life around."

Madeline snorted. "You're optimistic."

"I haven't had enough sleep or coffee yet."

We rode in silence for a few minutes. Traffic delayed us the farther we got into downtown Baltimore. All lanes were filled with cars turning into parking garages. Sidewalks bustled with men and women in suits headed into tall monuments of glass and steel. I watched a few of the women with some interest. As we sat at a light not far from the morgue, Madeline spoke again. "Will you go with me?"

"Go where?" I said.

"To see Karla."

I couldn't generate interest in going to see the spectacle. However, Madeline wouldn't ask if she didn't need the support. "Sure," I said.

"Good. We'll go when we leave here, if you don't mind."

"Sure." Might as well blow all the fun out in one wild morning.

I pulled into an available parking spot. Madeline took a couple deep breaths and got out. We walked in together. Dr. Hunt was still on duty and waved us to the waiting area. A few minutes later, we followed Hunt into the morgue. He'd set a smallish body on a slab, covered with a plain white sheet. I lingered back a few steps while Madeline approached.

"Are you ready?" Hunt said.

"Is anyone?" she said.

"Not really, I guess." Hunt held the top of the covering. He checked with Madeline; she nodded. As Hunt pulled the sheet down, the body looked more like Libby than before. He'd done a good job of cleaning her up and making her look more like she had in life, at least judging by the photos I saw. Madeline's head slumped forward. Her small nod told Hunt and me everything we needed to know.

Hunt replaced the sheet. "I'm sorry for your loss," he said. He must have said it a lot, but he managed to inject some sincerity into it.

"Did she suffer?" Madeline said.

"How much do you want me to tell you?"

"Everything. I'm a grown woman."

"All right." Hunt paused, probably considering how to say his piece without upsetting Madeline, grown woman status or not. "There are signs of drug abuse. I don't have a tox screen yet, but I would expect it to come back positive for meth . . . at least. It looks like this young woman experienced a lot of sex shortly before she died, and it was . . . rough."

"She was sexually assaulted?"

"Almost certainly . . . and repeatedly." Hunt paused as Madeline closed her eyes and sighed. "Sorry. She also has bruises and cuts consistent with getting into a fight."

"How did she die?" I said.

"She was strangled," Hunt said after another pause.

"Could it be the fight she was in?"

"Maybe. I checked for DNA under the fingernails and didn't find any."

DNA under the fingernails caught a lot of people. It's possible there never was any, but it was also possible someone savvy enough in criminal proceedings knew to check for it and remove it.

Another point for Judge Wilson.

"Thank you, Doctor," Madeline said. "Will her body be released to me?"

"Whoever's listed as her next of kin," Dr. Hunt said.

Madeline nodded and sighed. She started for the door, and I followed. On her way out, she grabbed a couple of tissues.

* * *

WE DROVE to Essex to see Karla Parsons. Madeline didn't say a word the entire trip. She dabbed at her eyes with tissues a few times. I didn't feel right saying anything. Madeline did all she could—including hiring me—to try and keep Libby alive, and nothing worked. Going in, I figured my odds of finding Libby and bringing her back alive were poor, but I still felt like I'd failed. Any words I might have spoken would have been cold comfort.

Karla Parsons' community looked as dilapidated and uninviting as ever. I drove the Caprice here the first time. Now I hoped the Audi didn't end up on blocks while Madeline and I spent a useless visit with her sister. I turned down her street. We wouldn't have to go inside Karla's filthy trailer after all. Despite the temperature being in the forties, she sat outside on a lawn chair threatening to fall apart. As I got closer, I saw she wore a bathrobe over sweatpants. Karla smoked something I hoped was only a cigarette. Madeline shook her head as I parked the car.

She got out first. I followed and lagged a couple of steps behind her. My role was moral support—a job I felt less than qualified to live up to, all things considered. I didn't want Karla Parsons to see me as someone else attacking her and shut down as a result. "Jesus, Karla," Madeline said, "it's cold out."

Karla looked at Madeline, then at me, then back at Madeline. I didn't see recognition dawn in her dim eyes. "Don't feel so bad," she said.

"I'm here about Libby."

"Ain't seen her."

"She's dead, Karla."

Karla's reaction consisted of staring ahead and dragging on her cigarette. I waited for something else. It never came. Madeline ran out of patience.

"Did you even hear me?" she said. "I just told you Libby is dead." Her voice cracked with emotion. "She's dead. Your daughter is dead!"

I expected some kind of emotional reaction here. Tears,

yelling about the grand unfairness of things . . . hell, I would have settled for a sniffle. Nothing. Karla kept staring ahead. "When?" she finally said in her usual flat tone.

"A while ago," Madeline said. "They just . . . they just found the body recently." Her voice cracked again. It annoyed me Madeline was a lot more broken up at Libby's death than Karla.

"I gotta pay for a funeral?" Karla said.

This must've been Madeline's tipping point. She marched to Karla and slapped her hard enough to knock her out of her shabby lawn chair. "She's dead, damn you," Madeline yelled at her fallen sister before slapping her again. "All you care about is getting high and paying for a funeral. I should have taken her from you! I should have called the state!" Madeline bent with both hands to slap Karla again and again. Tears came and reduced the rest of her shouting to inarticulate rage. Karla lay on the grass and covered her face. I pulled Madeline back. She kept yelling and fought to break free. I maintained my grip on her arms.

Finally, Madeline stopped struggling. She turned to look at me. Tears covered her face. She sank into me and sobbed. I put an arm around her. Karla stood, an intricate process she abandoned a couple times before making it to her feet. She tried to summon some dignity as she sat, but the bathrobe spoiled it. Karla looked at me as if seeing me for the first time. "Who the hell are you?" she said.

"We spoke before," I said. "I was trying to find your daughter."

"Mmm. Maybe you shoulda looked harder."

Madeline mumbled something into my chest. I didn't want to get into a game of should-have with a junkie mother who didn't seem to care her daughter died. "Let's go," I whispered. Madeline nodded. I kept a hand on her back for support as we walked to the car. She got in. I got in. We looked at Karla.

She lit another cigarette.

We drove away.

CHAPTER 20

I DROPPED MADELINE OFF AT HER HOUSE. SHE summoned a smile before bidding me adieu. I don't know if I could've done the same in her place. After Madeline went inside, I took my tablet out of the glove compartment, connected to my server, and looked for what the BPD learned about Libby and her murder. With the case being nascent, they showed little information. They knew the location of the body, however, which King didn't tell me before. I drove there.

Someone found Libby's remains in an alley behind a women's hair salon. None of the salon workers remembered seeing a corpse when they closed last night. Presuming they would have seen it, this meant someone dropped the corpse there several hours after she died. Trash and random bits of junk covered the alley. One area looked much cleaner than the rest. It had to be where someone found the body and the police setup their crime scene.

I nosed around, figuring I would find nothing useful but needing to try anyway. Between the BPD doing a good job processing crime scenes and Libby being dumped here post-mortem, I didn't find a lot to work with. I nosed around for several more minutes and discovered nothing. Anything interesting at the scene must have left in BPD evidence bags. Unable to think of anything else to do for Libby, I drove home. Madeline Eager had smiled when she got out of my car, but she hadn't thanked me. I understood. She had nothing to thank me for.

* * *

I CHECKED the case file a few times and found nothing new in it. Madeline might tell me my involvement was over. She'd hired me to find out what happened to Libby. We knew the answer. I wanted to find out how and by whom. The question of why could be a matter for the jury, if this mess even resulted in a trial.

Later the same night, I went to bed and slept fitfully. I even rejected Gloria's advances, which only served as a sign of serious sickness to this point. For the second night in a row, my ringing cell phone interrupted my sleep. This time, Rich called at several minutes before three. "We got another one," he said.

The haze lifted as I thought about what he told me. "Another what?" I thought I knew the answer, but I'd welcome being wrong.

"Another dead girl."

I closed my eyes and rubbed the bridge of my nose. I wasn't wrong. "Where?"

"Cecil County."

"They're expanding their empire."

"I'll text you the address."

"Sounds like you want me there."

"It's all hands on deck at this point."

"I'll be on my way in five minutes," I said.

* * *

THE ADDRESS RICH sent belonged to a pizza shop in the old town part of Port Deposit. A phalanx of police cars representing several jurisdictions cordoned the area off. I parked as close as I could, showed my badge to a Cecil County deputy, and got waved in. Voices came from the area behind the restaurant. I walked back there. Rich came out to greet me.

"Looks a lot like the Libby scene."

"How old is the girl?" I said.

"Don't know yet. No ID on her, of course. We're guessing sixteen at this point, but we don't know for sure."

"How long has she been dead?"

"The coroner just got here. He thinks this one is fresh, though."

"Not like Libby." We walked behind the restaurant. Casey Norton inclined his head at me as we approached. Everyone else dressed in Cecil County colors. We couldn't have been high on their list of favorite people at the moment. A middle-aged man with a very large leather bag beside him examined the body. I walked close. The girl was blonde and must have been pretty in life. The estimate of sixteen years old struck me as accurate. I took out my phone and snapped a picture of her face. The black eye and cuts would make identification difficult.

"We think this girl was killed tonight," Casey Norton said.

"But not here," the coroner added.

"Two girls in two nights," I said. "Both times, she was killed somewhere else."

"A lot of miles between the crime scenes."

"Doesn't mean the same people weren't involved both times."

Norton nodded. "I know. You still like the judge?"

"As a suspect or whatever you want to call him, yes. As a person, I think I'd pay good money to watch him get eaten by wolves."

"I think I'd contribute."

We took a few steps away. "When do you think you'll know something?" I said.

"Should be soon," Norton said. "I asked the coroner to move this to the front of the line."

"Good. You'll let me know what he finds?"

"Either me or Rich."

"OK," I said, "thanks."

"What are you going to do now?"

"I told Rich earlier I was going to pull on some threads until something unraveled. It's still my plan."

"You have a thread in mind?"

"As a matter of fact, I do," I said.

I HAD a few hours to kill. It's best not to break into the homes of armed men in the middle of the night. Better to wait until the light of day for such things. I left the crime scene and got some mediocre coffee from a convenience store. It was hot and fresh enough I didn't want to spit it out right away. Call it a victory at this hour. I took my middling java and drove to the closest hotel I could find. I didn't want a room; I wanted to use their wi-fi.

A slow drive around the parking lot found the greatest signal strength. I needed more speed than a cellular connection in the sticks would provide. I used my tablet to open a secure connection to my server. From there, I tunneled into the BPD's facial recognition program. I uploaded the picture of the dead girl for comparison, set criteria based on age and obvious characteristics, and chose to cast a wide net. No one knew who the girl was or where she came from.

While the program spun its wheels, I reclined my seat and took a nap. Experience taught me facial recognition doesn't produce results as fast as TV would like us to believe. Using a wi-fi connection didn't help, so I grabbed the opportunity to rest. I remembered the clock in my car telling me it was four-forty-five.

I woke up a bit before six. The program spat out a result: Donna Frank. Donna recently turned sixteen, attended Havre de Grace High School in nearby Harford County, and owned a record free of run-ins with the law. She'd been reported missing by her mother four days ago. Libby Parsons lived a troubled life which spiraled into drugs. I saw nothing to indicate Donna Frank shared those problems. How she got consumed by this mess would require more investigation.

In the meantime, I called Rich. "You're still awake?" he said.

"I took a power nap."

"Of course you did."

"Not so fast, dear cousin," I said. "While I slept, I figured out who the dead girl behind the pizza shop is."

"What? The coroner doesn't even know who she is yet."

"Rich, are you surprised I'm smarter than some guy from the sticks who may not even be a doctor?"

"Do I want to know how you found out?"

"Probably not," I said, "but I'll bet you want to know her name."

Rich sighed. "I do."

"Donna Frank." I took a screen capture of the relevant info on Donna, pasted it into a document, and emailed it to Rich. "Check your inbox. I just sent you the basics on her."

"Got it," Rich said after a delay of a few seconds. He paused again to read the data. "This girl was a lot different than Libby."

"But ended up the same way, probably by the same people."

"We're going to have to talk to her parents," he said.

"We?"

"You wanted to be cut in on this."

"She lived in Harford County," I said. "Let their deputies break the news. I have other things to do."

"Like what?"

"Like finding out exactly how untouchable some people are."

"Be careful, C.T. We have two dead girls we know of. These guys aren't playing around."

"Neither am I."

We hung up. It was still too early for what I had in mind. I did a little more reading about the late Donna Frank, found little of interest, and settled in for another snooze to while away the downtime.

Finding Deputy Connors' address had been easy. Austin Connors—I was surprised he wasn't named Billy Ray—owned a small house more than a century old in Port Deposit. It sat a scant few blocks from where Donna Frank turned up dead the previous night. It didn't make him a suspect, but it was certainly a coincidence. Experience taught me not to like coincidences.

Connors' road featured similar residences. I didn't see a lot of activity other than people leaving. I sat in my car across the street and a house down. It gave me a good view of his

198 / TOM FOWLER

home and some of his back yard. If Connors were looking, he could see me, too, but I would take the chance. He didn't strike me as the vigilant type.

About a half-hour into my surveillance, a dog appeared in the backyard. It was a brown mutt of indeterminate breed, looking to be about fifty pounds. The dog puttered around the grass. I got out of the car, walked up to the house, and rapped on the front door. Connors didn't have a peephole. I made sure to stand off to the side so he couldn't peek out the window and see me.

I heard the locks turn and assumed a ready stance. Connors cracked the door open. I kicked it in, staggering him back into the room. "Morning, Connors," I said.

Connors recovered his balance and lunged toward a table. "Ah-ah," I said, holding my .45. "I'd like to keep this a pleasant conversation. At least, as pleasant as I can have with an asshole like you."

"I got nothing to say," Connors said. He glanced at the gun a couple times. I hadn't raised it yet.

"Sure you do, Connors. What kind of host are you? Make some coffee, and we can just be two guys having a conversation."

Connors looked between me and the gun a couple more times. "Fine," he said. I followed him into the kitchen. I didn't know where he might have a gun, so I didn't put the .45 away. Connors poured water into the machine, added coffee and a filter, and started the brewing process. A minute later, the sweet smell of caffeine permeated the kitchen air.

I sat at the small table. Connors kept a messy kitchen. It wasn't dirty, just cluttered. He left pots and pans on the counter, along with bread and boxes of snacks. The room didn't want for pantry or counter space; he just didn't use it. To my surprise, the place smelled neutral rather than rancid food. Connors played the dutiful host and waited for the java to finish before pouring two cups. "How do you take it?" he said.

I tried not to think about the other contexts in which Connors may have asked the question. "Milk is fine if you don't have creamer," I said.

Connors brought a quart of half-and-half to the table along with the two mugs of coffee. I added some creamer and plucked a stirrer from a box. Connors splashed some creamer in his, stirred the coffee, and frowned at me. "What do you want?"

"What do you think I want?"

"You're still looking into the girl."

"Libby. Sort of. You see . . . she's dead." I watched Connors' frown deepen for a second before he recovered. "Now I'm trying to figure out who killed her."

"Wasn't me."

"I wouldn't think so," I said. "You don't have the stomach for it. There's also another girl, found dead not far from here last night."

"Another one?" he said.

"Yes. Found behind the pizza shop down the street."

Connors shook his head. "I wondered what all the police lights were about."

"I'm surprised your pedo friends didn't tell you."

"Hey, I'm no pedophile."

"No, you just enable them."

Connors fell silent.

"The girl's name was Donna Frank." I didn't see a reaction from him. "It's too early to tell, but I'll bet she was sexually assaulted quite a few times before she died. Just like Libby was."

Connors didn't say anything. I pressed on.

"Donna just turned sixteen. Libby was even younger. These girls never had a chance. They got used, abused, and killed by a bunch of sick fuckers who don't care anything about them." No reaction. "There's no difference between the people who kill these girls and the people who help make it happen."

Now Connors squirmed. At least I got a reaction. I could probably beat a confession out of him, and while it would be satisfying, I decided against it. This case was about two (and maybe more) dead girls, not my satisfaction. "You're already suspended, Connors. When this all blows up, you're looking at a lot worse. Make it easy on yourself. Tell me what's going on. Tell me who's involved."

Connors stared at the tabletop. "Or what?"

"I could beat it out of you," I said. He looked up at me and frowned. "I'd rather keep this pleasant, though. You joined a law-enforcement unit. I'm sure you did it for good reasons. You wanted to protect people like Libby and Donna from perverts who would abuse them and kill them. You still have a chance to help them now."

I waited. Connors sighed and stared at the tabletop some more. After a few more seconds, he looked up at me. The frown had gone, replaced with a heavy-lidded weariness radiating defeat. "Fine," he said. "I've been carrying this shit too long."

"Let's hear it," I said.

"There are men who . . . like children. Girls, mostly, but some boys, too. They tend to like teenagers. Don't ask me why."

"I wasn't going to."

"Some of them live up here," he said. "The rest are scattered."

I wondered if the scattering extended beyond the

confines of Maryland. The feds getting involved at this point wouldn't help. "How do they find the kids?"

"I don't know. Sometimes, deputies would help."

"Rakin ever help?"

Connors nodded. "A lot. I don't know for sure, but he probably found the girl who just died."

I steeled myself for the next part of the conversation. "What would happen when these people . . . found a kid?"

"They'd get together at someone's house. A big house. Teenagers are defiant. I think some of these guys liked it. If the girl didn't play ball, they had roofies on hand. Either way, they'd basically spend the weekend . . . well, you know."

I closed my eyes. It lined up with what I expected him to say, but hearing it drove it home. A group of men deliberately ruined the lives of children, and sometimes ended those lives. "Then what?" I said.

"It's tough to just drop a kid off afterward. They talk. Hell, these days, they tweet and Snapchat. It's hard to have a secret ring of kid touchers when people are talking about it."

"So they kill the kids?"

Connors shook his head. "This is new. I don't know why it started. Usually, they drug them enough they don't remember what happened."

"What about when they go to the police?" I said. "To the doctor?"

"It ends up reported to us. Doctor, school shrink, whoever . . . they're going to call the cops. They have to."

"But it doesn't matter, does it?"

"No," he said. "It's hard to point a finger at anyone when the kid doesn't remember who did it."

"And if someone does point a finger?"

"Then these men are protected."

"Rakin said I couldn't touch them," I said.

"He was right," Connors confirmed with a nod.

"Judge Wilson."

"He's probably not the only one."

"If a case comes up in another city or county, there needs to be someone who can quash it."

"Yeah," he said. "It's messed up. They chew these kids up and spit them out."

"And the system designed to protect them is working against them." Another mark against it. "Why did you go along with it, Connors?"

"Money."

"They paid you?" I said.

"Yeah. I ain't proud of it. I knew it was bad money. But when you need cash, it's all green, and all I did was mess up some paperwork."

"This is a lot bigger than a couple of corrupt deputies."

"Good thing you got a state boy working with you," he said.

"It is." I paused. "Anything else? Anyone else you can point me to?"

"No," Connors said. "I told you what I know. It ain't a lot, but it's a start."

"Thanks. You ended up doing the right thing."

"I hope you find them. They've ruined a lot of lives." He flashed a rueful smile. "Mine, too."

"You're helping now. It matters."

"You'll need a lot more," he said.

CHAPTER 21

I GOT HOME AND WANTED TO CATCH SOME Z's. MY
couple snoozes earlier didn't make up for the sleep I lost
traipsing to Cecil County. Gloria greeted me with a cup of
hot coffee and a kiss, both of which I appreciated. We sat at
the kitchen table. "You look tired," she said.

"There's a good reason," I said, sipping the coffee.

"What happened up there?"

I told her about the body of Donna Frank, how I
unearthed who she was, and my chat with deposed Deputy
Connors. "Wow," she said. "It sounds like you stumbled into
something really large."

"I think I have."

"Be careful." Gloria grabbed my hand and squeezed it.
"Whoever these men are . . . whatever they've created . . . it's
swallowing up children and ruining good men. Don't you get
swallowed up, too."

"I won't," I said, squeezing Gloria's hand.

"I'll hold you to it."

I smiled. "Deal." My ringing cell phone interrupted a
pleasant moment. Caller ID pegged it as Melinda. "You

talked to a girl not long ago," she said after opening pleas-
antries. "T.J.?"

"I remember her."

"She heard what happened to Libby. She wants to help."

"She came to see you?" I said.

"Sure did. Told us you said the foundation could help
her. We're doing our best."

"Good. I'm glad she stopped in. I'm not sure how she can
help with what happened to Libby, though."

"Well, she wants to try, and I think it would be good for
her. Humor her. Can you meet us?"

My nap would need to wait. I sighed. "Sure. Where are
you?"

"My house. Can you come by in a half-hour?"

"I'll see you then." We hung up.

"No rest for the wicked?" Gloria said with a grin.

"Not yet." I told her about the phone call.

"Do you think she can help?"

"I don't know," I said. "At this point, it doesn't hurt to
try."

"Will you go to bed when you get back?"

"That depends . . . will you come up with me?"

Gloria fixed me with her best lascivious stare. It was
almost enough for me to tell Melinda I'd be very late. "If I do,
you won't get to sleep for a while."

"Exactly what I had in mind," I said.

I GOT to Melinda's house thirty-five minutes later. For me, it
was prompt. She let me in. T.J. sat on the couch, wearing a lot
more than she did the first time we chatted. Like Melinda,
her time off the streets restored a little color to her appear-

ance. She wore jeans and a plain sweater in the same fashion of her hostess but with a different color scheme. "Should I make some tea?" Melinda said after I sat on the couch opposite T.J.

"I'll take any caffeine I can get at this point," I said.

Melinda smiled. "OK, I'll be back in a couple minutes." She disappeared behind the kitchen door. I glanced around. This marked my first time inside Melinda's house. She'd only moved in a couple weeks ago. The place was pretty small—downright tiny compared to her father's palace—but for one person, it was perfect. Whoever furnished and decorated it did yeoman's work.

T.J. stared at me. I didn't say anything. She flicked her eyes toward the kitchen then back. I shrugged. She frowned.

"What?" I said.

"How thick are you?"

"What do you mean?"

"Melinda likes you."

"Of course she does."

T.J. rolled her eyes. "No, I mean she *likes* you."

"Oh. Really?"

"Really."

"She told you?" I asked.

"She doesn't have to tell me."

"I'm flattered, but I have a girlfriend."

"Pity," she said.

"I don't think so."

I got spared the rest of this conversation by Melinda emerging from the kitchen. She carried a serving tray with three mugs of hot water, an assortment of teabags, three spoons, and a small dish of sugar. She set it on the table, put a mug on a coaster for me, did the same for T.J., then sat on the couch with me. T.J. winked at me. Melinda hadn't plopped down on the cushion next to me, but I expected she would sit with T.J.

She brought a nice selection of tea. I selected an oolong and let it steep in the hot water. "We were very sorry to hear about Libby," Melinda said as an opener.

"Yeah," T.J. said, "I was hoping we'd helped you."

"You did," I said. "Just because Libby ended up dead doesn't mean you, Alex, and Velvet didn't provide support. I know more about who the guilty parties might be now, and I wouldn't without you guys."

"I want to do more."

I thought about what she might be able to provide. "OK, but this might be a little gruesome," I said. I used my phone to connect to my server and pull down pictures of the alley scene.

"I've seen gruesome," T.J. said.

"Still." I passed T.J. the phone. She frowned as soon as she saw the photos.

"This is Libby's crime scene?" she said as she scrolled through them.

"Yes."

"What is she going to tell you about that?" Melinda said.

"I don't know much about it. I never got to see it in person."

"How do you have the pictures on your phone, then?" said T.J.

"The BPD likes sharing things with me," I said.

Melinda frowned at me. T.J. swiped back and forth and scrutinized the pictures. Recognition lit in her eyes. "I think I see something familiar," she said.

"What is it?" I said. Melinda and I both leaned close.

"The blanket she's wrapped in. It's green on one side and blue on the other. I know where that's from."

"Where?"

"The Deluxe Plaza Motel," T.J. and Melinda said in unison.

* * *

I KNEW the place better than I cared to. When I first took Melinda's case, I found her there. It is exactly what you would expect of a no-tell motel: cheap and dingy with oily employees and a vibe to make any lucid person want to sprint for the shower upon departure. I'd hoped never to approach it again. Now it factored into Libby's murder.

I stopped at home to read the updated police report on Libby and to change cars. Only insanity or desperation would compel me to take the Audi to the Deluxe Plaza. I headed up Pulaski Highway, past the Gentlemen's Gold Club, and into a depressing slice of the city. Empty buildings and failing businesses were common sights. I pulled into the parking lot of the dreaded motel, took a deep breath, and got out.

Despite its name, the Deluxe Plaza Motel is at the opposite end of the spectrum from deluxe and can boast of no visible plaza. The genesis of this misnomer would always be a mystery no one cared enough to solve. I walked into the shabby lobby. Several manners of condoms were available for sale at the front desk. A small gift and snack shop sat off to the side. Behind the counter, a greasy fellow in a stained T-shirt peered at me. His creepy smile revealed a couple of missing teeth. I shuddered and yearned for a shower. My bathroom seemed a world away now.

"Help you?" the man said, keeping the strange smile on his face. When most customers paid by the hour, they didn't mind a side of creepy with their room.

"I'm looking for information," I said.

"I don't want no trouble with the cops," he said right away.

"I'm sure you don't. I'm not a cop." I showed him my badge and ID, holding them far enough away so his aura couldn't taint them.

"Why should I talk to you, then?"

I looked at the greaseball and gave him a slow smile. "Because you'll be wearing your monitor as a hat if you don't."

He looked at the old CRT monitor on the desk, then at me. "I guess I can talk."

"Two weeks ago, an underage girl came here with a man," I said.

He held up his hands. "Whoa, man. I don't know about illegal shit."

"I'm not here to bust your balls about it. The girl is dead. She was found in a blanket from here."

"Damn."

"Yeah," I said. "I'm going to need to see your guest logs."

He fetched a fat spiral notebook. If the motel still checked guests in by hand, I didn't want to know what purpose the computer served. "Two weeks ago exactly?" he said. I bobbed my head. "I was working the night shift. Any idea when this guy would have come in?"

"None." I queued up a picture of Libby on my phone. "This was the girl."

He squinted at the photo. "I remember her."

"You remember who she came in with?" I said.

"Not offhand. You got any other pictures?"

On a lark, I did a search for Judge Wilson and found a nice official picture of him to show the clerk. "Yeah, he was with her." He searched the notebook and tapped his dingy finger on an entry. "This is them." Wilson signed in as W. Clement. Not very stealthy.

"You remember anything else about them?"

He pondered the question for a minute, then nodded. "Yeah," he said, "I remember they weren't alone."

"Another young girl?"

"No," he said. "Another guy. Looked even older than the dude on your phone."

I hung my head. "There was another man?" I said.

The clerk nodded. "Sure was."

"And you're positive they were together?"

"Sure am."

"Shit," was all I could say.

"Didn't know about the second guy?"

I changed course. "The girl who came in wasn't even sixteen, and she didn't look older. You were working. You let two assholes get a room with a girl who looks underage?"

"Hey, we all gotta eat. Ain't like they dragged her."

"They pay you?" I said.

"For my silence."

"Doesn't seem to have bought them very much."

He shrugged. "I see a lot of shit, man. I've learned to look past most of it. Some girls or pimps pay more. Cops come around sometimes." He shrugged. "You get used to hearing about bad shit going down."

"I'm sure you do," I said. I needed to keep him on point and not lose him in the minutiae of his job. "Do you remember what the other man looked like?"

Instead of answering, the clerk took a step to stand before the monitor. He used a mouse I wouldn't have touched through three gloves. "I do," he said, "but I'm seeing if we have tape from the night you're asking about."

I looked around at the ceiling. In addition to water marks

and paint someone should have refreshed early in the Obama administration, I saw the telltale dome of a security camera. "You have a system?"

"Hell, yeah," he said. "I told you, man, we get some bad shit. The office has one and so does the walkway to the rooms outside."

A basic camera system wouldn't get me to change my impression of the Deluxe Plaza Motel—the place would remain mired in the red—but it bumped the score up toward zero a tick. I waited while the clerk hunted for the footage I needed. A few minutes later, I saw his gap-toothed smile again. "Got it," he said.

"Both cameras?" I said.

"Yep."

I took out my keys. For years, I carried a small flash drive on my keyring. I was about to take the drive off the keyring when I remembered where the computer was. Who knew what horrors and malware lay on a hard drive at a place like this? "On second thought, I can FTP it to myself," I said. I pointed at the keyboard. "Can I use it for a minute?"

"We normally don't let people, but sure." He moved over, and I walked around. Stains I hoped were from coffee and other beverages pockmarked the keyboard. Times like these made me glad I was a fast typist. I opened a command prompt, connected to my server via FTP, and sent the files to myself. Total time soiling my hands with the keys: about a minute.

"Thanks," I said when I finished.

"Sure, man," the clerk said. "Totally fucked up what happened to the girl. I hope you catch those two."

"I'm sure as hell going to try." I walked back to my car. Before starting it, I made sure to apply a copious amount of hand sanitizer.

* * *

INSTEAD OF DRIVING BACK HOME, I went to my office. Might as well get some mileage out of my rent. As I walked down the hallway, I noticed the blood and vomit gone from my encounter with the three goons I still didn't know who sent. I made a mental note to look into it. I unlocked the office, sat behind my desk, and found the files I transferred.

I needed to fast-forward through a bunch of boring footage to get to Libby, Judge Wilson, and the mystery man arriving. A few people came into the office, rented rooms, walked down the walkway outside, and went behind their doors. I slowed the footage when Judge Wilson and his asshole friend arrived with Libby. The video was in color and far less grainy than I expected. I waited for Judge Wilson's friend to face the camera. So far, I'd only seen him in profile and to the side. Wilson signed the guest registry. Money changed hands. They turned to leave.

The other guy looked at the camera.

I paused the video and took a screen capture.

On TV, forensic and video technicians will blow up a picture and it will magically become clearer in the process. In reality, doing this only pixelates the image more, making it less sharp and thus, much harder to discern a face. Simple magnification was never the answer. I owned a program which might get me closer to the answer. Digital images are made up of picture elements—or pixels. Blowing up the image exposes the limitations of those pixels. Well-designed programs can take what's already in the image and fill in gaps. It's not an exact science, but it makes some very good guesses. I used such an app to enhance the picture of Judge Wilson's friend.

I could tell right away the other man was definitely older

than Wilson by at least a decade. I let the program do its magic. At the end of its process, it produced a pretty good rendering of a man who may have killed Libby Parsons. I connected to the BPD's network and fed the picture into the facial recognition software. Now I hoped the photo I input would be good enough to lead to a match.

The program churned. I didn't know if the quality of the input picture made a difference. A proper photograph would be easier to compare. My search parameters consisted of Caucasian men over fifty I didn't want to add any other exclusions. As the software kept working, I got a bottle of water from the office fridge. I wondered if my work on the photo made it unusable. When I pondered hanging up my editing shoes, a potential match popped up on the screen.

The program made most of its matches with over 98% certainty. This one checked in at 90%. I chalked up the delta to having to tweak a security camera screen capture to make it usable. Ninety percent was good enough for me. I didn't expect this to swing a court case, so I didn't care about the missing percentage points. When I saw the name associated with the picture pop up, I did a double take.

Conrad Milburn II.

CHAPTER 22

I KNEW I DIDN'T LIKE THE MILBURNS THE FIRST TIME I met them. The fact I now knew the two Conrads I met were the Third and the Fourth just cemented my dislike. Family pomposity increases in direct proportion to the number after someone's surname. I'd been around enough snooty families in my day. What I now wondered was how Conrad the Eldest related to Judge Wilson? I did some poking around and discovered they were cousins on the judge's mother's side. What was Milburn II's story?

Right away, I discovered his story was ugly. He'd been arrested on seven different occasions for crimes involving children. Somehow, he only got convicted once, and it later was expunged from his record, no doubt with help from Cousin Clem. This guy had been abusing children for years and carried a free pass to keep doing it by virtue of his cousin's ability to protect him.

This needed to stop.

I dug deeper on Milburn. The Cecil County Sheriff's Office as well as other law enforcement bodies throughout the state listed him as a person of interest on nine separate occasions in the last few years. None managed to stick. I copied the records of all the cases to my server, so I could peruse them later. I also looked more into the Milburn family. Conrad the Eldest had a sister who married and produced a few children. One served in the Cecil County SO.

His name? Philip Rakin.

* * *

I took a shower when I got home. The stench of the Milburns, the Deluxe Plaza Motel, and others clung to me. After stepping out and drying off, I didn't feel tired anymore, but I lay in bed anyway. The last couple nights played hell with my sleep. Gloria joined me after a couple minutes. "You were gone a while," she said.

"I stopped at the office to run something down," I said. I filled her in on what I learned at the motel and the office.

"You think you'll wrap this up soon?" Gloria said as she snuggled next to me.

"I hope so. The longer this case drags on, the dirtier I feel."

"I'm sure you do. What's your next move?"

"I'm not sure, actually. We need to take the judge down. When he falls, these assholes lose their protection."

"What about the guy who had all the charges against him?" she asked.

"I saved those files to look at later. There will be a lot of angry parents I'll need to talk to."

"What are you going to do?"

"Find out as much as I can," I said. "Then take these sick fuckers down. It's about time someone ruined their lives."

"You're hot when you're crusading," Gloria said with a grin. She ran her hand over my chest.

"Only then?" I said.

"Well . . . some other times, too."

"Am I crusading now?"

"You are."

"It sounds like we should capitalize on my hotness, then. Wouldn't want it to pass."

"No, we wouldn't," Gloria said before she kissed me.

* * *

AFTER GLORIA WORE ME OUT, weariness took over. I slept until eight the next morning. I'm normally loath to wake up so early, but falling asleep early balances this out. I left the still-sleeping Gloria upstairs and went downstairs to make breakfast.

Priority one: coffee. From there, I surveyed the refrigerator and pantry. My kitchen muse must have remained asleep. I heated a skillet and put sausage on to cook, then threw bread in the toaster. Even this simple breakfast lured Gloria from the bedroom. A few minutes later, we each enjoyed a mug of coffee and a plate full of toast and sausage. It wasn't gourmet, but it would get the day going.

"Still planning to go after the judge today?" Gloria said.

"I'm going to call Rich," I said. "He's on some task force working this case. I'll see what he thinks."

"You're going to defer to Rich?" Gloria looked at me as if I'd grown a third eye in my forehead.

"We're going after a judge. He's a lowlife but not a garden-variety one. We need to take him down the right way."

"Wow. I didn't think this case would make such an upstanding citizen out of you." Gloria winked at me.

"It's not," I said. "I still plan to unload on the Milburns with both extrajudicial barrels."

"There's the man I love."

We finished breakfast. Gloria handled the kitchen cleanup and I walked into my spare office. I emailed Rich a few things and then called him. "You're up early," he said.

"After the past couple days, I felt decadent sleeping past four," I said.

"Do you have something?"

"You'll need to check your email. But basically, I know where Libby's body came from."

"You do? Where? And how?"

"The Deluxe Plaza Motel," I said. "A couple of working girls IDed the blanket. Guess who signed the guest book the night Libby was killed?"

"Who?"

"Judge Wilson."

"You saw the guest book?" Rich asked.

"And the security footage."

"I'm surprised such a shithole has a camera."

"I thought they might use them in the rooms."

I almost heard Rich shudder through the phone. "You want to go after the judge?" he said.

"It's why I called," I said. "You were right earlier . . . we have to have everything in order to nail this prick. I'll defer to you on the best way."

"You sure you're feeling OK?"

"Positive."

"I'll look over what you sent," he said. "If it's good, I'm sure we can get something going on the judge."

"The sooner, the better. Once he falls, everyone else loses the protection they've been relying on."

"I'll keep you posted," Rich said and hung up.

Rich would take care of making sure all the ducks walked in neat little rows. It left me time to contemplate how to take down the Milburns. First, I needed to see if Conrad II passed down his love of violating children to his son. Conrad III had been arrested twice for inappropriate contact with a minor but never got convicted of anything. Conrad IV had a clean criminal record, though I remembered his love of partying with girls like Libby. It didn't take long to learn where he went to school, and it took even less time for me to get into the school's network. Conrad the Youngest had been suspended earlier in the year for "questionable conduct with female students," though he was never charged with anything.

This family needed to be stopped.

* * *

I WORKED on building a case against the Milburns. Nine families saw their children abused by the eldest Conrad, only to watch him skate on the charges. I looked them up. Two moved on from Maryland, but seven remained. Lacking a better system, I started alphabetically with the Andersons, Rick and Jean. "Hello?" a female voice said.

"Mrs. Anderson?"

"Yes, who's this?"

I introduced myself and told her a little about why I called.

"Of course I remember that sicko," Jean Anderson said. "I recall everything Rachel told us. I remember the look on his face . . . like he didn't care. Like he would just do it again."

"He did," I said.

"I'm not surprised."

"He faced allegations a total of nine times."

"Nine?" she said. "Good God, why didn't someone stop him? Why make all our families suffer?"

"He had a protector in the legal system . . . one the police and I are working to remove. With him gone, men like Conrad Milburn won't be untouchable, and they can finally pay for what they did."

"I'd love to see that son of a bitch pay."

I turned an idea over in my head. "Mrs. Anderson, if I could arrange it so you and Milburn were in the same place at the same time, would you be willing?"

"I'd relish it," she said. "Hell, I'm tempted to pay you to make it happen."

"I have an idea, but it will take a little time, and there's a legal domino we need to topple first. I'll keep you posted."

"Please do," she said. We hung up.

Next, I called the Coopers, Peter and Nancy. Mrs. Cooper answered the phone. After my introduction, her story was similar.

"I'll never forget that son of a bitch," she said. "Our Tim is still messed up about the whole thing."

"Tim?"

"That's right."

"I'm sorry," I said, "your case is the first I've heard where Milburn assaulted a boy."

"Creeps like him don't have boundaries."

"Mrs. Cooper, I'm working with the police to take down someone who's been protecting Milburn. He's skated past nine allegations. We're hoping to put a stop to it."

"What can I do to help?"

"You may need to testify later. Shorter-term, though, if I could arrange for you to be in the same place at the same time as Milburn, would you want it?"

"More than anything else."

"I'll see what I can do and get back to you."

"Please do."

The other parents I managed to reach—all mothers— shared similar tales of grief. Milburn violated their children, sometimes with others of his ilk, sometimes more than once. He never cared about the charges he faced because he knew Judge Wilson kept a gold-plated *Get Out of Jail Free* card at the ready. With any luck, it would be going away soon. Getting old charges to stick against Milburn might be dicey. My plan might at least give the families satisfaction, and could possibly indict or as a minimum, ruin the Milburns.

I just needed to get good news from Rich first.

* * *

A COUPLE HOURS LATER, Rich called back. "I hope you have something good," I said.

"We're going after Wilson," he said.

I pumped my fist. "Took a while to get a warrant?"

"We had to make sure this one was solid. Wilson could get off the hook if we messed anything up."

"When are we leaving?"

"We?"

"I'll break into your fucking car if I have to."

Rich chuckled. "Relax. You're coming along. You, Norton, and me."

"When do we leave?"

"We'll pick you up in a half-hour."

"I'll be ready."

CHAPTER 23

WE RODE IN AN UNMARKED BUT STILL OBVIOUS POLICE
car. Norton drove, and Rich sat up front, which relegated me
to the backseat. At least this car didn't have a cage. I noticed a
few other vehicles following us too. "How many more are
with us?" I said.

"I recruited a few people I trust," Norton said.

"Expecting a few pedophiles to give you a fight?"

"Some of these men can be violent. We've seen it
already."

"True," I said. "I think it might be different when they're
not facing a teenager."

"It never hurts to be prepared."

"You would have made a heck of a Boy Scout."

"I did," Norton said with a smile in the rearview.

We made good time up I-95, through Baltimore and
Harford Counties and across the Susquehanna River into
Cecil County. In my youth, I heard people tell stories of how
Cecil County was its own world. It was as if the
Susquehanna warped reality and something dark and sinister
lay on the other side. For the most part, I found Cecil County
to be normal and pleasant if a bit rural for my tastes. The

men of interest in this case, however, did not do their home county any credit.

Judge Wilson lived in a large house at least a century old. He owned enough land to seclude himself from his neighbors. A fence and poor lighting in the yard only helped. These factors also made his home a convenient place to bring teenagers. I shuddered on the bench seat. Norton flipped the headlights off as we got closer. Wilson's driveway was paved, and the cars inched forward so no one would hear our approach.

Norton stopped about a hundred feet from the house. He left our vehicle near two others, one new and one much older. Norton, Rich, and I waited as the other six state troopers fanned out around the house. Norton got a signal in his earpiece and waved us onward to the front. It was white with a pretty new paint job and dark red shutters. The square footage could hold three of mine and still have enough room for a wet bar and man cave. Lots of rooms to hide a teenager from prying eyes.

Rich pulled the storm door open and banged his fist on the heavy metal one. We waited a few minutes. Norton held his gun, and—never one to be left out—I drew mine, too. Rich banged again. From inside, footsteps approached. It took a few seconds, but three locks disengaged, and the door swung open.

Judge Wilson stood before us. Sweat lingered on the edges of his hair. His rumpled clothes looked like they had been pulled out of a pile and thrown on with some haste. The sweatpants he chose to wear did a poor job of hiding his erection. Wilson looked at each of us in turn. "What the hell are you doing here on a Saturday?" he said.

Norton thrust a document at him. "Judge Wilson, we have a warrant to search this house and property," he said, shoving his way in. Rich followed, and I brought up the rear.

"What's the meaning of this?" Wilson said.

"You're a lawyer," I said, "read the goddamn warrant."

Rich and Norton moved toward the back of the house to let everyone else in. I nosed around. Let the pros do their thing. The judge owned old furniture to match his aged house. The clutter cried out for a maid service. I looked for closed doors and listened for sounds of distress. If Wilson answered the knocking with a boner, I figured there had to be someone here being violated by him and maybe one or more of his sick friends.

I nudged an opening and saw stairs leading down. From below, I thought I heard a muffled curse. Another door opened. I hustled down the steps and looked for a light switch. Somewhere ahead of me, I saw a person moving. I flipped the light on and raised my gun.

Rakin stared back at me.

He was even more disheveled than Judge Wilson. His sweatshirt appeared tossed on crooked. His jeans were unbuttoned and I could tell he hadn't bothered looking for underwear. I shook my head. "Where is she?" I said.

"Who?" said Rakin.

"Her, him—I don't care. Whoever you and the judge have been down here raping. Where is she?"

"I don't know what you mean."

"Maybe you missed the fact I have a gun pointed at you."

"If you wanted to shoot me, you woulda done it already."

"OK." I took a step to the side and set the gun on a table. "There's no gun. Now I get to beat it out of you."

"I knew you were an asshole when we had you in a cell," Rakin said.

"I'm not in handcuffs now," I said.

Rakin smiled and rushed me. I grabbed his arm and spun him away from me and the gun. His back hit the wall hard and he bounced off looking angry. "That your best?" he said.

"Not even close."

Rakin stepped forward and threw a punch. He got a lot behind it. He was short but knew how to drive with his hips. I blocked this swing and the next one. Rakin tried a body blow, which I blunted by lowering my elbow. He went up high again to no avail. I drove my head forward and aimed for the nose. Rakin saw it coming and backed up enough to avoid a broken septum, but I still staggered him.

I followed it with a punch to the midsection. Air blasted from Rakin's lungs as I slugged him again. He took a wobbly step back. I drove my right elbow into his face. His cheekbone snapped with a satisfying crunch. The force sent him into the wall again. I pursued him, forsaking defense to rain body blows into his midsection. Rakin struggled to breathe. He slumped forward. I backed up and kneed him in the face, sending his head crashing into the wall. He sagged to the floor and coughed a few times as his lungs gulped in the air denied them.

"Where is she?" I said.

Rakin coughed something sounding like an insult.

I rolled him onto his back, raised my foot, and stomped on his groin with all the weight and force I could muster. He folded in half. I did it again, ignoring the hands he used to try and protect himself. Then I kicked him in the face, breaking his nose and putting him flat on his back once more. Rakin looked like a mess. I couldn't summon a whit of sympathy.

"Where is she?" I said again.

"Slider . . . in the . . . wall," Rakin choked out.

I looked at the wall. Whoever built the entry took care to

hide the outline. I had to look closely to see it. "How do I open it?"

Rakin coughed weakly in reply.

"How, goddammit?" I said, kicking him in the gut.

He sputtered some more. Blood ran from his lips. "Plaque on . . . the wall," he said.

I followed his gaze and saw it. I fetched my gun from the table and then stared at the inscription. In a perfect bit of irony, it commemorated Judge Wilson for his work with young people some years ago. I grabbed the award and tried moving it. It slid to the left. The door clicked open. Rakin groaned, so I kicked him in the face. He lapsed into unconsciousness.

I pushed the panel open slowly. A small lamp on a night-stand provided dim light in a small room maybe twelve feet by ten. It smelled mustier in here than in the main basement. A queen bed dominated the center. A young girl who did not appear eighteen was naked and tied up, her wrists bound to the bedposts with what looked like scarves. She moaned inco-herently. Her eyes rolled around and didn't focus. I rushed out of the room. "Guys, down here!" I said. "I found a girl."

A minute later, Rich, Norton, and a female trooper came down the stairs. Her nameplate identified her as Cutler; I waved her inside. "Call an ambulance," I said to Rich as I walked away.

"Already did," he said.

Norton crouched beside Rakin and checked his pulse. "Jesus, you did a number on this one," he said.

"Meet Rakin," I said. "He's a deputy involved in all of this. He's also related to the judge. He wouldn't tell me where the girl was."

"So you beat it out of him?"

"He started it."

Norton regarded Rakin and shook his head. "Son of a bitch deserves it. If I were down here, I might have killed him."

The female trooper poked her head out. "It doesn't look good," she said. "This girl has been drugged, and she's definitely been raped."

"Jesus," Rich said. "We caught them with a girl here. The brazen bastards."

"Who knows what they might have done with her?" I said.

"Judge Wilson is in cuffs," Norton said. "I think we've cut the head off his little pedophile ring."

"Maybe," I said. "Now the body should die. There are a couple pieces whose demises I'd like to hasten, though."

"Fill me in."

I took out my phone, found the email I sent to Rich, and forward it to Norton. "All the details are in your inbox," I said. "They don't live very far from here. It's kind of like one-stop shopping."

"Who doesn't love a bargain?" said Norton.

* * *

"We need to keep this hush-hush," Rich said. He, Norton, Cutler, and I sat around Judge Wilson's dining room table. The ambulance already left, taking Rakin and the girl with no ID to the hospital.

"A prominent judge gets arrested?" MDSP Corporal Elena Cutler said after tying her short blonde hair back. "People are going to talk."

"Probably," I said. "But we can try to keep it out of the papers and off the local news. If Wilson's friends don't know he's in jail, they might keep playing their sick games and lead us to them."

"We have to get the feds involved," Norton said. "Freel found some pictures of this girl, some other girls, and even a few boys."

"Actual pictures?"

"Yeah. Not Polaroids . . . these are digital prints. Makes me think they're on computers, too."

"Probably being traded around the Internet," Rich said.

"You know the feds are going to cut us out," I said. "They're going to take this over, focus on the kiddie porn, and we'll lose Wilson and his creepy friends."

"Let them rot in the federal system," Cutler said with a shrug.

"FBI doesn't fuck around," Norton added.

"But involving them makes it more likely the story gets out," I said.

"You think one of them would blab?"

"I think they'll attract more attention. This house is pretty secluded, but it's not invisible. Wilson's neighbors will see bright yellow *FBI* on blue windbreakers piling out of vans and start talking. It's inevitable his friends will find out."

"We can't just *not* report this," Norton said.

I sought some middle ground. "Can we *not* do it right away?"

"You want to bust the rest of Wilson's group," Rich said.

"Damned right I do. If they get wind of the feds sniffing around, they're gone. We won't find them. They'll just pack up and go somewhere else, then begin all this again. Maybe they'll even find another judge to keep letting them off the hook."

Norton sighed. "We all need to make careful notes about this, but reports don't need to be filed immediately." he said.

"Wilson is a judge. People must be used to seeing cops come and go from here, so a little police presence won't draw attention. It's Saturday. I'll probably kick this upstairs Monday afternoon, and the brass will probably decide to get the feds involved."

"So we basically have forty-eight hours to bring everyone else down?" I said.

"Yes."

I grinned for the first time in a couple days. "Challenge accepted."

* * *

"You're sure you want to stop there?" Norton said to me when we were back in the car.

"Positive," I said.

"What's there to gain?"

"I'm not going to tip our hand. I'm simply going to inform the Milburns Libby is dead, maybe try to ask Conrad the Fourth a few more questions about her."

"He might have been part of all this," Rich said. "And then they might tell the old man everything is falling apart."

"I doubt it," I said. "If we act like we're in the dark, they can't assume we've figured any of this out. They'll think they're still golden."

"I hope this doesn't blow up on us."

"It won't. Trust me . . . I know their type."

We drove to the Milburns' house. I checked an app I wrote for my phone as we crested the driveway. We exited the car and approached the door. As before, Norton did the knocking. Conrad the Third came to the door. He glanced at Norton and Rich, then recognized me and fixed me with a glower. "What do you want?" he said.

"We need to speak to you and your son, Mr. Milburn," Norton said. He and Rich showed their badges.

"What about?"

"A missing girl."

"I already talked to him," Milburn said, pointing at me.

"Things have changed," I said. "We can discuss this inside, or we can make a big show of dragging you to a state police barracks."

"Fine," Milburn said with a scowl. "My wife's not home. I'll get my son." We walked in and sat three abreast on the couch. The father went upstairs. Then, both of them came down to join us a minute later. The father took out his phone, texted someone, then tossed the phone onto the coffee table. Well within range for what I wanted to do.

Bluetooth has been a ubiquitous technology for years. It's very convenient, and the convenience comes paired with security often implemented as an afterthought. Compromising phones and similar devices via Bluetooth is trivial. I launched my app. It found Conrad the Third's phone, cracked his Bluetooth security code in less than a second, and left a little piece of code behind. The compromised phone would send its text logs and audio recordings to me every hour. The limited range of Bluetooth didn't matter when the phone itself had been infected. As long as it found a cellular or wi-fi signal, I owned him.

The younger Conrad looked around at everyone. His eyes lingered longer on Rich and Norton. They looked more official than I did, and I was fine with it. Conrad acted like a nervous teenager before, and only I sat here then. I hoped Rich and Norton might be able to coax something more out of him. In light of his grandfather's proclivities, Conrad's party invitations to Libby now looked suspicious.

"Let's get this over with," the elder Conrad said as if he were in control of the situation.

"It will take as long as it takes," Norton said.

"I can ask you to leave anytime."

"What are you going to do if we don't," I said, "call the cops?"

"Eat shit."

"Mr. Milburn," Norton said, "you know why we're here."

"Some girl."

"Her name was Libby Parsons," I said.

"Whatever. Wait . . . was?"

"She's dead," Rich said. "Found in Baltimore."

"Libby's really dead?" the son said.

"I'm afraid so," I said. "She died at least a day before anyone found her." Conrad the son shook his head a few times.

"Do you think we had something to do with this girl's death?" the father said.

"Here's what we know," Norton said, turning to face both of them. "Judge Wilson was involved with a bunch of pedophiles. We know your father," he nodded toward Conrad the Third, "was mixed up in it, too. We know Libby used to come here under the pretext of parties. Add it all up, and you have to admit it looks mighty suspicious."

"My grandfather was never here with Libby," Conrad the Fourth said.

"Good to know," I said. "But tell me . . . were these really parties? Or was Libby here only so you could screw her?" I turned to the father. "Maybe so you could screw her, too."

"I'm a married man!"

"Right. Married men never cheat."

"This is ridiculous." The elder Conrad crossed his arms

under his chest. If we were in a cartoon, steam would have poured from his ears.

"A lot of things get handed down from father to son," I said. "Some of them are normal. Others are disgusting. Maybe you liked underage girls, too. Hell, maybe you liked underage boys."

"Hey, I'm no faggot!"

I ignored his slur and focused on why we came. "No? Just a rapist like your old man?"

"You have no proof," he said.

"There's something an innocent man would never say."

The younger Conrad got up and paced the room. He glared at his father, who lost color in the face. "Dad, this is bullshit," he said. "She's dead. Libby's dead." Conrad stalked toward his father. "Did you and your sick friends have anything to do with it?" The father couldn't look at him. "I liked Libby," the shaken boy continued. "She was a nice girl. And you ruined her, just like the others. Did you kill her, too?" Conrad the Third remained silent. "Did Grandpa kill her?"

Still no response. Conrad the son became my favorite person of the day when he balled up his fist and clocked his father in the face. The older man fell over on the couch. Rich pulled the younger Conrad back before things escalated.

"I think we'll need to go to a state police barracks anyway," Norton said.

CHAPTER 24

Conrad the Third lawyered up right away. Norton and Cutler talked to him and his mouthpiece in one of the interrogation rooms. The attorney had a round face and a rounder body, and what I could hear of him made me think he belonged in used car sales. Rich and I sat at Norton's desk along with Conrad the son, who'd said very little since we arrived. It couldn't have been easy for him knowing what his father and grandfather did and trying to live with it. Everyone has a breaking point.

"How many girls?" I said after a few minutes of silence.

"A few." Conrad shook his head. "They tried to get me to go in with them. Said I was young, so it wasn't really illegal. Because doping a girl up and tying her to the bed was legal." He rolled his eyes.

"You do it?" Rich said.

Conrad didn't say anything. His nostrils flared as he breathed. "Once," he said in a small voice.

"Why?"

"I was sixteen. The girl was probably fifteen. She looked eighteen. I wanted her real bad. It was . . . just so easy." Conrad let out a deep breath. "Afterwards, I tried to tell myself she was into it. She was into *me*. I tried to make myself feel better." Tears rimmed his eyes. "In the end, I'm no better than they are."

I grabbed some tissues from Norton's desk and handed them to Conrad. "You *are* better," I said. "You knew what you did was wrong. You knew, and you cared. I'm not sure they even know, and if they do, I'm positive they don't give a damn."

"You spooked my dad when you came around asking about Libby. He said he had to get you off the case."

A connection clicked in my head. "He sent three goons after me."

"He did?" Rich said.

I nodded. "They came to my office."

"What happened?"

"I didn't drop the case, did I?"

"What's going to happen to my dad?" Conrad said.

"He has a lawyer," Rich said. "He'll probably get released for now. Formal charges will come soon."

"They should pay for what they did."

"Are you willing to testify against them?"

Conrad thought a long moment. "I want to say yes," he said. "They did some really bad things. I don't know about any girls ending up dead, but I saw they got girls to the house, gave them drugs, and . . . took them to the basement."

"Your mom know about it?" I said.

"Hell, no. I'm not sure how she didn't discover it. I got the feeling she suspected something."

"Maybe she couldn't bring herself to admit it," I said.

"Conrad, I have to ask you something," Rich said. "It's an uncomfortable question, but considering everything, we have to know. Did your father or grandfather ever . . . touch you? Do anything bad to you?"

"No," Conrad said, shaking his head. "For a long time, I thought they were normal. When I got old enough to start noticing girls, I thought something was odd. I saw a glimpse of a girl downstairs once. I asked what was going on, and my grandfather said she was selling something for her school. I didn't believe it." Conrad closed his eyes. "Jesus, they were with her down there. I was in the house and I didn't know about it."

"Judge Wilson built a hidden room in his basement," I said. "Did your dad have something like it?"

"He had his mancave, he called it. He always kept the door locked. I don't even know where he kept the key. If they took girls to the basement, it must be where."

"You have a walkout basement?"

He nodded and winced in disgust. "The door comes in right near the mancave. They didn't even have to try very hard."

"Do you know how they kept the girls quiet afterwards?" Rich said. "Even if they were out of it at the house, they'd have to come to later and realize something terrible happened to them."

"I don't know for sure," Conrad said. "I overheard them talking once. I think they drugged the girls again afterward before getting them out of there. Then they'd just leave them off somewhere."

Rich and I both shook our heads. "The girls certainly went to the police," Rich said. "They must've gotten rape kits done. No DNA?"

"I'm sure they have rubbers down there."

The interrogation door room swung open. Conrad the father and his fat lawyer walked out. "What are you doing?" the father said, pointing at Rich and me. "You can't talk to my son."

"It's a free country," I said.

"What did he tell you?" Conrad glared at the youngster, who looked away. "What did you tell them?"

"He told us you're an asshole. We already knew."

Conrad took a step toward me. I stood my ground. "You were supposed to find Libby," he said. "You failed. Why don't you go let someone else down?"

"What are you going to do if I don't . . . send another three shitheads after me?"

"Those are serious accusations," the lawyer said. I expected him to tell me about the features of the car I wanted to buy.

"Well, your client is a serious piece of shit," I told him.

Conrad the father fumed but made the wise choice to walk away. He grabbed his son by the arm, said, "Let's go" through clenched teeth, and headed for the door. The lawyer followed them. Rich and I watched them go. Norton and Cutler came out of the interrogation room. "You guys learn anything from the kid?" said Norton.

"Yeah," I said. "We really need to find the old man."

"I wish I understood when you speak geek," Rich said as we drove back.

"It's simple. Bluetooth security is a joke. I put something on the father's phone. I'll get his texts and his phone calls."

"And he won't know?"

"Nope."

"You think he's going to contact his father?"

"He pretty much has to," I said. "Their world is crumbling. We've kept Judge Wilson's arrest hush-hush, but they're bound to find out eventually. At some point, they have to circle the wagons."

"And when they do?" said Rich.

"Then we'll grab as many of them as we can."

"These guys might be modern. I don't think they're sitting around trading Polaroids. They're online."

"When did you learn so much about the modern pedophile?" I asked.

"When I linked up with the Staties to start working this."

"They figured pedophiles were involved?"

"Sort of," Rich said. "We knew a girl was missing. We heard rumors of connections between Cecil County and Baltimore covering multiple girls. By this point, pedophiles became a logical conclusion."

"I probably should have thought of it sooner, especially when you and Norton got involved."

"You were looking for Libby," Rich said.

"Fine job I did."

Rich looked at me. "Don't beat yourself up over it. She had problems long before you started looking for her. Then once she fell in with these assholes, she was as good as gone."

I didn't say anything. A thought turned over in my head. Conrad the son said his father and friends would drop the girls off somewhere after a fresh round of sedatives. Between the girls not remembering anything and the lack of DNA evidence, no one came under suspicion. Why kill Libby, then? What was so different about her they couldn't simply drop her off like everyone else?

"What are you thinking about?" Rich said.

"Libby," I said.

"I told you to ease up on yourself."

"No, I'm wondering why they killed her."

"Hmm." Rich frowned in thought. "It's an outlier, isn't it?"

"They've killed two girls we know of. Before, they must have gone through several. Like little Conrad said, they'd dope them up and ditch them somewhere. First Libby was different and then Donna Frank, too. Why?"

"No idea."

"They relied on the girls not remembering," I said. "The initial drugs, maybe booze, then a second round of meds to keep them out of it. What made Libby so different . . ." I trailed off.

"What?" Rich said.

"Libby was a druggie."

"So?"

"Maybe whatever they gave her didn't have the same effect. Maybe she was more lucid than they expected. They couldn't take the chance, so they killed her."

"But they checked her into the motel."

"The clerk said she looked out of it," I said.

"She could have simply been stoned."

"Or dosed on whatever they gave her."

"And the second girl?" Rich said.

"Maybe she built up a similar immunity."

Rich pondered the idea. "It's a theory," he said.

"I wish we had more than theories and malware on some sicko's phone," I said.

* * *

SOMETHING ELSE BUGGED me about this case. A lot of things bugged me about it—mostly the people involved—but one item in particular picked at me. Conrads the Second and Third, and whoever else was with them, would take girls into

Third's mancave and sexually assault them. Condoms would explain a lack of DNA. What about evidence from the rest of the room? A fiber from the carpet? A string from the blanket?

The lack of evidence required professional cleaning, like hospital grade.

So Conrad the Third used a specialized service. It would take me a while to find which one. If I knew where the Milburns did their banking, I could start there, but I didn't. I needed to get Mrs. Milburn in on this to save time. I wondered what she knew and how much she had to deny to herself. Being married to a monster has to take a toll. I hoped she wanted to unburden her soul.

I couldn't call the house. Either Conrad would recognize my voice. I asked Gloria to do it instead. "If a man answers, play the wrong number card," I said. "If it's a woman, hand me your phone."

"OK," Gloria said with a nod. I gave her the number, and she dialed it. The Milburns might have been eating dinner. Or maybe Mrs. Milburn started drinking herself to sleep while her husband violated another girl in his basement. Gloria sat beside me; I heard the phone ringing in her ear. We got lucky; a female voice answered. Gloria passed it to me.

"Mrs. Milburn?"

"Yes, who's this?"

"I hope you remember me, and I need you to hear me out. This is C.T. Ferguson."

"The investigator?"

"Yes."

Her tone sharpened. "Haven't you done enough?"

"Mrs. Milburn," I said, "I need to talk to you. Alone."

"I don't think so."

"It's very important. Two girls are already dead. Two we

know of. I don't want the number to climb any higher, and I don't think you do, either."

"My husband didn't have anything to do with that," she said.

"I think we both know it's not true."

"I shouldn't be talking to you." Her voice lost its edge.

"I'm sure your husband told you not to."

"He did."

"This time, I need you to ignore what he told you. We need to talk, and the sooner, the better. Are you alone?"

"Yes, my husband and son are out. I don't know when they'll be back."

"Good," I said. "Meet me somewhere, then. Someplace close to you."

"How about the Pizza Tower on Route Two-twenty-two?"

"Your husband won't look for you there?"

"He hates the place, so we never go."

"I'll meet you," I said. "Give me about forty-five minutes."

I MADE IT IN FORTY-TWO. The Audi knows how to get up and go. I walked into Pizza Tower and found Autumn Milburn sitting in a booth nursing a soda. She looked up, saw me, and didn't smile. The first time I met her, she lounged about the house in style. Today, she wore jeans, a pair of brandless tennis shoes, and a North Face fleece. A heavier jacket lay next to her in the booth.

"Thanks for meeting me," I said.

"I wish I knew what this was about," she said.

The smell of pizza wafted over me as a fresh pie made its

way to a table on the other side of the restaurant. The décor was typical pizza shop: booths along the walls, a few tables in the middle, paper placemats and napkins, and a counter and soda fountain on the left side. "Are you hungry?" I said.

"I'm sorry?"

"Are you hungry?"

"Oh. Actually, I am."

"Me, too. Pepperoni OK?"

"Sure."

I went up to the counter and ordered a large pepperoni and an iced tea from a teenager who could have been called "pizza face." Appropriate he worked here, at least. I took my drink back to the table and sat across from Autumn.

"Thanks for buying," she said.

"I'm sure it'll be well worth it."

She sipped her soda through the straw. Autumn hadn't put on any makeup. A few lines in her face told me she was a woman of about forty. With good cosmetics, she could have passed for early thirties. She wore her blonde hair pulled back in a ponytail. Her green eyes studied me. Autumn Milburn was blessed with fine features and would be in bounds for any definition of pretty and most definitions of beautiful. It was probably sexist of me, but I couldn't understand why a man would pass her up for a drugged teenager. "What are you thinking about?" she said.

"Unfortunately, a missing girl who was discovered dead has consumed a lot of my thoughts," I said. Pizza Tower didn't have a large dine-in crowd. I didn't talk loudly, but I didn't feel the need to whisper.

"That girl you came to the house asking about?" I nodded. "Conrad didn't tell me she was dead."

Of course he hadn't. "She was found in Baltimore."

"That's terrible. I'm just not sure how I can help."

"Mrs. Milburn, what can you tell me about your husband?"

"Conrad's a good man. He's worked hard for what he has." She looked away. "I'm not certain what you're looking for here."

"Is there anything unusual about him?"

"Unusual how?"

The pizza arriving at the table spared me an explanation for the moment. The same kid who took the order brought the pie, along with two plates. He set the pan on a metal tower and used the triangular spatula to put a slice on each. Never let it be said Darren at Pizza Tower didn't try to class up the joint. Autumn and I were both hungry, so we each tore into our first slices. I picked up the spatula and raised my eyebrows at her. She nodded and I put a second on her plate, then one on mine.

"I don't know why my husband doesn't like this place," she said.

"Another mystery about him," I said.

"What did you mean before about something unusual?"

I put my pizza down, took a sip of tea, then dabbed at my mouth with a napkin. "There's no easy way to say this, so I'll just come out with it. Mrs. Milburn, I'm pretty sure your husband is a pedophile."

I expected a strong reaction. I'd prepared myself for anything from screaming to crying to Autumn trying to stab me with the spatula. She sat there and stared at me. Much like choosing not to decide was still a choice, this constituted a reaction. It wasn't one I expected, but maybe it shouldn't have surprised me.

"That prick," she said.

"You don't seem surprised."

Autumn set her pizza down and looked at me. "You ever

know something was off about someone, but you don't want to think too much about it . . . don't want to confront them with it?"

"Sure," I lied.

"I knew something was funny about Conrad. I've suspected for years. Him and his father both. They're a couple of odd ducks."

"Have you ever been in your husband's mancave downstairs?"

She chuckled at the idea. "No. Conrad makes sure to tell me the key word in mancave is man."

"I really need to see the room."

"Why?"

"According to your son, your husband and his father and maybe some other men . . ." I paused and sighed. "Uh, they would take teenaged girls down there and . . ."

"Rape them?"

"Yes."

Autumn Milburn closed her eyes and shook her head. I saw a tear escape her closed eyes and run down her cheek. When she opened them, I handed her a paper napkin. "How did Little Conrad find out?"

Another thing I didn't want to tell this woman. "They invited him to participate once."

"Did he?"

"I think you should talk to your son."

"Jesus, he did." Autumn wiped at her eyes. Some new tears streamed down her face. "What a fucked-up family I married into, huh?"

"Mrs. Milburn, I need to see this mancave."

"OK. Christ, I don't even want him to touch me anymore. I don't want him to look at me. Whatever I can do to help."

"Thanks."

She looked at her pizza. "I shouldn't be hungry anymore after hearing that, but I still am. Crazy, huh?"

I shrugged. "We all gotta eat."

"Can we go after we finish the pizza?"

"Sure," I said. I hoped her desire to help proved sincere. If not, she could be leading me into an ambush.

CHAPTER 25

I FOLLOWED AUTUMN MILBURN BACK TO HER HOUSE. IT took us about ten minutes to get there. I hoped she didn't call her husband or call some other enforcers he knew to have a welcoming committee waiting for me. I carried a gun just in case. Her heavy-heartedness at hearing the news about her husband struck me as genuine. This was a woman who had suspected something awful and lied to herself about it for some time. She wouldn't want to have his goons ambush me. There were no cars in the driveway. I parked on the street so Conrad wouldn't see mine if he returned.

We walked around to the back of the house and went in. "There it is," she said, pointing to a door on the right down the short hallway. Autumn turned the lights on. I tested the knob: locked. As always, I carried my special keyring with me. I got to work on the lock. Conrad chose a good one to keep people out of this room. It took me almost two minutes to massage the tumblers to the point I could open the door.

I walked in, slipped on a pair of thin black leather gloves, and flipped the light on. Autumn Milburn entered behind me. The carpet of the hallway yielded to plain linoleum tile. No wonder no one ever found any fibers. A white hypoallergenic blanket covered the bed. I pulled it back and saw a sheet and pillows to match. It explained no random strands of fiber from the bedding.

Autumn looked at the setup and frowned. "It's so . . ."

"Clinical?" I said.

"Yes." She nodded. "It's so clinical."

"By design, I'm sure. A tiled floor means no carpet fibers. This bedding means no random strands of fabric. There can be no physical evidence from here found on any of the girls."

"Conrad always was smart. I just wish he didn't use it for . . . this."

I couldn't detect a trace of dust in the room. Even the bedframe was pristine. Whoever cleaned this room did a hell of a job. If the technicians didn't take money from a piece of shit like Conrad Milburn, I'd want to hire them to clean my house. A large nightstand sat on the right side of the bed. I opened the top drawer. Four boxes of condoms. Autumn came up behind me and glanced in as well. She sighed and turned away.

I opened the bottom drawer. On one side, a bunch of syringes in wrappers were arranged neatly. Small paper cups were stacked behind them. On the other side lay dozens of small medical bottles, no doubt filled with a sedative. If they couldn't get the girl to drink the roofie, they'd inject it into her. I wondered where they got the drugs. These weren't the kind you could buy from behind the counter at CVS. "Has the room always been like this?" I said.

"At first, it was an extra bedroom," Autumn said. "Conrad converted it into a mancave a few years ago."

"How many, would you say?"

She frowned. "Five, I guess."

"So, for five years, he's been bringing girls down here."

Autumn shook her head. "His father suggested the

remodel. Said some bullshit about a man needing a room he could call his own."

"Who did they hire to do it?" I said.

"Conrad did most of the work himself, actually."

"Did anyone help him?"

"His dad did a little. Oh, and his brother."

"Does the brother work in construction?"

"No," she said. "He works for a hospital."

* * *

THE PIECES STARTED FITTING TOGETHER. The Milburns' mancave had been constructed to look hospital clean because one of the builders knew all about it. Keeping it to those standards would be another matter entirely. "You don't know who cleans this room?" I asked Autumn Milburn.

"You think it's professionally done?" she said.

"Look around. It must be. There's never a bit of evidence originating from this place. Part of it is the build. The rest has to be in the maintenance."

Autumn studied the room. "Wow," she said. "I'd eat off of any of these surfaces."

"Knowing what goes on down here, I wouldn't. Who does the finances in your house?"

"I do."

"Can you check your account for payments to a cleaning service?" I said.

"I think I'd know if we were making a payment like that."

"Could your husband get to a checkbook?"

"Yes, but I balance it every month. There are no checks to a cleaning company."

I nodded. "Then your husband is paying the bill himself out of some separate funds."

"No," she said, shaking her head. "Conrad doesn't have a separate account."

"Are you sure? I don't mean to be indelicate, Mrs. Milburn, but I think today has shown you don't know your husband as well as you thought."

This left Autumn at a loss for words. She nodded and welled up before she could speak again. "You're right," she said, her voice cracking. "He must have a second account."

"Do you bank online?"

"We have for years."

"Your husband, too?" She nodded. "Do you know his login?"

"I could probably guess it."

"Could you try?" I asked.

She went upstairs to fetch a laptop. I locked the dungeon and followed her.

* * *

"Son of a bitch," Autumn said when I joined her at the kitchen table.

"You found a second account?"

"Yes." She shook her head. "He's had it for years and hidden it from me the whole time. That prick." Autumn wrote something on a piece of paper and handed it to me. It was information about a cleaning company.

"You couldn't have known," I said.

"I still think I should have." Autumn grabbed a tissue and dabbed her moistening eyes. "How much of this is my fault? I enabled a monster. I liked the way we live, and I ignored things I should've seen all along."

"You can't blame yourself," I said. "Men like your

husband are very good at hiding what they do. They have to be. He probably learned the ins and outs from his father."

"That old creep is never coming into this house again. Jesus, I wonder if he did anything to Conrad."

"Your son said he didn't," I said. "We asked him. It's an awkward question, but we needed to know."

"That's a relief," she said. "The rest sucks." Autumn looked at me. "What am I going to do?" Tears rolled down her cheeks.

"You're going to carry on," I said. "You'll find strength you didn't know you had. I'm sure you'll be OK."

She smiled at me around her tears. "I know what you're trying to do, and it's sweet. I hope you're right." She paused. "What about for now, though?"

"You'll have to act like everything is normal."

"I don't know if I can."

"Your husband got a shock today," I said. "He might back off his creepy campaign for a while. Or he might keep going like nothing happened. It's impossible to say. We don't want him spooked, though. If he is, whatever evidence we might be able to get would be gone."

"All right." She bobbed her head. "I'll do my best."

I gave her a business card. "Don't hesitate to call me if it gets too hard," I said. "I'll do what I can to help."

"I'll make sure Conrad doesn't see this." She studied my card and then tucked it into the back pocket of her jeans. "What's your next stop?"

"I need to look into this cleaning company."

"I doubt they're open now."

"I have a feeling the owner will want to talk to me," I said.

* * *

I SPENT a few minutes in the car, using my tablet and an SSH connection to my server to look up information about Like New Cleaning. They specialized in houses and small businesses. And pedophiles, too, but they didn't proclaim it on the website. I matched the name of the listed website owner with a man who lived in the area. He seemed reluctant to talk to me at first but agreed to meet me at a bar inside the Hollywood Casino.

The casino opened almost a decade ago as part of Maryland's attempt to capitalize on the slots and table games available in neighboring states. Despite a fondness for poker and other pursuits, I'd never been there, choosing to stick to the two closer gambling halls. Now I walked in to meet someone who may have enabled a pedophile. The stools at the bar were sparsely populated, and I recognized the owner from his LinkedIn picture. I'd hoped he would have come to his senses and ditched the John Lennon glasses and hipster beard. No such luck. People like him give the rest of us millennials a bad name. I might like avocado toast, but I have standards when it comes to grooming.

Taylor Miller opened his company five years ago. Online reviewers praised them with high star ratings and positive reviews. Miller employed a couple handfuls of women who did the cleaning. His company was trusted enough to maintain keys to houses and small businesses without a whisper of theft. I wondered what providing cleaning services to a pedophile would do for the trustworthiness of the business.

I sidled up to the stool on Miller's left and sat. The bartender greeted me right away. They had an IPA on draft, and I went with it. He dropped off the mug, and I put a five on the counter. He didn't ask if I wanted change. I sipped the brew and admired its hoppiness. Miller didn't say anything to me, instead nursing his piña colada. I gave him a moment, and he didn't take it. "You're awfully quiet," I said to break the silence.

Miller drained his colada and ordered another. He still hadn't said anything to me. When he got the second drink, he started in on it right away.

"You know, I could just run with what I have," I said. "I can guess the rest. The publicity will sink your company."

"Don't," he said.

"It speaks."

"I don't know anything about what you mentioned."

"Your company cleans Conrad Milburn's house, right?"

"Only the basement," he said.

I took another sip of the IPA. "Any room in particular?"

"We're contracted for the whole basement." He fell silent.

"For someone whose ass is in the fire, Taylor, you don't seem to care a whole lot."

"I'm just kind of shocked, you know?"

"I can guess," I said. "But you need to talk to me. You said you're contracted for the whole basement. Cleaning services take special instructions all the time. Did Mr. Milburn leave any?"

Miller nodded. "He asked us to pay special attention to a certain room down there. It needed to be pristine."

"Did Mr. Milburn explain the purpose of this room?"

"He said he had a sick relative stay with him on occasion. It needed to be as close to clean-room standards as we could get it."

A convenient and clever lie. "Has the same woman worked his house?"

"I've assigned Shirley to it for . . . I guess about three years now."

"I might need to talk to Shirley."

"You mentioned something bad went on there." Miller finally turned to look at me. "What happened?"

This called for another sip of my IPA. The bitterness would help carry me through the conversation. "Let's characterize it as awful," I said.

"So terrible I don't want his business?"

"Depends on your ethics, Taylor. What do you think of pedophiles?"

Miller's eyes went wide. It took him a moment to find some words. "You mean, he uses the room to . . . to . . . "

"Yes," I said, "it's exactly what I mean."

"Jesus Christ." Miller pounded most of his drink. After this news, I expected him to need another.

"Here's the thing," I said. "I don't want Milburn to know something is amiss. He's been spooked once already. If it happens again, he might be gone. These assholes are good at disappearing."

"I don't want his money."

"I wouldn't, either. Don't deposit his check. Light it on fire if you want. When he goes down, you can rest easy."

"OK," Miller said with a nod. "How soon do you expect all this to happen?"

"Hopefully in a day or so."

"Good. The sooner, the better."

I polished off my IPA. "Thanks for meeting me," I said. Now to find the old man.

CHAPTER 26

I ARRIVED HOME TIRED. FINDING DEAD GIRLS AND chasing pedophiles messed up my sleep. I wanted to find Conrad Milburn II. The grandfather must have been the worst of them all. He'd been doing this the longest. How many lives did he ruin? How many children grew into damaged adults because of him and his friends? How many had they murdered? I hoped no more would be added to either tally before I could blow the lid off this whole operation.

Even with the rise of surveillance and the ebb of anonymity, it's possible to disappear online. Pedophiles have proven good at remaining invisible. In an era where everyone updates friends and followers about mindless minutiae, people like Conrad Milburn II left scant digital footprints. Whatever they did put online couldn't be used to figure out the secrets they hid. It could be argued only the stupid or sloppy ones got caught.

My work began with the assumption Conrad Milburn and the rest of his sick friends used the dark web. Commercials like to scare people into thinking their credit card data is being passed back and forth there. It may be, but illicit porn gets traded far more often. There were a bunch of places they could go, however, and I had no way to know where. I knew the eldest Milburn's email address, however. Why try to do all the work myself when I could let him do it for me?

In my most revolting Google search ever, I found a picture of a girl of legal age—I triple-checked—made up to look younger. A fellow like me has many anonymous email addresses. I used one to send an email to Conrad Milburn II, with the picture attached. The picture, of course, carried some extra payload, a little piece of malware which would execute when he opened the image. I sent the email. A listening port would tell me when someone downloaded the file and thus executed the bonus code.

In the meantime, I checked my other malware, the one I put on Conrad the Third's phone. He'd sent texts to his father, telling him people were sniffing around the operation. The father encouraged his son to relax, they were anonymous, and their protector had their backs. He sent the latest affirmation an hour ago. So far, we'd kept the news of Judge Wilson's arrest quiet. I hoped our good fortune could continue another day.

I waited another half-hour, but Milburn didn't take the bait. The point at which I grew tired was long in the rearview mirror. I went upstairs and found Gloria already asleep. I got ready for bed and crawled in beside her. She stirred and mumbled briefly and then went right back out. I joined her about a minute after my head hit the pillow.

* * *

AFTER I WOKE UP, I headed downstairs to the office. Milburn opened the file. My listener was active and providing me regular reports. I went into the kitchen, made coffee, and came back. The dark web houses a lot of darknets —encrypted parts of the Internet requiring special software or authorization to access. Most people used Tor, but other applications did similar work. Milburn and his friends used a darknet to talk to one another and distribute their smut. I didn't recognize the name, but like many, it required a software installation.

How far down this rabbit hole did I want to go? I could get the required file, create a new virtual machine, and install it. This would get me onto their darknet. I could destroy the VM when I finished. My problem was I didn't want to join it in the first place. I didn't want to be exposed to these men and their perversion and their penchant for ruining lives.

The clincher was I needed to think about those lives. Libby had already been murdered. Donna Frank, too. How many more kids did these perverts kill which we hadn't discovered yet? How many more lives would they ruin? I needed to install the software. I spun up a new Windows virtual machine. While I waited for it to finish the usual setup, I went back to the kitchen to make breakfast.

I got the iron out, whisked a small bowl of batter, and put a waffle on to cook. While it bubbled, I tossed a couple handfuls of blueberries in a pot, added a little butter and maple syrup, and worked on a sauce. The smells wafting from the kitchen roused Gloria from her slumber, and she joined me. She yawned, gave me a minty-fresh kiss, and poured herself a cup of coffee. When she sat at the table, I plated her waffle and topped it with some of the sauce.

I put a second on and started a small skillet of turkey bacon. In a few minutes, Gloria and I sat at the table with waffles, my terrific blueberry syrup, turkey bacon, and coffee. The four breakfast food groups.

"How's your research going?" Gloria said between bites of her waffle.

"It's getting to the point where what I'll see will disgust me," I said.

She frowned. "If this stuff ends up on your computer . . ."

"Don't worry. It's a VM. I'll destroy it and wipe the hard drive when this whole mess is done."

"Your cooking really makes up for the times you sit there and talk nonsense," Gloria said with a grin.

"I need to have a redeeming quality somewhere," I said.

I ended up putting a third waffle on, which Gloria and I split. "How long until you've wrapped it up?" she said.

"I hope by tomorrow."

"So soon?"

"The Judge Wilson arrest will have to make the news at some point," I said. "And the feds will have to get called. We're trying to tie everything up and catch these assholes before both those clocks run out."

"And you think you're pretty close."

"I'll get closer after breakfast."

After I finished eating, I trudged back into my office. The Windows VM sat ready. I joined it to my network, installed the darknet software, and read the text file telling me which ports on my firewall to open. I did so with some reluctance. I owned other defenses if these kid touchers discovered my outsider status and tried to attack me.

The software featured a large user interface meant for file sharing and chat. Two people occupied the chat room. I didn't enter. If I did, I would need to pick a handle, and then the other two would know I wasn't one of them. No reason to spook them now. I poked around the file-sharing piece. A slew of images—thankfully not in thumbnail view—greeted me. I hunted around for things other than pictures and found a list of members and bits of information about them.

I poked around for more documents and more non-image files but found nothing of interest. I logged out, scanned all data I nabbed for viruses, and moved them to my server. Once I finished, I destroyed the VM, re-enabled ports on my firewall, and started a script to reformat the hard drive hosting the VM thirteen times.

I had some light reading to do.

* * *

I CALLED RICH. "YOU HAVE SOMETHING?" he said.

"A lot, actually," I said. "These sickos are using a darknet to talk to one another and share files."

"You found your way onto it?"

"I'm kind of surprised you know what a darknet is."

"I watch TV."

"No help," I said. "Anyway, yes, I got onto it for a little while. Long enough to download a couple documents."

"And?" said Rich.

"I got a member list."

"They kept a member list?"

"Yep. Names, normal email addresses, darknet emails, chat handles, and regular Internet haunts they like to frequent. I guess they wanted to be sure they were only talking to each other."

"Wouldn't their software make sure of it?"

"You're not paranoid if they're really after you," I said.

"I suppose not. How many names are on it?"

"Enough. You'll recognize some of them, too."

Rich groaned. "Tell me it's no one in the BPD," he said.

"No one I know of. I'm emailing it to you and Norton now."

"You know this isn't a smoking gun, right?" he said. "So far, it's a collection of names with some maybe-incriminating information. We can't get warrants for these men."

"I know," I said. "I have a plan for adding smoke to the gun."

"Am I going to like it?"

"Almost certainly not," I said.

I DIDN'T THINK many people would care for my plan. It flagrantly skirted the law and would force someone to incriminate himself. These, of course, were reasons why I liked it so much. I didn't need a lot of buy-in, though, but what I did need started with Melinda, so I called her at the foundation. She sounded eager. "Did you make a break in the case?"

"I think so," I said. "I have a lot more information. Libby's killer is still out there, though. I don't know exactly who it is yet. I . . . I need a favor."

"From me? Anything."

"Actually, from T.J., but I figured I would need to run it by you first."

I heard Melinda sigh into the phone. "I'm not going to like this, am I?"

"You're the second person to ask me the same question in the last few minutes."

"I'll take that as a no," she said. "I don't want her to do it."

"Melinda, she's eighteen. She's an adult. T.J. can decide for herself if she wants to be involved."

"Are you going to be risking her life?"

"No."

"You're sure?"

"As sure as I can be," I said.

"What does that mean?"

"It means crossing the street can risk your life. I don't think I'll be putting her in any real danger. It's all I can promise you."

"Well, that's something at least," Melinda said. "Why don't you have lunch with us, and we can talk about it. Can you come to the foundation?"

"Is your father there?"

"No, he's out of town."

"Then I'd love to drop by," I said.

* * *

I BROUGHT lunch for everyone from The Abbey. No one could be in a contrary mood after eating one of their burgers. I carried one for each of us, a collection of sides, and some non-adult beverages into the Nightlight Foundation. Melinda, T.J., and I ate lunch in Melinda's office. It was the size of my living room, with a large desk and high-backed chair near the wall. Pictures of the city, of Melinda alone, and her with her father—both before their split and after their reconciliation—adorned the walls. T.J. and I sat in guest chairs. Melinda cleared her desk to give us room to eat.

The ladies devoured the burgers and helped me work over the chips, fries, and onion rings. After consuming a bunch of meat, grease, and soda, I hoped everyone would be in a good mood when I laid out my plan. "T.J., I'd like to ask a favor of you," I said.

She said, "Melinda told me you wanted to. What's up?"

"I've discovered a group of men who are responsible for

Libby's death. So far, I don't know which man actually did it."

"I'm in," she said. "Whatever you need to figure it out."

"Let's hear the details first," Melinda said, frowning at both of us.

"I was able to acquire the group's member list," I said. "It also came with certain other information, like what online haunts they use to find young girls to prey on."

"And you want me to chat with them?" T.J. said.

"With one man in particular."

"Will he want to meet me?"

"I guess it depends on your chatting skills but probably."

She paused. "Then what?"

"You'll meet him," I said.

"Wait, wait," Melinda said. "We just got T.J. out of a bad situation. Now it sounds like you want to put her back into one. Do you want to use her as bait?"

"Yes," I said.

"For a pedophile?"

"Yes."

"Who might also be a murderer?"

"Yes."

"No way," Melinda said.

"I'm in," T.J. said.

Melinda shook her head. "No way," she repeated. "It's way too soon to put you back into that situation."

"Melinda, I know you understand what getting out of these bad spots is like," I said, "but it's T.J.'s choice. She's old enough to make it."

"Whatever you need," T.J. said.

"I really don't like this," Melinda said. She glowered at me.

"I don't, either," I said. "However, our time is running out to catch these assholes. We need to set a trap and spring it on them."

"You know it won't be legal," said Melinda. "This guy will argue entrapment, and he'll probably win."

I smiled. "It's a popular defense. I considered it . . . it's why I wanted to make this a little more official. I'll need to make a phone call, but I have to know we're a go here first."

Melinda sighed and shook her head. "Will you be there to make sure nothing happens to T.J.?" she said.

"Me and at least one other person . . . probably more."

I watched Melinda stew over it. She felt protective of girls like T.J., girls the Nightlight Foundation rescued from lives (and probable deaths) on the streets. Her conflicting emotions played out on her face. Finally, she threw up her hands. "I still don't like this," she said. "T.J., he's right. You're an adult. It's your decision."

"I keep telling you . . . I'm in," she said. "Whatever it takes."

"I hope it doesn't take a lot," I said.

"It'd better not." Melinda fixed me with a glare.

"Let me make another call," I said.

CHAPTER 27

I BROUGHT A LAPTOP WITH ME, LOADED WITH ANOTHER fresh Windows virtual machine. I'd also modified a program to capture logs from Internet Relay Chat rooms and send them back to my server via an encrypted tunnel. T.J. sat at Melinda's desk and joined one of the chat rooms on the list I swiped from the darknet. None of the handles corresponded to members of the group. A couple people tried to talk to T.J., but she blew them off.

"I don't like this," Melinda said.

"We've been over it," I said.

"I mean this room. 'Older Gentlemen for Younger Ladies.' It's creepy. Why not just put up a sign saying it's for pedophiles? How can something like this be legal?"

"There's nothing inherently wrong with older gentlemen looking for younger ladies, so long as everyone's a consenting adult," I said.

"Do you really think that's what this chat room is for?"

"Of course not," I said. "But it's easy to claim, so it avoids getting the hairy eyeball from people who might try to shut it down."

Over the next couple hours, people came into and left the

virtual room. T.J. was cordial enough to anyone who tried to talk to her but gave them the cold e-shoulder at the same time. Melinda wandered in and out of the actual room, alternating between doing her job at the foundation and babysitting her young charge. T.J., for her part, rolled her eyes and chuckled at many of the lame come-ons. "This is fun," she said. "Old men are pervs."

"These old men in particular are," I said.

Another user entered the room. I looked at the name. Conrad Milburn II decided to grace us with his pedo presence. "There he is," I said to T.J.. "There's the man we need to catch."

T.J. grinned. "I'm on it." After a couple brief exchanges, she opened a private chat with Milburn. My program would capture these, too.

16&Ready> hey hot stuff

Burnin4U> hey yourself. U really 16

16&Ready> by a couple weeks yeah

Burnin4U> mmm that's a great age

16&Ready> how old r u

Burnin4U> old enough 2 b ur grandpa lol

16&Ready> lol i like my men older but maybe not that old

Burnin4U> i don't even need a blue pill

16&Ready> lol u better not

Burnin4U> u got a pic

T.J. looked at me. "It's your picture," I said. "As long as you're comfortable sharing it."

"Not really," she said, "but if it helps catch this creep, I'm all for it."

"Were you eighteen when it was taken?"

"Does it matter?"

"I'm logging this conversation. It matters to me."

She nodded. "By a week, yeah." A small smile played on her lips. "Shit, that wasn't so long ago. My life has changed a lot."

"For the better, I hope," I said.

"Definitely." She smiled. "And I have you and Melinda to thank for that."

"Me?"

"Yeah, you. You told us what happened to Libby, and you gave us the info about this foundation."

I shrugged. "Those aren't anything special."

"But you cared. I could tell. We all could. You didn't want to see anything bad happen to us. That's . . . rare to see. You've got a big heart, C.T." She paused and grinned. "That must be why Melinda likes you."

"After today, she's probably been cured of the problem," I said.

"I wouldn't be so sure." T.J. clicked around and found the picture we added.

Burnin4U> u there

16&Ready> yeah findin the pic be patient grandpa

*User 16&Ready transferred the file c:\pics\sexyme.jpg**

"You put a virus in that pic?" T.J. said.

"Not exactly," I said. "I added something to help the police track the computer he's using. If he shares it with his sick friends, we'll be able to find them all."

"Wouldn't he run some antivirus or something?"

"I'm sure he does. They're based on signatures, though . . . patterns in code, basically. I'm using something I think will avoid known patterns."

"If you can do all that, why are you a detective?"

"Keeps me off the streets," I said.

Burnin4U> damn ur hot def no blue pill with u

16&Ready> thanx lol
Burnin4U> i need to meet u
16&Ready> idk
Burnin4U> u said u wanted an older man
16&Ready> u sure im a lot 2 handle lol
Burnin4U> im sure ull see
16&Ready> ok but we gotta meet in public the 1st time. i gotta know ur not some psycho lol or a cop
Burnin4U> ok how about 2morrow morning
16&Ready> not today? im soooooo ready 4 u
Burnin4U> i wish i could 2day but i cant
16&Ready> ok tomorrow
Burnin4U> where
16&Ready> how bout patterson park near the rink
Burnin4U> ok can u meet me at 10
16&Ready> u want me to cut school lol
Burnin4U> ill make it worth it
16&Ready> u better
Burnin4U> ok ill be wearing a green hoodie and baseball cap
16&Ready> ok see u tomorrow
Burnin4U> u don't wanna cyber
16&Ready> i only want the real thing. u better give it to me good tomorrow
Burnin4U> u bet i will
User 16&Ready has left the room.

T.J. took her hands off the keyboard and sighed. "I feel dirty," she said. I shared the sentiment. She frowned at the screen. "I don't even want to think about what that sick old bastard is doing right now."

I shuddered. "Thanks for your help," I said. "You're OK to do part two?"

She nodded. "I'm in all the way."

* * *

WHEN I LEFT THE FOUNDATION, I called Sherry Hampton. "Hello?" she said.

"Mrs. Hampton, I hope you remember me. We talked in a Waffle House after . . . a certain day in court."

"You were the private investigator. Ferguson, right?"

"Yes."

"You have an update?" she said.

"I do. We're close to shutting these assholes down."

"You got the judge?"

I didn't want to tell her about Wilson. If word got out before we were ready for it, these assholes might go underground. "Not yet," I said, "but we've set a trap for a big man in the organization."

"What can I do?"

"You mentioned you keep in contact with other affected parents."

"That's right. Mothers, really. The fathers don't talk much about it."

"Perfect. Do you know where Patterson Park in Baltimore is?"

"Yes, why?"

"Mrs. Hampton, I think I need you to assemble the legion," I said.

CHAPTER 28

When I arrived home, I caught Gloria up on the events and plans of the day. "I'm glad you use your powers for good," she said.

"I just try to be on the right side of the ledger more often than not," I said.

"You're doing a lot of beneficial work, and you do it for the right reasons. Face it, C.T.—you may want people to think you're a badass, but you're a good man."

I put my hands on my chest and feigned pain. "You wound me," I said.

"I mean it. You're a great guy."

"Take thy knife from out my heart."

Gloria chuckled and slapped me on the shoulder. "Stop it.". "There's nothing wrong with being a good guy. The work you do is important, and the people you help need it." She smiled. "I wouldn't love you if you were a dick."

"I'm glad being a nice guy has paid off so well for me," I said.

Gloria grinned and put her arms around me. Her lips traced kisses on my neck. I felt my breath leave in a sigh. "Want to see how it pays off right now?" she said.

"Oh, yes."

We went upstairs, and she showed me.

* * *

THE NEXT MORNING, Rich and I sat in the Caprice parked on Patterson Park Avenue between Lombard and Pratt. Our spot afforded us an easy view of the pagoda. Leafy foliage receded enough in winter to let us see it with minimal obstruction. A few people milled about. Joggers lived up to their designation and jogged past. Rich and I observed a few of the women with interest. I glanced at my watch. Ten minutes until showtime.

I sipped my peppermint mocha. Rich enjoyed a plain old coffee. T.J. walked into view. She lingered around the pagoda, along with a few other people with nothing better to do on a Monday morning. I'd told her not to wave or draw attention to herself. If Milburn smelled a trap, he would leave.

"What are we doing here?" Rich said.

"Drinking festive drinks," I said. "Well, I am, at least. You're drinking boring coffee."

"We could do this anywhere. Your house. My house. The precinct."

"You should be thankful, dear cousin," I said.

"For what?"

"You're about to have a front-row seat to watch justice unfold."

"What on earth are you talking about?" said Rich

"You'll see in a few minutes."

"Is this something I want to see?'

"I should hope so," I said.

Among the people in the area, I spied Sherry Hampton. Seven other women clustered around her. They spread out a little and did some light stretching. A few others milled about. On this mild morning, a group of women limbering up wouldn't attract any undue attention.

"You said there would be a break in the pedophile case," said Rich.

"There will," I said.

"You know the Judge Wilson shit will hit the fan sometime today."

"It's why we're coming in under the wire."

Rich sipped his coffee and looked at me. "Why are you so dogged on this one?" he said.

"What do you mean?"

"I mean you've been going at this hardcore from the start. Especially after what happened before you went to Hawaii, I figured you'd try to ease back into it."

"Go hard or go home," I said.

"Look, I know you don't quit when you get your teeth into something. I'm just wondering why you're so determined to solve this. It's almost like it's something personal with you."

I inhaled the sweet, delicious scent of my peppermint mocha. Whoever first decided to pair mint and chocolate had not received proper credit for his or her genius. I took a drink of the hot beverage, leaned my head back, felt the beverage run down my throat, and let out a deep breath. The memory ran through my head a few days ago. Might as well share it with Rich. "Remember Sheila?" I said after a moment.

"Sheila?" said Rich.

"One of my good friends when I was a kid. We met in middle school."

"I think I remember her. Did you date?"

"No," I said. "Neither of us wanted to."

"What does she have to do with this?"

I closed my eyes and took a slow, measured breath. "Sheila killed herself in high school."

"Oh, my god," said Rich, "I remember now. Wow. Your sophomore year, wasn't it?"

"Yes."

Rich didn't say anything. Neither did I. Silence lingered in the car until Rich broke it. "Was she sexually abused?"

I nodded. "Her father. Her mother left, and her father had custody."

"How do you know? Did she tell you?"

"Not in so many words. I wish she did. It only made sense after she died."

"Wait a minute." Rich frowned. "I remember this. Didn't something happen to her father later? He got his ass kicked, didn't he?"

"And a bunch of money drained from his bank accounts."

I could feel Rich's eyes boring into my face. "You did it, didn't you?" he said.

"I can neither confirm nor deny any involvement," I said.

"Why not go to the police?"

"I tried. I found a private, unpublished LiveJournal Sheila maintained. She laid it all out there." I shook my head. "I tried to put the police onto it, and they said they couldn't use it. No one made a case against her father."

"So you took it into your own hands."

"Someone needed to," I said. "The system let her down."

Neither of us said anything for a minute. "It makes sense now," Rich said. "For what it's worth, I think you're honoring your friend."

I smiled. "Thanks."

Coming from the north, Conrad Milburn walked down

Patterson Park Avenue. I spied him before Rich did. Milburn walked deliberately, stopping to look around every so often. I sat lower in my seat and noticed Rich doing the same. After a couple minutes of puttering around, Milburn entered the park, took in more of his surroundings, and made a beeline for the pagoda.

Rich and I both sat up. "What's he doing here?" said Rich.

"I imagine he's looking for his next victim," I said.

"Did you have something to do with this?" Rich looked over at me. "Why do I feel your fingerprints all over it?"

"I didn't take enough semesters of psych to answer you," I said.

Milburn saw T.J. and approached her. He struck up a conversation. T.J. talked to him and did flirty things like twirling her hair around her finger. I watched Sherry Hampton. She and her friends took note of Milburn. They moved in his direction. Milburn, oblivious, kept chatting up T.J.. I wished I could have heard what they said. T.J. giggled, but I didn't know if she did it to play the part or as a legit response to Milburn's pathetic come-ons.

From Conrad Milburn's right, Sherry Hampton brought her purse back, then whacked him in the head with it. The old man staggered but didn't go down. Another bash from a different woman's handbag sent him to the grass. T.J. kicked the fallen Milburn, spat on him, and moved a few steps away. Sherry Hampton's friends formed a circle around Milburn. Others at the pagoda suddenly remembered they needed to be anywhere else.

"What the hell?" Rich said. He tried the door and found it locked. "Let me out!"

"No way," I said.

"I'm not kidding."

"Neither am I."

A few women beat Conrad Milburn II with their purses. The rest kicked him. One woman stood to his side and stomped his groin with her high heels. They all yelled at him. I again wished for an audio feed.

"What is this?" Rich said. "They're going to kill him."

"No, they're not," I said.

"How do you know?" He yanked on the door handle again and again.

"I don't, I suppose."

"And what if they do?"

I shrugged. "Then I have no doubt eight juries of their peers would acquit them. Your precious system in action."

"Let me out, C.T. Right now."

"Rich, you have two ways out of here. You can try to break the window, but you should remember they're made of bullet-resistant glass. Your fist or your elbow will break first. The power lock control is on my door. You can try to reach across me and use it." I smiled. "But I wouldn't recommend it."

"Goddammit!" Rich kept yanking on the handle, maybe hoping ripping it out would cause the door to open. "What are you trying to prove here? A bunch of women beat up one pedophile. Good job. Nice justice. What the fuck is going to happen when they go to court?"

"I think they'll be OK in court." I watched Sherry and her friends continue to pound away on the fallen Milburn. The one woman's heels must have reduced his genitals to pulp at this point.

"You're insane." Rich glared at me.

I let him seethe for a moment. "The girl he talked to is a former hooker," I said. "She's been pulled off the strect by the Nightlight Foundation. She chatted with Milburn last night in a logged session, and she's wearing a wire right now."

"A wire?"

"Yes. Makes it official, right?"

"You got her a wire?"

"Not by myself," I said.

"You didn't call me."

"What would you have said?" Rich kept on glaring. "Exactly. I needed to call someone whose moral compass doesn't always point due north."

As if on cue, I saw Paul King dash across the park toward the pagoda.

"You called King?" Rich said.

"Narcotics and vice work in tandem a lot," I said. "And I knew he would have the ethical flexibility required."

"You set all of this up." Rich shook his head. "Unbelievable."

I unlocked the doors. "Go make the arrest for your task force," I said.

Rich bolted from the car.

* * *

AN AMBULANCE CAME for Conrad Milburn II. The EMTs said he suffered a bunch of cuts and bruises, a concussion, a few obviously broken bones, and a lot of blood in his pants. He deserved it all. Rich, Paul King, and a few other members of the BPD corralled Sherry Hampton and her friends. I heard the riot act being read. The ladies stood with their hands on their hips or their arms crossed under their chests. One played with her phone until Rich singled her out with his yelling.

"The righteousness in the air is thick," I said to T.J.,

She smiled. "We really did it."

"We really did, and you were great."

She wrapped me in a big hug. "Thank you," she said. She clung to me longer than I felt comfortable, but I didn't fight it. T.J. had been though a lot, including the loss of a friend. I was glad she cared enough to want to help.

"What are you thanking me for?" I said when she had let go.

"For not giving up."

"When I take a case, I don't quit. The loud one over there is my cousin. He'll tell you a lot of bad things about me—maybe a few more after today—but even he will tell you I'm not a quitter."

T.J. shook her head. "I'm not talking about the case. It's about Libby. Everyone gave up on her . . . her mother, whatever homes they put her in." T.J.'s voice cracked. "You didn't give up on her even when you knew she was dead. And you didn't give up on me, either." T.J. cried in earnest, and I couldn't understand anything else she said past her tears. I put my arms around her, and she sobbed on my shoulder.

After a few minutes, T.J. composed herself and wiped at her eyes. "So many people have given up on me," she said in a quiet voice.

"Melinda won't," I said. "And now I think you won't give up on yourself."

"I'm trying to hand you some credit here."

I smiled. "I appreciate it."

She nodded toward the scene behind us. "What's going to happen to that piece of shit?"

"Between the logged chat from yesterday, the conversation from today, and whatever gets found on his computer, I think he won't see the light of day again before he dies."

"Good. The hell with him."

"By now, the police should be moving in on his associates."

"We took out the whole ring?"

"It's my hope."

"That's pretty awesome."

"Some days, I really like my job," I said.

CHAPTER 29

"I WISH YOU WOULD INVOLVE ME IN THESE THINGS," Rich said. We both sat at Casey Norton's desk at the State Police Barracks.

"You know why I didn't," I said.

"Of course I wouldn't have gone for it. It was reckless. You put a man's life in danger." Rich cut me off by holding up his hand. "I know . . . you're going to tell me he's not worth protecting." I figured a nod might earn me the heave-ho, so I refrained. "I'm telling you we don't get to make those decisions."

"No, *you* don't get to make those decisions."

"You can't invent your own rules and then play by them."

"It's worked pretty well so far," I said.

Rich shook his head. "What about the girl? What if something happened to her?"

"You and I were right there."

"And if Milburn had a knife or a gun? It could have gone bad really fast, and she would have been dead before either of us got out of the car."

I hadn't considered such a grim possibility. We didn't know who killed Libby or Donna Frank. It might have been

Milburn for all any of us knew. "She's an adult, Rich," I said. "I told her the risks going in, and she jumped at the chance to do this. She wanted to do it for Libby."

"Did you tell her she might die?"

"Come on. You might die every day. You might die every time you cross the street or whenever you drive your car. You can't refuse to do something because there's a nonzero chance you may not survive."

"You don't get it," he said. "You took a chance with people's lives. It paid off this time. Maybe probability was on your side. I don't know. Maybe you got lucky."

"Maybe I did."

"Luck doesn't last forever," Rich said.

"I know what you're getting at. You might even be right, but look at the big picture. The girl I put at risk helped us bring down a pedophile, who will lead us to his creepy little friends one way or another."

"One way or another? What do you mean?"

"He'll roll over on the group to get a deal," I said.

"What's the other way?"

"These assholes share files all the time," I said with a casual shrug. "Who knows what malware they might contain."

"You're . . . I don't know if there's a word for it."

"I'll settle for 'awesome,'" I said.

I JOINED Rich and Norton in the interrogation room. Conrad Milburn II had been treated for his injuries and released. We passed the few hours with mediocre coffee and Rich's occasional attempts to continue lecturing me. Norton shot me a look when I walked in, telling me he didn't want me in there.

He and Rich must have talked chapter and verse from the police handbook. Milburn sported bandages on his face, and his right arm was in a sling. I didn't want to imagine what treatment the hospital devised for the groin stomping.

Norton and Rich sat at the table across from Milburn. They occupied the only three chairs. I considered bringing another one in but didn't want to push my luck. Rich probably insisted I be here over Norton's objections. If the table didn't look so cheap and flimsy, I would have sat on it. Instead, I parked my butt on the ledge just below the one-way mirror.

"I got nothing to say," Milburn said before anyone even asked him a question. Rich and Norton flipped through the file folders before them. Milburn's eyes darted between them. "I said I got nothing to say." Rich and Norton continued to ignore him. He stopped looking at them and turned to me. I maintained radio silence.

Milburn kept quiet once it became apparent neither Rich nor Norton would indulge him while they riffled paperwork. I craned my neck to peek at what they looked at in there, but their bodies blocked most of what I could see. They whispered back and forth, looked at their papers some more, and whispered again. If one had passed a note to the other, it would have been high school all over again.

"You and your friends are in trouble," Norton said after a few minutes of silence.

"Is that a fact?" Milburn said. The handcuffs around his wrists and the signs of injury ruined the effect, but he tried to look nonplussed as he leaned back as much as the cheap metal chair would allow.

"It's a fact."

"I don't think so."

"Why?" Rich said.

"W . . . I am protected," Milburn said with a smile.

"You mean Judge Wilson?" Norton said.

The question erased the smile from Milburn's face. "You know about the judge?"

Rich put a few pictures on the table. I stood to get a better look at them. "This is your buddy getting arrested," said Rich. "Two days ago."

"Two days?"

"Yes. Were you wondering why you didn't hear from him?"

"Not really," Milburn said, shaking his head. "Clem wasn't around all the time like some of us. He was just always there when we needed him."

"Not anymore," Norton said.

"Got anything to say now?" asked Rich.

Milburn sighed. "Not really."

"How about after this?" I said. "We have your member list. I was on your little darknet." Milburn looked up at the mention, his eyes wide. "Oh, you didn't think it could happen, did you? Open any good attachments recently?"

"A few."

"Yeah, well, you shouldn't have opened one of them."

"This is entrapment."

I laughed. "Do you think anyone would believe you wouldn't open a picture of a girl who looked underage? Seriously? Everyone in your sick little group would double-click it in a nanosecond, and you'll never convince anyone otherwise."

"What do you want?" Milburn said, staring at the cuff bar. He couldn't meet our eyes. His shoulders sagged, and not only with age.

"The whole thing," Norton said. "Every person who

helped you, everyone you talked to, all the girls you hurt, and especially all the girls you killed."

"We know of two," Rich said.

Milburn shook his head. "I didn't kill anybody."

"You and your friend the judge checked into a motel with Libby," I said. "Right after, someone killed her."

"You know about that?"

"We saw the video. Don't try and deny it."

Milburn didn't deny it. He didn't say anything, in fact. He sat there and stared. We waited him out. It got boring. Maybe he was waiting us out, too. Norton and Rich sat with their arms crossed. They were used to doing things like this with suspects. I, on the other hand, was used to running into people in disreputable places, roughing them up, and getting quicker answers the hard way. After a couple minutes of silence, Milburn said, "I got nothing to say."

"Fine," Norton said, "stew in silence, then." He and Rich got up. I did the same. We all walked out and slammed the door.

* * *

JUDGE WILSON SEETHED in the next room. He glowered when the three of us entered. "What is the meaning of keeping me waiting like this?" he roared.

This room featured three chairs opposite Wilson. I'd get a place at the grownups' table. Norton, Rich, and I sat down and stared at the judge. The other two didn't say anything, and I followed their lead. Wilson glared at each of us in turn. "Aren't you going to offer me a lawyer?" he said.

"You *are* a lawyer," Rich said.

"And I know better than to say anything to you."

"We don't need you to say much," Norton said. "We already know a lot about you and your circle of sick friends."

"And we know about Libby," I said.

Norton looked at me. He must have wanted to sit on the fact a while longer. Oh, well.

"Who's Libby?" said Wilson.

"The girl you and your friend Milburn are on video with, checking into some seedy motel in Baltimore."

"She was a sweet girl." Wilson had the audacity to smile. I fought the urge to leap across the table and punch him.

"Is it why you killed her?" I said.

"I never killed this girl."

"So you killed other girls?"

"I didn't say I did."

"Someone killed her, Judge. You and your buddy Milburn were on tape with her. Are you trying to convince us someone came by the room and murdered her later?"

Wilson looked at me but didn't answer. He glanced at Rich and Norton but found no sympathy in their stares.

"You might as well tell us what happened," Rich said. "We have the member list for your little pedophiles' club. We saw the darknet where you predators talked and traded pictures." I decided not to pipe up and point out Rich's use of the royal *we* at this point. "While you sit there wasting our time, Maryland State Troopers are rounding up your friends and their computers."

"What do you think we're going to find?" Norton said. "Any of those pictures travel across state lines?" Wilson's shoulders slumped at the question. "You pricks ever travel into another state for a kid? Now you're looking at the feds." Norton spread his hands palms-up. "I can't do anything once they get involved. Whatever they find out, you're looking at federal prison."

"They're going to set everyone in your little group against one another," I said. "The first one to spill the beans about what the authorities don't know will win the lightest sentence. The rest of you . . . well, I'm sure you've heard the stories of how men like you fare in jail."

"You can't send me there," Wilson said. He looked between us quickly with large eyes. "Please."

"Like I told you, it'll be out of my hands," Norton said with a shrug.

"Unless I tell you everything right now."

We all nodded. Rich readied a legal pad and a pen. Wilson took a deep breath. "I don't even know where to begin," he said.

"Let's start with something simple," I said. "Who killed Libby Parsons?"

"I was there, but I didn't kill her. It was Milburn."

"Why did he kill her?"

"Conrad has always been . . . jealous of attention. It's something he passed on to his son. We often had two or three of us in a room with one girl. If Conrad felt he didn't get the most attention, or if the girl did something to someone else but not him, he would get angry. Sometimes, he got violent."

"This is what happened with Libby?" I said.

Wilson nodded. "Yes. She . . . preferred me, for whatever reason. Conrad didn't react well to it. He started throttling her. At first, I thought it was . . . well, you know." We all grimaced. "Once I could tell he was really strangling her, I tried to stop him. He shoved me away, and I hit my head."

"It knocked you out?" Norton said.

"I wish it did," said Wilson. "Rang my bell pretty well, though. I was too dazed and foggy to get up and do anything. I was conscious, though, and I watched Conrad kill the poor girl." His voice got small. "He choked the life right out of her. Kept it up at least a minute after she'd obviously died."

"What about the roofies?" I said.

We waited a minute for Wilson to collect himself before he answered. Recounting Libby's death troubled him. I almost felt a twinge of sympathy for him before I reminded myself who he was and what he'd done. "We gave them to the girls," he said. "College boys roofie girls enough to knock them out. We used a lighter dose. We wanted the girls to be awake and . . . involved but affected enough to be pliable and uninhibited. Afterward, they'd get a larger dose."

"Where did you get the drugs?"

"Conrad's brother. He works in a hospital. He gave them to us and suggested the right amounts."

"And he knew what you'd be using them for?" Rich said.

"He knew very well. He even participated a few times."

"We'll have to bring him in, too," Norton said.

This grew so much bigger than only Libby Parsons. A bunch of men conspired to drug, rape, and sometimes kill teenagers, most of them girls. The FBI would be taking over because the crimes crossed state lines. We still didn't know how many girls and boys these sickos killed, and we could only guess at the number of lives ruined in the name of perversion. I wanted this case to be over, and I felt relieved we sprinted toward the finish line. And it all started with one girl's concerned aunt.

At this point, I felt I needed to talk to Madeline Eager. Rich and Norton could finish questioning this piece of shit. I excused myself to make a phone call. I left the interrogation room, headed downstairs, and stood in the lobby to call Madeline. Her voice sounded tired when she picked up. "Madeline, it's C.T. Ferguson."

"Mr. Ferguson, I was wondering when I would hear

from you." One of these years, I needed to get better at keeping clients in the loop. "Did you make a break in the case?"

"We broke it wide open. We found the man responsible for Libby's death."

Silence was my only reply. As it persisted, I thought the connection had gone dead. Then I heard the faint sounds of crying. "Are you all right?" I said.

"Mm-hmm," Madeline said before weeping some more. I gave her time to let it out and compose herself. "I'm sorry," she said a minute or so later.

"You have nothing to be sorry for."

"You caught the man, you said?"

"Yes." I gave her some of the details of the pedophile ring.

"That's awful," she said. What a bunch of worthless, disgusting people. I hope all of them die in agony."

"Considering the way men like them get treated in prison," I said, "you may get your wish."

"What's going to happen now?"

"Now the state police are rounding up everyone else we know to be involved. Forensics people will analyze all the computers. Before long, the feds will sniff around and get involved."

"They'll go to federal prison?"

"It's a little bit above my pay grade," I said, "but I'm sure some of them will."

Madeline took a few slow, deep breaths. "Thank you, Mr. Ferguson. You've helped us close this chapter."

"I wish I could have done more. Libby's story didn't have to end."

"You did what you could. You caught the lowlifes responsible." I even nabbed a few peripheral assholes along the way, like Douglas Mann, who'd be dragged in before long. "I think

Libby's story even affected Karla. She called me yesterday and said she wants to go to rehab."

"Wow . . . good news."

"It is. I'm not sure how I'm going to afford it after the last time, but I'll figure something out. Thanks for letting me know you caught these men. I'll be sure to tell Karla."

Madeline hung up. I did the same. As I put my phone away, I watched a couple of troopers bring Conrad Milburn III in from a squad car. His face looked like he had gone a couple rounds with them and lost. Both were bigger than I was, and their scowls indicated the lack of patience they maintained for dealing with scum like the Milburns. I smiled as they approached. "Looks like it'll be a family reunion in here, Conrad," I said.

"What are you doing here?" he said.

"We were talking to your father earlier."

"My father's here?"

"I'm sure you'll have a lot of company before long." The troopers herded The Third in through the doors and toward a desk at the back of the building. I heard him boast he knew a judge. I wanted to see the look on his face when he saw Clem Wilson in handcuffs. Norton and Rich didn't need me for any of this, however. The rest of the ring would be brought in and questioned.

Let Rich and Norton have the late night.

I went home.

* * *

THE DRIVE REMINDED me this case played hell with my slumber schedule over the last few nights. I still had some sleep debt to repay. By the time I got home, Gloria was in the middle of planning dinner, which meant she pored over menus and online reviews. If this constituted 21st-Century meal planning, it worked for me. Gloria wrapped me in a tight hug I let linger. "You look tired," she said.

"It's been a long few days."

"You caught the bastards who killed that poor girl?"

"We did." I told her about the morning Rich and I spent at Patterson Park, the gang of mothers kicking the tar out of Conrad Milburn II, the arrest of some key players, and what would likely happen in the next couple of days.

"Wow," said Gloria. "It sounds like you broke up the whole ring."

"An interstate syndicate, most likely."

"That sounds even more impressive."

"It'll look good in the articles and sound good on TV," I said.

"You're going to become a celebrity."

"God, I hope not."

"I trust you'll still have time for the little people when you're rich and famous," Gloria said, poking me in the ribs.

"I have time for you right now, missy," I said.

"Whatever will you do with me?"

"Come upstairs, and I'll show you."

Gloria grinned.

I FOLLOWED the case over the next couple days. The police made two score arrests, including Vincent Brown, Aaron Jameson, and Pat McHugh, who counted among those set free by Clem Wilson at some point. The members of the ring stretched from West Virginia to southern New Jersey. Newspapers in all the affected states ran with the story. I got interviewed by *The Sun* and by a smaller paper in Pennsylvania.

Every little bit helped. Despite my love of pontificating about yours truly, I always felt like I whored myself out to the press. However, when one runs a free detective service, one needs to get free publicity.

After reading one punchy article about the busted band of pedophiles, I got the phone call I'd been expecting. "Hi, Mom," I said.

"Coningsby, what a bunch of awful men," she said.

"You don't know the half of it. Necessity forced me to sit in the same room with some of them. I've never wanted a hot shower more."

"I'm sure, dear. You did some great work on this case. Your father and I have been following the stories all over the area."

"It all started with a missing girl," I said, "and an aunt who couldn't stop worrying about her. I worked hard for this one, and it took me to some places I'd just as soon not have gone."

"You know, you could always choose a new line of work. Your father and I just want you to help people. You don't need to risk yourself so often to do it."

I smiled. "I've thought about it a few times. This is what I do, Mom. I'm good at it. I didn't like it at first because the reality didn't match how I thought I could do the job. I've adjusted. I like it now."

"It's dangerous, Coningsby," she said. "These people were killers."

"How many killers do you think you've passed on the street in your lifetime?"

"Hmm. I'd rather not think about it like that. We want you to be safe."

"I'll be as safe as I can."

"Please do, dear. Your father and I will transfer twelve

thousand into your account tomorrow." It constituted a nice raise over the usual rate. Maybe Gloria and I could go back to Hawaii next year. The timeshare weeks would be available again.

"Thanks, Mom."

"You're welcome. You and Gloria need to come by for dinner some night."

"Some night," I said.

* * *

LATER THE SAME DAY, Rich called. "We've rounded them all up," he said.

"Good," I said. "Seems like it took a while."

"A couple of these assholes lived pretty remote."

"Convenient for what they do, I suppose."

"We got them all, though. Everyone on the list, plus a few people who were enablers. The realtor, too."

Good. "The feds move in?"

"They've taken over a lot of it," he said. "It's all interstate stuff now—the picture trading, some of the kids involved. It's a mess. I'm kind of glad I don't have to slog through it all."

"What about Wilson?"

"He gave up a lot of people. We figured a judge would be harder to crack, but he sang fast and loud. He's going to be tried locally. A jail around here will be easier on him. All the rest are looking at federal cases."

"A job well done all around. How did you like working on the task force?"

"It was . . . different," Rich said. "I'm used to being assigned a bunch of cases, often more than one in the same day. This task force kept me focused on just one thing. I'm not sure which I like better."

"When are you leaving the BPD for the state police?"

Rich didn't say anything at first. "Has anyone talked to you?" he said.

"So you *are* doing it."

"I don't know." Rich sighed. "I'm thinking about it. Norton made the offer. I guess I expected him to. Now I have to decide if I want to take it."

"Why wouldn't you?" I said.

"Bigger organizations mean more bureaucracy. The Army had a lot of it. The BPD has some of course, but I can live with it most of the time. I'm not sure I want to add more into my life."

"Whatever you decide, I'm sure it'll be the best call."

"If I went with the state, you'd have to find someone else to feed you information from the BPD."

"You know I can get it from your network, right?" I said. "You'll have to start a new shelf for the next round of commendations I'll help you win."

Rich snorted. "I know you love taking credit for things. How many interviews have you done?"

"Enough."

"Will I need to ask for your autograph soon?" Rich said.

I tried to steer the conversation back on track. "When's your deadline for making a decision?"

"I don't have one. I don't want to drag it out, though. It wouldn't be fair to anyone involved."

"Especially you."

"I suppose," Rich said.

I knew Rich would make the right decision. He always did. I figured the odds were even he would stay with the BPD. He'd made a nice career for himself there after the Army, and a bright future lay ahead of him.

After lunch, I went to my office. My voicemail brimmed

with messages. A few must have been regarding the pedophile cases. Some were bound to be requests for my services. It had been a few days. I might as well see what messages piqued my interest.

THE END

Do you like free books? You can get the prequel novella to the C.T. Ferguson mystery series for free. This is exclusive to my VIP readers. Just go here to get your book!

If you enjoyed this book, I hope you'll leave a review. Even a short writeup makes a difference. Reviews help independent authors get their books discovered by more readers and qualify for promotions. To leave a review, go to the book's sales page, select a star rating, and enter your comments. If you read this book on a tablet or phone, your reading app will likely prompt you to leave a review at the end.

The C.T. Ferguson Mystery Series:

- The Reluctant Detective
- The Confessional (novella)
- The Unknown Devil
- Land of the Brave (novella)
- The Workers of Iniquity
- Red City Blues (novella)
- Already Guilty

- Daughters and Sons
- A March from Innocence

While this is the suggested reading sequence, the books can be enjoyed in whatever order you happen upon them.

Connect with me:

If you're into social media and book sites, you'll find me. I have an author page on Facebook and a profile on Instagram. For new release notifications, you can follow me on BookBub or Amazon. And, of course, there's good old-fashioned email.

This is a work of fiction. Characters and places are either fictitious or used in a fictitious manner.

"Self-publishing" is something of a misnomer. This book would not have been possible without the contributions of many people. The professionals credited at the beginning have my gratitude for making this book look and read better. Big thanks to my advance readers, The Fell Street Irregulars, for their sharp eyes and swift feedback.

Made in the USA
Monee, IL
21 December 2019

19379435R00171